"I can't understand why you want to hurt me so much," Tori said.

"Hurt you?" He looked a bit stunned by the accusation. "Why would I ever want to do that?" He reached out to touch her cheek.

She twisted away. "Because I'm a Langford," she replied. "You've resented my family for years, and now you're using me to get back at them."

"That's crazy! You're way off base, Tori."

"Am I? Wasn't that the real reason you made love to me? Just to somehow even the score?"

Serge stepped back as if she'd struck him, and his icy-blue eyes glittered with anger. "I made love to you because I found you very lovely. Very fascinating," he told her in his deep, husky voice. "How can you accuse me of using you, dammit? I didn't even know your name!"

Dear Reader,

Sophisticated but sensitive, savvy yet unabashedly sentimental—that's today's woman, today's romance reader—you! And Silhouette Special Editions are written expressly to reward your quest for substantial, emotionally involving love stories.

So take a leisurely stroll under the cover's lavender arch into a garden of romantic delights. Pick and choose among titles if you must—we hope you'll soon equate all six Special Editions each month with consistently gratifying romantic reading.

Watch for sparkling new stories from your Silhouette favorites—Nora Roberts, Tracy Sinclair, Ginna Gray, Lindsay McKenna, Curtiss Ann Matlock, among others—along with some exciting newcomers to Silhouette, such as Karen Keast and Patricia Coughlin. Be on the lookout, too, for the new Silhouette Classics, a distinctive collection of bestselling Special Editions and Silhouette Intimate Moments now brought back to the stands—two each month—by popular demand.

On behalf of all the authors and editors of Special Editions,
Warmest wishes,

Leslie Kazanjian
Senior Editor

BEVLYN MARSHALL
The Pride of His Life

Silhouette Special Edition

Published by Silhouette Books New York

America's Publisher of Contemporary Romance

To my lovely and gracious mother, Y.D.D.

SILHOUETTE BOOKS
300 East 42nd St., New York, N.Y. 10017

Copyright © 1988 by Bevlyn Marshall Kaukas

ISBN: 0-373-09441-8

First Silhouette Books printing March 1988

America's Publisher of Contemporary Romance

Printed in the U.S.A.

BEVLYN MARSHALL,

a Connecticut resident, has had a varied career in fashion, public relations and marketing but finds writing the most challenging and satisfying occupation. When she's not at her typewriter, she enjoys tennis, needlepoint, long walks with her husband and toy spaniel, and reading. She believes that people who read are rarely bored or lonely because "the private pleasure of a good book is one of life's most rewarding pastimes."

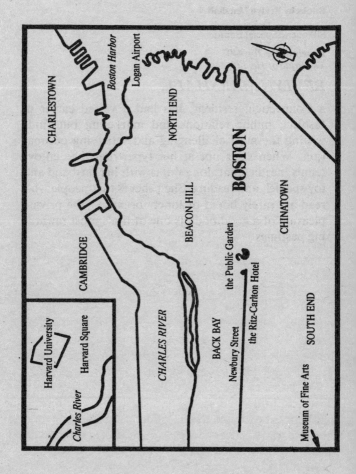

Chapter One

Spring came to Boston reluctantly, after March snow-storms and a wet, bone-chilling April. Victoria Langford welcomed its arrival with an expectant heart as she strolled through the Public Garden on a balmy May morning. As the sun warmed her back and a light breeze caressed her neck, the joy of simply being alive bubbled up inside her. She had a strong desire to kick off her shoes and run through the lush, dewy grass. She stifled the urge, though; Tori was not one to act on impulse.

Her constant companion, Mr. Jiggs, twitched his flat nose and rolled his lustrous brown eyes with obvious pleasure as he took in the rich scents and sights all around him. He was a brown-and-white English toy spaniel whose chief purpose in life was to give and receive affection.

Jiggs had been content to cuddle close to his mistress all winter, but now he was anxious to explore. He tugged on his lead so hard that the leather dug into Tori's soft palm.

She bent and unleashed her indulged pet. She didn't think there could be any harm in letting him run free for a while. Jiggs was a timid little creature and never strayed too far away from her.

A gentle smile softened Tori's lips as she watched the spaniel trot off, his white plume tail waving like a flag of newfound freedom. She sat down on a nearby park bench and kept an eye on him as he sniffed around a bank of blooming red tulips. His thick fur glowed in the sunlight.

As she sat so still and calm, ankles crossed and pale hands folded in her lap, the breeze fluttered a few tendrils of hair that had escaped her carefully coiled chignon. It tickled and teased her neck like a playful lover's kisses. She could feel the deeper, more heated kiss of the sun, too, and relaxed under the warmth it produced.

Soon Tori's thoughts began to drift as aimlessly as the fluffy clouds floating across the delft-blue sky. She stopped paying attention to Mr. Jiggs, and her eyes wandered in the direction of the sparkling pond beyond. She noticed that the swan boats had been put out—a sure sign of spring. A pair of real swans was gliding through the water, too. Tori had a special fondness for swans; she had read somewhere that they mated for life.

The weeping willows along the shore were fuzzy with tender new leaves, and the cherry trees were blooming in gaudy glory. The grass all around was so bright a green it almost brought tears to her eyes. Tori was very sensitive to color. In fact her acute visual perception was one of her chief assets as an art dealer. It also made her highly sensitive to some of the less attractive aspects of everyday life in the city; she noticed things other people were lucky enough to be blind to, and often wished she could view the world with a less critical eye.

But as far as she could see, this day was quite perfect. Weeks of rain had transformed the Garden into a verdant oasis in the middle of city concrete. Tori always found this annual metamorphosis a magical and enchanting experience even though she'd witnessed it every spring for the twenty-seven years of her life. So. had generations of Langfords before her. Her family had been prominent in Boston long before there was a Public Garden—or paved streets, for that matter.

As her attention wandered from Jiggs it was snagged by the sight of a man in a dark blue T-shirt and white shorts who was running along the path by the pond. A large gray dog followed in his wake. The man was taller than average, with the innate grace of an athlete in perfect control of every muscle movement. He loped along with such ease that he seemed to be floating a few inches above the ground. Miss Victoria Langford certainly wasn't in the habit of ogling attractive men, and she observed this one without realizing she was staring so boldly. He was so perfectly proportioned that he reminded her of an animated Greek statue. But unlike the cold marble figures Tori had often admired in the Museum of Fine Arts, the runner's skin was golden, his muscles pulsing with life. A bemused smile flitted across her full lips.

Serge Zhdanov noticed her noticing him. Funny, but she didn't seem the type who would give a man such a blatant once-over. He was still too far away to make out her features clearly, but she appeared rather old-fashioned to him. Her light brown hair was parted in the middle and severely pulled back into a bun. The high lace collar of her orchid dress fluttered in the breeze.

Maybe she was an apparition from the past, Serge thought, a ghost who appeared in the Garden on a certain date each spring when the tulips sprang up. It was a fanciful thought—the kind Serge wasn't used to thinking. He was a practical man who had no patience with dreamers. He himself was a doer and prided himself on his no-nonsense approach to life.

So he considered the direct approach of running right up to her and introducing himself. She was obviously interested in him. Lately he'd been so wrapped up in his work that he hadn't had much time to socialize. As much as he enjoyed the company of women, he disliked the silly little dating games they seemed to expect. The rituals of flowers and phone calls and candlelit dinners irritated him. He often wished men and women could be straightforward with each other from the start and get down to the business at hand: the satisfying business of physically enjoying each other. At thirty-five, Serge Zhdanov had been in lust many times before; but never in love. This didn't particularly bother him. He doubted that he'd ever be ready to settle down. At certain times, though, he did realize that something special seemed to be lacking in his life, despite all his success. What Serge didn't realize at the moment was that his dog, Duke, was no longer following him.

Tori heard her own pet's plangent cry for help, and to her horror she saw that her precious little Jiggs was being chased by what appeared to be a big gray wolf. She leaped up from the bench, unbuckled the ankle straps of her high heels, kicked them off and sprinted across the grass to save her little darling.

It surprised Serge to see the proper young woman discard her shoes and shoot off like that. He noted how nicely the thin material of her dress clung to her thighs as she ran. And then he noticed what Duke was up to. Swearing under his breath, he joined the chase.

Tori had almost caught up to Jiggs—the monster hot on his heels—when she tripped on an exposed tree root and crashed to the ground. She blinked away the stars in front of her eyes and sat up slowly. Nothing seemed to be broken, although her bones still vibrated from the jolt. She vaguely felt something warm and strong press against her back.

It was Serge's hand. "Don't stand up yet," he cautioned softly in her ear as he knelt beside her. The heat of her flesh through her dress was pleasant against his palm. Such a hot-blooded ghost, he thought. "That was quite a fall you took," he said. "Are you all right?"

"My dog's in trouble," she managed to gasp. "Don't worry about me. Help him!"

Serge stood and whistled sharply. Duke gave up his pursuit of Jiggs and ran right to him. "Good boy," Serge said, rewarding him with a pat on the head. "Duke didn't mean any harm. Did you, pal?"

Tori, still sitting on the ground, was eyeball-to-eyeball with Duke and shivered inwardly. The dog's eyes were a cold, eerie blue. She found his stare extremely disconcerting and, rather than suffer it, she raised her gaze to his master's face. He, too, had vivid blue eyes, she discovered. Thick dark eyebrows and lashes accented their piercing frostiness.

With a great effort Tori pushed herself up, ignoring the hand he extended to help her. Although she was taller than average, he still towered over her. Being barefoot made her feel very vulnerable, but Tori refused to let it show that she was the slightest bit intimidated by the large man or his dog.

"That beast of yours attacked my dog!" she accused.

Serge didn't appreciate having his best friend referred to as a beast. Like most dog owners, he thought his was beyond reproach. "Hey, Duke was just trying to be friendly," he objected. "He didn't harm a hair on your pooch's brainless head."

"Jiggs happens to be very intelligent. And extremely sensitive." Having set the record straight, Tori hurried to her pet, who was a few yards away, afraid to come closer. She had to coax him to her, and when she scooped him into her arms she could feel his little heart pounding fast and furious. She cooed soft reassurances into his floppy brown ear as her own heart tightened with pity for him.

Serge watched her closely, wanting to make sure she was all right. She seemed to have bounced back very nicely from her fall. He decided she wasn't as fragile as she looked. Her pale, translucent skin looked as delicate as fine porcelain—the kind that could shatter easily.

As Tori clutched Jiggs to her chest he whimpered softly, as if to express what an ordeal he'd gone through. She was infuriated that her beloved pet had been so badly frightened. She turned to the jogger. "I intend to report this incident to the park authorities," she informed him. "Your dog should have been leashed."

Serge found her superior tone offensive. He didn't much care for the way she raised her chin in such a disdainful manner, either—a chin he considered too sharp. Who did she think she was, anyway? Queen of the Public Garden? He hadn't appreciated how she'd refused to take his hand when he offered to help her up. Serge was sensitive to the smallest slight.

"That mutt of yours wasn't leashed either, lady," he reminded her and stuck out his own chin, which was as blunt as hers was sharp. He stood before her, arms folded across his broad chest.

Tori wasn't an argumentative person by nature, and rather than risk unpleasantness she usually sidestepped a confrontation. Unless there was a principle at stake, that is. Or unless the person addressing her had an overbearing manner, a belligerent stance, and was so obviously in the wrong.

"My dog is hardly a 'mutt,' " she informed him. "He's a purebred and knows how to behave in a public place. He would never dream of attacking another animal and doesn't need to be restrained like your flea-bitten mongrel."

Tori threw a contemptuous glance in Duke's direction. He was scratching himself with great gusto at the moment. His eyes were half shut in ecstasy, and his tongue lolled out of the side of his black-rimmed mouth. Tori's expression made it obvious that she did not consider Duke a pretty sight.

This realization hurt Serge to the quick. Where did she get off looking down her nose at such a handsome animal? A rather long nose at that, Serge noted critically. He preferred women with cute little upturned noses. But he gave Duke a nudge with the tip of his running shoe to make him stop scratching so vigorously in front of her.

"You obviously don't know much about dogs if you can't tell a champion Siberian husky from a mongrel, lady," he stated flatly.

Tori was not impressed. "That's where he belongs. Back in Siberia. He's not fit for civilized society." She could easily envision Duke's owner in Siberia, too. Those icy blue eyes of his could freeze over a continent.

"Where'd you get your overstuffed animal?" he asked her. "At a toy store? That pampered piece of fluff is a pretty poor excuse for a dog."

Jiggs, as if understanding he'd been insulted, let out a protesting snort. Tori shifted him in her arms. Perhaps he was a wee bit overweight; and ever so slightly spoiled. But there was no cause for this rude stranger to ridicule him. Poor little Jiggs was completely innocent of any wrong doing. He'd been sniffing tulips and minding his own business.

"I can see I'm wasting my time waiting for an apology from you," she told the jogger. "I'd as likely receive one from that bully dog of yours."

"Oh, is that what you're waiting for? An apology?"

Serge had to smile. She sounded like a stuffy Boston dowager although he guessed her age to be a few years under thirty. She wasn't bad looking, either. Actually, despite her long nose and sharp chin, she was downright attractive if you liked that type—which Serge didn't. She was too thin for his taste. And too humorless. He liked curvy, good-natured women.

Still, he liked the way her intelligent, wide-set eyes changed from hazel to green and then back again. He found that completely fascinating. And he had to admit that Duke had scared her silly dog out of his wits—if he'd had any to begin with. She herself had taken a pretty hard fall but wasn't moaning and groaning about it. At least she wasn't the whiny sort. So would it kill him to apologize to this Miss Manners if that's what she wanted?

"Okay, okay, I shouldn't have let Duke run loose," he admitted. "But since I did, I should have kept a closer eye on him. You're right. I'm completely in the wrong. I'm sorry it happened." As sincere as Serge was, his slightly lopsided, rather boyish smile made him look less so.

It was really more a smirk than a smile, Tori decided. She found everything about the man abrasive. He simply rubbed her the wrong way. She resented that he made her so acutely aware of him physically. His bare, muscular arms and legs gleamed in the morning sun and upset her sense of propriety. Sure, there were other joggers in the park—some wearing even less than he was—but Tori hardly noticed them. She couldn't help thinking how this one would look stark naked, though. His brief white shorts and thin, chest-clinging shirt left little to the imagination. It was obvious to her that he took pride in keeping his body fit. He was probably quite smug about it. She was sure he was the type who could never pass a mirror without pausing for a brief nod of self-approval. Then she realized that she was gawking with approval herself.

"I accept your apology." She paused. "For what it's worth," she couldn't help adding. And without so much as a goodbye she walked off, clutching her dog to her chest.

Most people knew better than to dismiss Serge Zhdanov so abruptly. He didn't like it one bit. He stood in surprised silence as she headed toward the path and watched her straight, unyielding back with narrowed eyes. Maybe *she* thought their conversation was over, but as far as he was concerned it wasn't. Women didn't usually get away from Serge without giving him something—a smile at the very least. He started running in her direction, telling himself that he really wasn't chasing her.

"Hey," he said when he'd caught up. "Didn't you forget something?"

She gave him a wary, sidelong glance as he fell into step beside her. "I don't believe so," she replied cautiously, although she knew she'd forgotten her manners with him. Her curt departure hadn't been very gracious.

"Shoes," he reminded her, grinning.

Tori stopped in her tracks and looked down at her unshod feet. Her fall must have rattled her brain. Feeling foolish, she smiled and shook her head over her own absentmindedness.

Serge decided that it was a smile well worth waiting for. It was such a slow, gentle one and it sweetened the aloof severity of her features. Humor twinkled in her large serious eyes. And at that instant, she became beautiful right before his eyes. Like magic, he thought.

"I kicked them off by the park bench over there," she said, waving in that direction.

Without a moment's hesitation Serge ran to the bench to find and fetch them for her. His dog Duke couldn't have performed the task with greater enthusiasm, he thought. He warned himself to cool it. He wasn't going to lose his head over a smile. Despite this prudent advice to himself, he was completely charmed by the sight of her dainty high heels lying askew in the grass. He plucked them up by their ankle straps. As he carried them back to her, they dangled from his big strong hand like fragile ornaments.

When he placed them down in front of her Tori slipped her narrow feet into them. But when she bent to buckle the straps Jiggs wriggled in her arms, making the simple task much more difficult.

"Why don't you put him down," Serge suggested. Her suspicious glance at Duke, panting nearby, told him why she wouldn't. He was a little hurt that she still didn't trust the husky. He almost took it personally. But then again, who could blame her? Duke looked a lot more dangerous than he was. "Oh, hell, I'll buckle them for you," he said.

Before she could object he was kneeling in front of her, one hand encircling her slender ankle. It prevented Tori from stepping back. Then he began working the thin strap into the tiny gold buckle, muttering under his breath at his own clumsiness.

As his fingers brushed against her silk-sheathed legs Tori experienced a sweet melting within her. She longed to run her fingers through his thick thatch of dark brown hair as she gazed down at the top of his head. Ruffled and unruly, to her it looked as soft and tempting as puppy fur. She refrained from such a familiar gesture, though. The situation was much too intimate as it was—a strange man was kneeling attentively in front of her.

She endured her discomfort silently. The proper thing to say at such a moment eluded her. His fingertips were as light as butterfly wings as they brushed against her legs. She could also feel a fluttering of butterflies in her stomach. He made her very nervous.

As uncomfortable as she was, she was almost disappointed when he'd finally managed to fasten both shoe straps. Mission accomplished, he stood up to tower over her once more. Even with the advantage of her high heels, she was still much shorter than he was.

Tori liked that. She had a penchant for tall men. When she was an awkward adolescent she'd towered over all the boys in her exclusive dance class and they'd seemed to dislike her for it even though she hadn't done it on purpose. She'd never quite gotten over the experience of being too tall, too thin, too gawky. What she'd needed so much at the time was a mother to reassure her, to tell her the story about the ugly duckling who became a swan. But her mother had died when she was thirteen.

Standing in front of the jogger now, she judged that her chin would just graze his broad shoulder if they embraced. Not that they ever would, of course. It surprised her to even consider it. He was a total stranger.

Yet his simple, almost humble act of kindness had managed to disarm her. Her initial antagonism toward him had completely dissolved the moment he knelt down to buckle her sandals. At first she'd been put off by his rugged sexiness, his bold, frosty stare. But no longer. His thoughtful action had proved to her that he was a true gentleman.

As she was imagining him a chivalrous knight, Serge was having rather more down-to-earth thoughts about her. He hadn't missed the opportunity of taking in the length of her sleek, curvaceous legs and was now picturing how good they would look against the blue sheets of his bed. He was also wondering how long it would take him to get her into it. At least a week, he estimated, if he gave the project his complete attention. Maybe longer. She seemed the type who expected some romancing.

He reminded himself that he didn't have too much time to spare right now. He was closing a big deal out in California. But her legs were really pretty spectacular. He decided to give it a shot.

"What's your name? I'll give you a call," he offered with offhanded generosity.

A little too offhanded to suit Tori. She knew nothing about this man except that he kept himself in good shape and was fond of his beastly dog. "I don't usually give out my name or number to strangers,' she informed him.

Her schoolmarmish tone grated on Serge a bit. So did her clipped Boston Brahmin accent. It reminded him of grudges that went back a long way. The people who'd first employed his parents when they came to America spoke like that. Still, the pleasing shape of her long lean legs made it possible for Serge to find it in his heart to forgive her aristocratic accent and prim manner.

"Listen, I want to see you again," he said.

Tori considered his request. His demand, actually. She regarded him carefully as she thought it over. His features were hardly refined. His mouth was too wide. His cheekbones too prominent. And his icy blue eyes slanted a bit, making him look sly and dangerous and foreign. His nose was short and blunt, a little crooked if you looked closely enough. Maybe he'd broken it—or someone had broken it for him. He looked like a man who wouldn't sidestep trouble when he saw it coming.

She wondered if he was a professional athlete. Maybe a rough-and-tumble hockey player. That would account for the broken nose. Tori had little interest in sports, but her brother Gordon had once dragged her to a Bruins game. She could easily picture this runner as one of those fierce gladiators swerving hell-bent around the ice rink.

Sweat darkened the front of his faded navy T-shirt. There was no team or college name emblazoned across it, no commercial logo or tasteless phrase. It was an unadorned billboard advertising nothing but the man's own broad chest. Tori approved of that. She approved of his body in general. He was muscular without being musclebound. Lean but not thin. And despite his large size he moved with a certain grace. He was no lumbering lug of a man. Yes, definitely an athlete, she concluded.

Serge was becoming acutely uncomfortable under her unblinking scrutiny. "I'm beginning to feel like some bug under a microscope," he told her. Used to being the one who appraised others, he didn't like having the tables turned on him.

"Oh, I don't mean to be rude," Tori said quickly, brushing a filmy strand of hair from her forehead. She laughed self-consciously. "But you're rather pleasant to look at, you know." She stated this as simple fact.

Serge was taken aback by her remark. He was used to compliments from women, but hers was so artless and unexpected. Was she coming on to him? Or leading him on? He couldn't figure her out. One moment she was aloof, the next she was as open as a child. Either she was naive about the games men and women played, or she was a master of them.

"You haven't answered my question yet," he reminded her. "I'd like to see you again."

"That's hardly a question," Tori pointed out. She was stalling. She didn't know what to do. She sensed she was poised on the edge of some exciting adventure but couldn't get up the nerve to jump.

Serge was irritated by her reply. He disliked coyness. He felt inclined to drop the whole thing but the flickers of green in her serious eyes held his attention. He decided to try another approach rather than give up on her quite yet. Once he'd set his mind on anything, he hated giving up on it.

"So tell me your dog's name if you won't tell me yours," he said in an easy, sociable tone. He couldn't have cared less about her dumb dog, but he wanted to keep her talking.

"I call him Mr. Jiggs," she said, relieved he'd changed the subject.

Better to call him Stupid, Serge thought. "Cute," he said. That was an understatement. The fuzzy-muzzled pooch was almost too cute to bear. Serge liked *real* dogs, not stuffed toys. But he decided it wouldn't hurt to make friends with the little cartoon creature. "Would Mr. Jiggs mind if I petted him?" He almost choked making this request.

"Not at all," Tori assured him enthusiastically. "Jiggs is very friendly. And gentle as a lamb." Unlike your beast, she added silently.

Since permission was granted, Serge reached out to give the dog a pat on the head. The little spaniel's response to this friendly overture was immediate and emphatic: Jiggs dug his tiny sharp teeth into the stranger's proffered hand.

Serge was too surprised to even swear. He quickly pulled back his hand and examined his nipped finger. At least "gentle," lamblike Jiggs hadn't drawn blood. Duke, sensing his master had suffered some kind of subtle injury, laid back his pointed ears and growled.

"Easy, boy," Serge said calmly, as if nothing at all had happened.

But Tori was aghast. If it hadn't happened right before her very eyes she would never have believed Jiggs capable of biting anyone. "Good Lord, did he hurt you?" she cried.

"Not as much as he wanted to." Serge's feelings were more hurt than his finger. Animals usually took to him immediately; he prided himself on having a way with them.

"I don't understand what came over Jiggs. He must have been trying to protect me," Tori said, attempting to find an excuse for her sweet pet's behavior.

Serge's laugh was more like a bark. "Protect you from what, lady? Me? Or men in general?"

Tori ignored his question. She didn't need Jiggs to keep men at arm's length. She'd developed more subtle strategies. "Let me take a look at that finger," she said.

But there was nothing much to see. She was thankful the skin hadn't been punctured. His fingernails, she noticed, were extremely well manicured. She found this surprising only because she assumed macho jocks paid little attention to such fine points of grooming.

A warm ray of pleasure traveled through Serge's chest as she examined his injured finger with such diligent concern. It made him smile to see his large tanned hand being cupped by her pale delicate one. He was almost glad her silly dog had bitten him.

"I think you'll survive," she diagnosed. "It may comfort you to know Jiggs had his rabies shot."

"Is that all the comfort you're willing to give me?" He pulled a long face. "That nip didn't exactly tickle, you know. The least you can do is kiss it and make it all better."

"You want me to kiss your finger?"

"I'm sure it would help ease the pain."

The absurdity of his request amused her. Playing along with the joke, she slowly brought his hand to her lips and softly pressed them against his long, strong finger. Then, on an impulse too sudden to stifle, she flicked out her tongue to taste his skin. It tasted salty and good.

He hadn't expected that sexy little flick of her tongue. It made his nerve endings tingle. His sharp eyes fixed on her mouth. He hadn't noticed how sensuous it was until now. He was especially captivated by her plump bottom lip, which protruded slightly in a delicious pout. The rest of her features were rather austere, but she had a mouth that dared a man to kiss it. Serge could rarely pass up a dare.

Without a moment's hesitation he placed his palm on the nape of her neck and swiftly lowered his lips to hers. He knew he was taking a big risk. He half expected her to push him away and slap his face. Worse yet, that treacherous mutt she was holding might take a chunk out of his cheek. But Serge liked risks. He made his living taking them.

Tori, completely taken by surprise, was caught with her defenses down. She gasped as his mouth came down on hers, but she didn't twist away. Vaguely, as if from a great distance, she heard her dog's muffled growl as he was pressed against her soft breasts and the man's hard chest. Then there was no room for thought, only sensation. The man's sun-sweetened athletic fragrance was as heady and intoxicating as the rich moist scents of spring in the fresh morning air.

Tori swayed slightly in an answering rhythm as his mouth brushed back and forth across her sensitive lips. He took his time and ease, skimming the surface of her mouth, tasting but not invading. He was a hungry but never a greedy man. This had a lot to do with his success in life.

Her scent, he discovered, was lilac. That seemed natural and right and perfect. Like a tender bud unfurling, her lips opened for him, and he accepted the invitation.

Tori drank him in. It was an unconscious reaction, a desire to quench a long-neglected thirst she hadn't even realized she'd had until now. And his mouth, his tongue were as sweet as nectar.

Her passionate response almost threw Serge off balance, like a streak of lightning bolting through him. He'd intended a teasing brush of lips, not this intimate soul-kiss. Using all his self-control he broke away from her; but instantly longed to feel her persuasive yielding mouth melded to his again. Who and what was she?—some magical spring nymph disguised as a demure, proper Bostonian? Stepping back to look at her, he almost believed it was possible. Her pale face was now flushed and her serious eyes blazed green. She'd been transformed into a desirous, desirable sprite. He was sure she'd cast a spell on him. The only thing that seemed to matter to him at that moment was that he wanted her.

His apartment was close by. He considered simply picking her up and carrying her there. Undisturbed, they could finish what they'd so clearly started in this very public place. Later they could celebrate with champagne. Did wood nymphs drink champagne? Serge wondered.

But as Serge contemplated carrying her away, Tori was wishing she could vanish into thin air. Catching that knowing glint of arousal in the stranger's ice-blue eyes, she felt the heat of embarrassment spread through her. What on earth had come over her to make her behave so uncharacteristically?

She'd completely lost all sense of who and where she was. Had she become as balmy as the weather? That was it, of course. She blamed it on the season. People with spring fever did odd things.

Her heart jumped when he gripped her upper arm with strong, sure fingers. "Come on. We'll go back to my place," he told her softly but confidently.

She shrugged off his hand and raised her sharp Langford chin. She would have to set things straight with him immediately. "I've given you the wrong impression," she said crisply. Although her face was burning, her voice was cool.

"I hope not. Because I'm very impressed." He tried his best to sound casual. One false note, and he was sure she'd disappear. "Don't you think it's time you told me your name, Lady Green Eyes?"

Feeling a fool, she shook her head. All she wanted to do at that moment was to escape from his knowing gaze. How could she have allowed herself to let down her guard with him like that? A complete stranger, no less. "I'm sorry," she mumbled. "I have to go now." She spun around and began walking away from him.

This time he didn't go after her. His mobile face became a mask of disinterest. The glint of desire in his eyes dimmed as they glazed over. These kinds of games bored him. She was no spring nymph after all. She was just a teasing witch. He found nothing magical in that type of woman.

As Tori hurried down the path she began to wonder what exactly it was that she was so intent on fleeing from. A tall, sexy stranger had kissed her, she'd enjoyed it, but she was running away. What sense did that make? Her head was spinning. Nothing was making much sense to her. In her confusion she stopped dead in her tracks. Would the man still be there if she turned around? She promised herself that if he was, she'd go back to him, taking his staying as a sign that it was time to make some changes in her life, to be a little daring for once. She glanced back. She was both relieved and terrified when she saw that he hadn't moved.

He didn't budge or so much as blink as she hesitantly walked back to him. Stiff as a statue, arms folded across his chest, he watched her return with the same cool detachment as he'd watched her retreat. What's she up to now? he asked himself.

She laughed her light, nervous laugh when she reached him. "Could you possibly meet me here tomorrow morning?" Her voice was breathless, tentative. She hadn't exactly thrown caution to the wind with that question, but it was still a bold step for Tori.

Serge tried to keep a hold on his anger. But it was fading fast in the light of her shy, lovely smile. She looked so damn guileless and sweet, standing there clutching her dumb little dog. He'd never come across a woman who could seem so plain and ordinary to him one moment, and so enchanting the next. She changed with the color of her eyes.

"I'll be here," he promised despite his better judgment. "Same time, same place, Lady Green Eyes. By the bench where I found your shoes."

Chapter Two

The art gallery Tori owned and managed was located on Newbury Street, only a few blocks from the Public Garden. It was a street lined with pricey boutiques, chic beauty salons, fine china and antique shops, and sidewalk cafés. Back Bay Gallery was housed on the first floor of a Victorian brownstone. The art displayed inside, though, was boldly modern. And despite her reserved, almost old-fashioned appearance, Tori was a very savvy dealer with a reputation for discovering and sponsoring hot new talent. Her taste was avant-garde and usually right on the money. She devoted almost every waking hour to her business and never regretted a minute of it. She simply loved what she was doing and felt more comfortable in her gallery than anywhere else.

That's why her assistant Ginger O'Neil expressed surprise when Tori arrived late rather than early. Ginger was perched on a stepladder adjusting the spotlights on a large abstract painting when Tori walked through the front door.

"What happened? Did you get hit by a truck or something?" Ginger asked.

Tori did rather feel as if she'd been hit by a truck—or *something*. The expression on her face was slightly dazed when she smiled up at her friend. Ginger was a plump, pretty-faced free spirit who'd been Tori's friend since their student days at the School of the Museum of Fine Arts.

"Thanks for opening up. Sorry I'm late," Tori replied. "I got sidetracked on the way here." Remembering how brought high color to her cheeks. She bent down and unleashed Jiggs.

"Why, Victoria, I do believe you're blushing," Ginger said. "Now why is that?"

"I'm just red from exertion," Tori quickly explained as she tucked a wayward strand of hair into her sleek chignon. "You see, Jiggs and I were accosted by a wolf in the Garden."

"You're kidding!" Ginger scurried down the stepladder with the grace of a chubby kitten. "What kind of wolf? The four-legged or the two-legged species?"

"One of each, actually," Tori informed her with a straight face. Then she laughed at her friend's amazed expression. "It was really a Siberian husky that attacked poor Jiggsy. Luckily its owner was close by, and he called his dog off before it could do any harm."

"Was he cute?" Ginger wanted to know.

Tori smoothed her silk stocking and noticed a run. Real silk was one of the few luxuries she indulged in and she swore silently over the mishap, blaming the jogger rather than the tree root.

"As dogs go he wasn't bad," she said in reply to Ginger's question. "Not really my type, though. Much too big and rambunctious."

Ginger pursed her brightly painted mouth. "You know very well I was asking about the owner, not the dog."

"Not really my type. Too big and rambunctious," Tori repeated blandly.

Pretending little interest in the subject, she crossed the large showroom to the teak counter and reached behind it for a box of dog biscuits. She gave one to Jiggs, and as she watched him greedily gobble it up she recalled the jogger's description of him as an overstuffed toy. Maybe it was time to put Jiggs on a diet, Tori thought. But when he gazed up at her with those adoring brown saucer eyes of his, she gave him yet another treat. Tomorrow, she promised herself. She would put him on a diet tomorrow.

Ginger had followed Tori to the counter and was now giving her a disapproving look. "You'll never change," she proclaimed.

"I know, I know. I indulge Mr. Jiggs too often. I really must stop spoiling him," Tori said.

"I was referring to your attitude about men, Tori. I'm not surprised that this guy in the park wasn't your type. What man is? You're too damn picky, sweetie."

"No, I'm not," Tori protested. "You make it sound as if I turn away men in droves, which is hardly the case."

"What about that darling artist who wanted you to pose for him?"

"Which one was that?" Many artists had asked Tori to sit for them, rhapsodizing about her dramatic profile and pale cameo-textured skin. Tori took their flattery with a grain of salt. Although she considered herself attractive enough, she couldn't help but wonder whether they didn't just want to win her favor because she was an influential art dealer. Tori had been raised to distrust flattery.

"Which one?" Ginger looked shocked. "Don't you even remember the poor boy? The artist who followed you around like a lovesick puppy all last fall."

"Oh, him." Tori smiled gently. "He really was rather sweet, wasn't he? But much too young for me."

"He certainly didn't think so. But if age is your objection, then what about that charming, gray-haired banker you met at the charity auction last month?"

Tori's smile faded as she stifled a yawn. "Ah, Charles. Such a *nice* gentleman." When he'd kissed her good-night it had been like dry leaves brushing against her lips.

Ginger sighed. "So far, one was too young, one was too nice. What about that art collector from New York? Are you going to complain that he was too rich?"

"I admit he was very attractive," Tori conceded.

"That, my girl, is a blatant understatement," Ginger told her. "I swear I would have given my little finger to go out with him myself." After pausing a moment, she amended her statement. "Well, maybe not my actual finger. But my longest fingernail, for sure."

Coming from Ginger, even that was saying a lot, Tori acknowledged. Ginger had exceedingly long, pampered fingernails, which she painted a different color each day to either match or clash with her flamboyant outfits. Today they were purple. Her knit dress was orange.

Tori tried to conjure up the image of the man they were discussing, but his features had become fuzzy in her memory. He'd definitely been attractive, though. Sleekly elegant. And they'd shared the same avid interest in art. He'd wanted her to go to France with him for the summer and stay at his château. But the magic hadn't been there. Tori didn't know why—it just hadn't been.

"You know what I think the problem I had with him was, Ginger?"

"He was too perfect?"

Tori shrugged. "Maybe that, too. But the problem was that he kept sending me bushels of long-stemmed red roses."

Ginger let out a wail. "You poor thing to suffer such brutality. The man should be put against a wall and shot!"

"Seriously, Ginger. I loathe red roses." Tori leaned across the teak counter, intent on explaining herself. "That's the whole point, don't you see? He never took the time to consider what kind of flower I'd like. He just kept sending me the most expensive ones."

Tori threw up her hands, giving up her attempt to explain something she didn't really understand herself. Maybe Ginger was right; maybe she was too picky when it came to men. She'd managed to avoid having an intimate relationship with one for years now.

Ginger was shaking her curly head in puzzlement. "I worry about you, Tori. I really do. You'd think your heart was Fort Knox, the way you keep it so guarded. You've got to forget that some idiot jilted you ages ago and get on with your life."

"I have forgotten about that," Tori replied a bit stiffly, not appreciating the reminder of her broken engagement when she was twenty. "And I think I've managed to get on with my life quite well," she stressed, glancing around her airy gallery.

"I mean your love life, kid," Ginger said.

"Oh, that." Tori's expressive voice fell flat.

Ginger rolled her eyes to the ceiling, as if she had invisible friends hovering up there who were more in tune with her. "How can you be so blasé about *that*?"

"Well, you certainly seem to be," Tori retorted, and then wanted to bite her tongue. "I'm sorry, Ginger. That sounds so catty."

Ginger waved away her apology. "I admit I've had my share of affairs. I guess we're blasé about love in different ways. I play the field, and you sit on the sidelines. We're complete opposites."

Tori gave her friend a sad smile. "Maybe we're more alike than we think. Why are we so afraid of commitment?"

"Because we don't want to get hurt, of course," Ginger answered without missing a beat. "But you've already been there, Tori. You know all about it."

Tori smoothed her hair back from her crown. "That was almost seven years ago, Ginger. And looking back, I think I was more humiliated than hurt. He practically left me standing at the altar, after all. Poor boy. He assumed all Langfords were wealthy and was terribly disappointed when he learned that I wasn't an heiress."

Tori actually laughed now, but at the time she'd wanted to die. From her present perspective she could see that everything had worked out for the best. She thanked her lucky stars that she'd never married the man. A fine head of golden hair, elegant manners and an English accent quoting Shakespeare's sonnets didn't really impress her anymore. Besides, their lovemaking had left her sorely disappointed.

Ginger pushed up the sleeves of her neon-orange dress. "Men!" she exclaimed. "They'll always let you down in the end. The trick is to drop them first."

"Men have feelings, too," Tori reminded her a bit sharply, concerned about one man's feelings in particular.

"Don't worry," Ginger said, her expression becoming more serious. "I didn't drop your brother, Tori. And

Gordon didn't dump me, either, I'll have you know," she quickly added. "We just sort of let go of each other at the same time, if you understand what I mean."

Tori didn't understand at all. Ginger, who was usually so loquacious about her relationships, had kept her feelings about Gordon to herself. And Gordon never discussed his feelings with anyone, including his sister. All Tori knew for sure was that whatever her best friend and her brother had shared together had ended as abruptly as it had begun.

Since she abhorred people prying into her personal life, Tori wasn't about to pry into Ginger's or Gordon's. "I'm sorry things didn't work out between you two" was all she said now to her friend. She sincerely meant that.

Ginger lifted her padded shoulders. "Hey, that's the way the cracker crumbles."

Tori smiled. Her friend never got her clichés quite right. "You would have been so good for Gordon. He takes everything much too seriously," she told Ginger.

"Like brother, like sister," Ginger said. "You're too serious yourself. You've got to break out of that shell of yours and live a little! I think you should give yourself, body and soul, to the next handsome stranger who crosses your path."

Although she knew Ginger was just joking around, Tori avoided her eyes. She'd come too close to describing what had actually happened in the Public Garden a short while before. Tori picked up the morning mail on the counter and rifled through it as she considered telling Ginger about the jogger. She decided that it was better to keep the experience to herself. Her strong, sensual reaction to his kiss had amazed her. She was still a little dazed by the effect it had had on her, and she needed time alone to mull it over.

"I'll look at this mail in my office," she told Ginger, trying to sound casual. "Then I'm going to do some bookkeeping. Just call me if it gets too busy for you here in the showroom."

"I hope it does get busy," Ginger replied. "Meanwhile I'll get started on those invitations to the upcoming exhibition."

Tori thanked her and went down the long hall to her office in back. Unlike the large bright showroom, with its glossy expanse of hardwood floor and dramatic displays and lighting, Tori's office was small and cozy. In fact it was almost shabby. The gray file cabinets were dented, and her desk, retrieved from the attic of her family's Beacon Hill house, was scarred and water-stained. It happened to be a genuine Hepplewhite desk, though; a valuable antique despite its wear and tear. A white wicker basket sat beside it. Jiggs slept away most of his day in it, on a bright emerald cushion of the softest velvet. He curled up in it and yawned, his trauma in the Garden completely forgotten.

His mistress wasn't able to settle down quite so easily. Tori kept shuffling through the mail as if it were a deck of cards. There was a pile of paperwork on her desk, waiting to be delved into—work she'd been avoiding for days. As much as Tori enjoyed discovering and promoting artists, she disliked keeping books and balancing accounts. She was reluctant to reduce art to figures in a ledger. But she possessed a strong streak of Yankee practicality, and when it was necessary, she could always put her long Langford nose to the grindstone and deal with the nitty-gritty of running the business. Tori was well aware that "Art for art's sake" didn't pay the rent or electricity bills. She'd started Back Bay Gallery with a small inheritance left to her by her parents and had turned it into a modest but dependable living. Unlike her elder brother, she had come to terms with the necessity of supporting herself.

But today she was acting dreamy and vague. It was impossible for her to concentrate with the jogger's face looming in her mind's eye so vividly. She was amazed that she could remember every detail of it—every dark eyelash that shaded those ice-blue eyes. Remembering him made her feel warm all over. Yet she kept imagining him on some frigid, snowy plain where the wind howled and wolves bayed.

It wasn't the most comforting image. She blinked it away and got up to open the window behind her desk. Even though it faced the service alley, a waft of soft spring air drifted in. It brought back the memory of the jogger's scent—that heady mixture of sun and sweat and soap. There was nothing cold about that. Nothing cold about the way his kiss had seared through her, either. It had heated her very bones. Just remembering caused a melting in the pit of her stomach. Resting her arms on the windowsill, she breathed in deeply, hoping the fresh air would clear her head.

"Aha! Caught you daydreaming, didn't I, Victoria?"

Tori jumped at the sound of the unexpected male voice but turned from the window with a smile. "So you did, Gordon."

Her bother walked into the office and slumped down in the ladder-back chair across from Tori's desk. Very thin and loose-boned, Gordon could manage to slump anywhere. He was fair and aristocratic looking. His features were similar to his sister's but not as pronounced. Tori had often wished that he'd been the one to inherit the long Langford nose and strong chin.

"You do look a bit logy this morning," he told her. "I hope you're not coming down with a bad case of something."

"Just spring fever, no doubt." Not wanting to call attention to herself, Tori directed it at Gordon. "And you look absolutely exhausted. Did you stay up all night working again?"

With more concern than she wanted to show, she took in the dark circles under her brother's gray eyes, his pallid complexion and the tense set of his jaw. He'd been working too hard on his latest project. Tori had little understanding of it and even less hope for it. Gordon was a self-styled inventor, with more patents filed in Washington than he could remember. None had ever developed into anything.

He rubbed his weary eyes so hard that Tori had to use great self-control to prevent herself from ordering him to stop. She often had to remind herself that he was eight years older than she, not eight years old. Whenever she caught herself thinking he'd never grow up, she reminded herself that he'd come through for her when it had really counted. He'd fought long and hard to become her guardian after their parents had died in a boating accident. Tori could have ended up the ward of their dreadful Aunt Olive when she was thirteen if Gordon hadn't intervened.

Just after graduating from Harvard, he'd taken on the responsibility of his little sister. Tori knew that couldn't have been easy for him; Gordon wasn't the responsible type. But he'd done his best to give her a stable home life, and Tori would always be grateful to him for that.

They still lived together in the family town-house on Beacon Hill. It was a large, three-story house and sometimes days would go by without their having more than a brief glimpse of each other.

"I managed to get a few hours' sleep this morning," Gordon replied. He stopped rubbing his eyes and began massaging his temples.

"Then you did spend all night tinkering in your workroom," Tori concluded. "I wish you could learn to take better care of yourself, dear."

Irritation flickered across her brother's tired face. "I'm doing a little more than *tinkering*, Victoria. The project I'm working on now could turn out to be quite lucrative. I made a real breakthrough last night."

"That's wonderful," she said, putting as much enthusiasm as she could into her voice. Gordon had had many "breakthroughs" in the past, and she didn't ask him to explain this one. His replies were always too technical for her to understand. She had a vague idea that this project had to do with developing some kind of new racing oar. She wondered if there was a market for that sort of thing. Or was Gordon simply dwelling on his glory days of college crew?

"Yes, a real breakthrough," he repeated, abstractly rearranging everything on Tori's desk into an order more pleasing to him. Tori didn't stop him. She usually ignored her brother's oddities. "But I need a little time to work it all out," he continued. "I've decided to take off a few days and drive to Vermont. Mountain views are so inspiring."

"I think a rest would do you a world of good," Tori said. It was obvious to her that something was worrying him, but she didn't question him about it. Tori and Gordon managed to get along so well living under the same roof because they respected each other's privacy. "Don't forget to pack a warm sweater," she added lightly. "It can get cool in Vermont this time of year."

"What I'm hoping is that things cool down around here while I'm away," he muttered vaguely. But then the tension in his face eased, and he smiled fondly at Tori. "I'll pack that sweater you knit for me when you were a kid. Remember?"

Tori threw back her head and laughed. "That brown horror, you mean? Father called it your gorilla sweater because the sleeves hung way down past your knees."

"I still wore it, though."

Tori's eyes filled with warmth. "Not many brothers would be that considerate, Gordon."

He brushed a lock of his sandy hair off his high forehead. "I was proud to wear something my sister made for me." He stood up and stretched his thin body. "Well, I'm off. I'll be back from Vermont by Monday. Tuesday at the latest."

"Where will you be staying?"

"Some little inn or other. Whatever strikes my fancy along the road."

Tori hoped he didn't end up sleeping in his little sports car for lack of a reservation. "I'll walk you out to the front door," she told him, taking his arm.

"No, I'll leave the back way."

"But I want to show you some of the new art on display. You haven't dropped by the gallery for ages," Tori insisted.

Gordon gave her that flat Langford look of his—the one that said No Trespassing. But for once, Tori ignored it.

"Oh, for goodness' sake, Gordon. You can't avoid Ginger for the rest of your life, can you? Whether you like it or not, she not only works here, but she's my closest friend."

"You were raised to be more discriminating about the company you keep, Victoria."

It hadn't been so long ago that Gordon had found Ginger's company highly acceptable, but Tori didn't think it necessary to mention the obvious. "I like Ginger. I always have and always will," she countered simply. "Now come out to the showroom and be civil to her, dear." She tugged at her brother's arm, pulling him down the hall that led to the front of the gallery.

When they entered the showroom Ginger glanced up from the envelopes she was addressing at the counter. "It's been slow so far this morning," she told Tori. "A few gawkers but nobody serious. These invitations to the next show will be ready to mail tonight."

"Good. That should generate some traffic," Tori said. Although Gordon was standing right beside her, Ginger acted as if he were invisible. And Gordon remained as silent as a stone. Tori looked from one to the other but she was the only one making eye contact between them. "Gordon is leaving for Vermont today," she said to keep the conversation going. "Let's hope this fine weather holds up for him."

"The prediction is rain," Ginger stated flatly. "Of course, your brother has a knack for raining on his own parade without any help from the weather."

It appeared Gordon had suddenly turned deaf. He walked right past Ginger without acknowledging either her statement or her presence and showed great interest in a geometric canvas hanging across the room. "My life has been a lot less stormy lately." He appeared to be addressing the painting. "No more silly little plump clouds getting in my way."

"No more silver linings, either, I bet," Ginger said to her long fingernails as she examined them.

"No more stormy scenes. No more messy cloudbursts of emotion," Gordon intoned, still facing the painting rather than Ginger. "The general atmosphere of my life has become a lot more pleasant, believe me."

Ginger snorted to show she certainly did not believe him. "I've never been afraid of storms myself. But some people prefer living in an arid desert with no emotions. I have nothing but pity for people like that."

Gordon pretended a shiver. "How unpleasant the atmosphere's turned again. I think I'll move on to a better climate." He crossed the glossy wood floor to Tori and gave her a peck on the cheek. "I'll be back in a few days, Victoria. If I change my plans I'll call you." He strode out of the gallery without having glanced at Ginger once.

"Can't you two even talk about the weather without quarreling?" Tori asked her friend.

Ginger went back to addressing envelopes with a vengeance. "We could never talk about anything without fighting." She crossed a *t* with a harsh pen slash. "Your brother and I have absolutely nothing in common."

"There was a time when you two seemed to have plenty in common," Tori ventured to say.

"We were mistaken to think we did." Her pen tip poked right through the envelope as she forcefully dotted an *i*. "But why beat a sleeping dog?"

As fractured as Ginger's expressions were, Tori got the message loud and clear. Ginger had no intention of discussing Gordon with her—which was just as well, Tori conceded. She certainly didn't want to be caught right in the middle with allegiance to both parties. She gave her friend a sympathetic smile and went back to tackle the work waiting in her office.

But she could concentrate no better than before Gordon's visit. The stranger's kiss had completely discombobulated her, and she was beginning to resent his intrusion into her thoughts. She didn't like interruptions in her well-ordered life. That's why she directed her passion toward art rather than a lover. Tori much preferred the safe haven of her gallery to the emotional risks that lay beyond in the real world.

Then why in heaven's name had she asked the rude, swaggering jogger to meet her the next morning? Why, indeed! Tori slammed shut her account book in a spurt of irritation. She was annoyed with herself for having started something she wasn't sure she was prepared to finish. There was only one solution to the dilemma: she would take Jiggs for a walk by the Charles River instead of the Garden the next morning. She would never see the jogger again, and her safe, comfortable, predictable life would return to normal. Tori breathed a sigh of relief after making this resolution.

That night, though, she had trouble sleeping. She tossed and turned so much that she disturbed her snoring companion. Mr. Jiggs awoke and began licking Tori's face, as if that would soothe away her troubles. But it wasn't the sloppy affection of her little dog that Tori needed.

Throwing on her white robe edged in eyelet, Tori went down the steep dark back stairway to the kitchen to make herself a cup of warm milk. She was comforted to hear the patter of Jigg's paws close behind her as she felt around in the dark for the light switch. The big house seemed so lonely and gloomy with no one here but herself.

The kitchen was large and outdated, with glass-fronted cabinets and a pantry in back. More than any other room in the house, it was filled with pleasant childhood memories for Tori—not that she remembered her mother ever working in it. Cooks had come and gone, but there had been one who'd been very special. She would sing in a foreign language as she worked and was always giving Tori delicious treats to nibble on. It surprised Tori that she still thought of this woman, since she'd been quite young at the time. She couldn't remember the woman's features, only the wonderful scent of her breads baking and the sound of her cheery songs.

Tori poured some milk in a little pan and heated it on a low flame. She began to have doubts that it would do the trick of calming her. It wasn't insomnia that was keeping her up but rather a surge of extra energy coursing through her bloodstream.

She sipped her hot milk slowly from a thick blue-and-white mug. Jiggs scratched at the back door, and she let him out to the small enclosed garden. She stepped out herself, pulled by the force of the full, glowing moon. Her feet in their embroidered slippers moved silently across the yard.

She paused under the magnolia tree. Its branches were heavy with pink blossoms, and the petals shimmered in the moonlight.

"Why not?" a tiny but persistent voice pleaded deep within her. "Why not meet him in the morning and see what will happen next?"

Her strong-featured face remained immobile, but her heart began to beat faster. She stretched out her arms and sighed. Moonlight poured over her. Yes, she would go to meet him. It appeared that she had no choice in the matter—not if she ever wanted to sleep in peace again.

The aged brick of the Beacon Hill town houses lining the narrow cobblestoned street took on a rosy hue in the morning light. The sky was bright blue and cloudless above their chimneyed rooftops. His leash taut, Jiggs pulled Tori down the steep hill toward the park. She didn't try to slow him down. She was as anxious as he to get there. Anticipation tightened her stomach muscles as each step drew her closer.

She had dressed with special care that morning. She hoped the blue knit she'd chosen would meet with the jogger's approval. She wasn't in the habit of dressing to please a man. But as simple as this dress was, the knit fabric did show off her slender frame to advantage. The neckline, scooped a little lower than most of her clothes, accented her long neck.

As usual, her hair was parted in the middle and pulled back into a glossy, neat chignon. What wasn't so usual was the flamboyant decoration she'd added to it—a magnolia blossom. She'd plucked it from the tree in her garden and on impulse had tucked it into her bun before leaving. Normally she would have felt silly sporting a big flower in her hair. But for the past twenty-four hours she hadn't been acting at all normally.

He wasn't waiting for her by the park bench when she got there. Her large hazel eyes, a trifle anxious, scanned the area. He was nowhere in sight. All the better, Tori told herself; she needed a few minutes to catch her breath. She perched on the edge of the bench and kept Jiggs leashed, not wanting to risk another run-in with the wolfish husky. Tori felt that she was already risking enough by simply showing up.

Because it was a Saturday morning, there were many weekend athletes in the park. From a distance some of them resembled the one Tori was so eagerly expecting, but when she took a closer look she found these other men lacked his special appeal. ·

She didn't mind waiting for him at first. It was another beautiful day, and there was a lot of activity around her. But as the minutes began to add up to almost an hour, Tori's hopeful little smile and high color faded. She knew by then that he wasn't going to keep their date, yet she couldn't make herself stand up and walk away. Then the wind picked up, Jiggs started to moan with impatience and ominous-looking clouds began to drift in.

As if to bring herself out of a trance, Tori shook her head. The magnolia blossom fell from her hair and landed on the ground before her. She noticed it had wilted. So had her hopes of ever seeing the jogger again, she thought, crushing the blossom underfoot. It was obvious to her now that he'd been playing with her, amusing himself at her expense. It must have been difficult for him to contain his laughter when she'd suggested they meet here the next morning. What interest would a man like that have in her?

She stood up and threw her shoulders back. "What an idiot!" she said out loud, not sure if she was referring to herself or him. She walked out of the Garden without looking back, her head high, her step long and determined. Jiggs had to trot to keep up with her. She told herself that the tears burning behind her eyes were tears of relief, not disappointment.

Luckily it was a good day at Back Bay Gallery and Tori found solace in her work. She sold a painting and two pieces of sculpture to an influential collector; was interviewed by a reporter from a small but prestigious art magazine; and, best of all, met with a young artist whose work she thought had great potential. Not a bad day in the end, despite how badly it had started. Yet it didn't give Tori the deep sense of satisfaction it usually did. She was still restless and dissatisfied when it came time to close up shop, and she dreaded going home to that big, empty house. She told Ginger she would stay a little late and catch up on things.

"Not on a Saturday night!" Ginger protested. "Why don't you come along to this hot new night spot called the Fried Frogs' Legs?"

"Ugh!" Tori laughed. "For some reason that doesn't appeal to me, Ginger. And I hope you're not going there alone."

"No, I have a date," she replied with little enthusiasm. "Really a great guy," she added, pushing more energy into her voice. "He's very open with his feelings. And he never criticizes the way I dress or act—unlike some men I've dated who think they're so superior."

"You're referring to Gordon, aren't you? Sometimes he acts that way because he feels insecure, not superior," Tori said, truly believing it.

Ginger smoothed down her clinging magenta dress. "Whatever the reason, the effect is the same. Why'd he take off for Vermont, anyway? Is he visiting anyone special? Not that I could care less, mind you."

Tori heard the absolute need to know in Ginger's voice and wished that she could enlighten her. "Gordon never tells me anything about his private life, Ginger. I simply don't know why he took off on the spur of the moment like that."

"Well, that's par for the court," Ginger said, getting golf and tennis mixed up. "Gordon's too secretive for his own good." Shaking her curly head, she headed for the door. "Don't stay too late tonight," she advised Tori. "There's more to life than Back Bay Gallery, you know."

Tori nodded in agreement, although she wasn't sure there was. "I'll lock up after you. Have a good time tonight, Ginger."

"I'll try," Ginger promised without much optimism in her voice.

As fond as Tori was of Ginger, she was relieved to see her go. She always enjoyed being alone in her gallery. She especially liked it on this particular evening. She needed to bolster her ego by roaming around her showroom and assuring herself that she had something worthwhile in her life. What did it matter that some sweaty jock had stood her up that morning?

She paced the expanse of the showroom floor, now and then straightening a painting or moving a sculpture a few inches on its pedestal. The muscles at the base of her neck were tense, and she couldn't relax. She decided to go to her back office and direct her energy to something useful. A vague but unpleasant uneasiness had come over her. It was almost as if her every move were being observed.

Tori was poring over her account books when she heard the bell above the front door jingle. Realizing that she'd forgotten to lock up, she got up to see who'd come in after closing hours. She was saved the trouble, though. A man barged into her private office before she could leave it. Jiggs shot out of his wicker basket and growled at him. The man kicked at the little dog, just missing him with the tip of his fancy snakeskin shoe. No hero, Jiggs retreated under Tori's desk.

"How dare you try to kick him like that!" Tori cried, fury superseding fear. She'd never laid eyes on the man before.

His smile was as snaky as his shoes. "Sorry, baby. But I'm scared of dogs."

Although she tried not to show it, Tori was afraid of him. He certainly didn't look like an art patron. "We're closed for business," she told him. "Our hours are posted on the door."

"Yeah? Well, the door was open. I didn't break in. And I got some private business to discuss, Miss Langford."

It surprised her that he knew her name. She didn't like that. She didn't like anything about him. Not his mean little smile or his tight black pants or his purple silk shirt. She didn't like the way the shirt was unbuttoned to show off his pale hairy chest and yards of gold chain. She especially didn't like the way he was snapping his gum as he waited for her response.

"What business?" she asked sharply. "I'm sure I don't know you."

"You don't, but your brother Gordon does." Seeing her surprise, his smile twisted wider. "Yeah, me and Gordon are old pals. Matter of fact, he was supposed to meet me today. But he never showed up. I got worried and came looking for him."

"Well, he isn't here, so you'd better leave." Tori didn't believe for a minute that this man was any friend of her brother's. Gordon was very particular about the people with whom he associated.

"Sure, I'll leave." The man's voice was oily with false pleasantness. "Soon as you tell me where I can find him, sis."

"He's out of town."

"Okay. That's a start. Now why don't you narrow it down for me a little more, honey." As if trying to keep himself patient, he began stroking the dark hair on his exposed chest.

Tori noticed that he was wearing a diamond pinkie ring. It was hard not to notice. She'd never seen such a large diamond. But somehow she was certain it was real, as certain as she was that this man meant trouble for her brother. "I have no idea where he is." She raised her sharp chin. "And even if I did, I certainly wouldn't tell you."

Chomping on his gum, the man ruminated over her reply for a long moment. "I decided to believe you, doll.

This must be your lucky day,'' he said. Then he extracted the wad of gum from his mouth and stuck it on top of her Hepplewhite desk.

Tori's eyes filled with horror as she stared down at the gray glob. "Remove that immediately," she ordered, her body rigid with anger and distaste.

"But that's my calling card for Gordie. Don't fancy people like you leave calling cards when they go visiting?" He laughed at his own great wit. "That's to remind him that he's gumming up the works. You make sure you give him that message."

"Get out," Tori said, reaching for the phone with a trembling hand. "Get out or I'll call the police."

He snatched the receiver from her grasp as easily as if he were taking a rattle from a baby. She tried to make a dash for the door, but he grabbed her arm and yanked her back.

"You're not being very nice to me," he complained in a menacing voice. He was so close she could feel his hot breath on her face. "Would it kill you to be a little nice to me, sweetheart?"

Fueled by a rush of repulsion, Tori pushed her hands against his shoulders with all her might and shoved him away. Caught off balance, he backed into the desk and sat down hard on it. As he hissed an obscenity, Tori attempted to make her escape again, but her exit was blocked by another man standing in the doorway. She crashed right into his solid chest.

"What the hell is going on here?" Serge Zhdanov asked.

Chapter Three

It took Tori a moment to realize who he was. She had been picturing him in his brief running outfit all day, not in the conservative pin-striped business suit he was wearing now.

"Need my help, Lady Green Eyes?" he asked in his low, even voice as he took in her frightened face.

Relief flowed through Tori, flooding her heart. She'd never been so happy to see anyone in her life. It didn't matter that he'd stood her up that morning; all that mattered was that he was here at this very moment. She instinctively knew that he was friend, not foe. Somehow she connected with him, as if they'd shared a past together. And at that moment, at least, she trusted him completely. Too stunned to reply, she remained speechless as she unconsciously leaned against him for support.

Serge had no idea what he'd walked into, only that the situation was unpleasant. For all he knew the man sitting on the desk was her lover, and they'd had a spat. But that possibility seemed highly remote. A woman like her simply couldn't be involved with such a sleazy type. Not that he really knew what kind of woman she was. That was part of her fascination to him, the reason he'd come straight from the airport to the gallery. He decided to take control of the situation even though he didn't know what it was exactly. That's what Serge Zhdanov usually decided to do. He was a man who had built a business out of taking control.

His hands pressed protectively against Tori's back as he looked over her head at Purple Shirt. "Seems you've upset this lady," he said almost casually, as if observing the weather. But his light blue eyes were sharp and dangerous.

The snaky smile slid across the other man's lips but wavered under Serge's cold gaze. He raised his palms as if to demonstrate he was unarmed. "Hey, no harm meant, mister. My business isn't even with her but with another party."

Tori caught the elusiveness of his answer. He had made a point of not mentioning Gordon's name. Why? What kind of trouble was Gordon mixed up in? Whatever it was, she didn't want to be the cause of any more. She stepped away from Serge and made an attempt to look as if nothing were amiss. Not trusting the expression in her eyes, she avoided Serge's and turned to the man in the purple shirt.

"Weren't you just about to leave?" she asked him coolly, amazed that her voice was so calm.

Without moving, the man met her stare. He said nothing but his small mean eyes shot back daggers of menace. Serge saw the look too and stepped into the office, closer to Purple Shirt.

"You heard her," he said, looming over the other man and looking as tall as a skyscraper in his gray pin-striped suit. "Get out of here."

Purple Shirt decided that it would be a good idea to comply with this second request but when he made an attempt to stand, Serge pushed him down on the desk again. "You know, I can always spot a bully when I see one," he said in a conversational tone. "Usually they have a big yellow streak running down their back. Now let me see your back, buddy. Just to confirm my theory."

Serge didn't stop him again but allowed him to slink out of the office. Tori didn't see any yellow streak down the back of his silk shirt as he slithered out but she did notice that he was sporting a big glob of gum on the seat of his tight black pants. It must have stuck there when he'd plopped down on her desktop during their brief struggle. The sight of it made her burst into a fit of hysterical giggles that quickly turned into sobs.

Not knowing what to do about it, Serge did the only thing he could do. He took her into his arms and began stroking her slender back to calm her. His fingertips brushed against the softness of her thin knit dress. At that moment he thought her the most delicate, vulnerable creature he'd ever touched. Because of this he almost felt like crying, too.

"Hey, hey, hey," he whispered. "It's okay. He's gone now."

She regained her composure almost as quickly as she'd lost it. But he kept patting her back reassuringly. "Who was that jerk?" he asked gently. "Why did he upset you so much?"

Tori forced herself to leave the solid warmth of his comforting arms. This man was a stranger to her, too, she reminded herself. As much as she was tempted to trust him, she thought it best to say as little as possible. She was sure Gordon was involved in something terribly wrong, and she was worried.

"I don't know who he was, and he upset me because he was so rude," she replied as honestly as she could without being completely truthful.

"Level with me," Serge persisted. "Are you in some kind of trouble? Maybe I could help you." He often helped people in trouble and benefited financially from it when he did. But he wasn't thinking about profit now.

Tori gave him that closed-face look that Langfords were so good at giving. "Thank you for your concern, but it really isn't necessary."

It was as if a blank curtain had descended over her face, Serge thought. He had the impulse to either shake it or kiss it away. He did neither. "Suit yourself," he said easily. Unless she wanted it to be, it was no business of his.

Tori crossed the room and sat behind her desk to put more distance between them. Jiggs shifted to make room for her feet and then rested his fuzzy muzzle on the top of her shoe. His familiar presence comforted Tori, and she felt more in control.

"Tell me," she said. "Why are you here? It can't just be some great coincidence that you strolled into Back Bay Gallery this evening."

Serge sat down, too. He found the ladder-back chair extremely uncomfortable, but it was the only other chair in the room. "Greater coincidences have happened," he replied.

"Sorry, but I don't buy that."

Serge shifted his weight in his hot seat. He was reluctant to admit the truth. "I followed you here yesterday," he confessed. "I wanted to know where I could find you again if you didn't keep our date this morning."

"If *I* didn't keep it?" Tori laughed ruefully. "I ended up sitting on that park bench for nearly an hour in the hope that you'd come."

"You did?" A smile of satisfaction began to ease across Serge's wide mouth, but he contained it and did his best to look apologetic. "There was no way I could make it. I had to fly out to the West Coast on business. I would have called you last night, but you refused to tell me your name, remember?"

He enjoyed reminding her of this. That's what she got for being so coy with him. Not that she was being that way now: how many women would be open enough to admit waiting so long for a man who never showed up?

"You could have called the gallery," she reminded him. "You just told me you followed me here yesterday morning." It was Tori's turn to contain a little self-satisfied smile.

"I was more or less heading in the same direction that you were, anyway," Serge replied a little gruffly. He didn't want her to imagine him chasing after her. Because he hadn't. Not really. He'd simply made sure to keep her in sight after she'd left the park. He was a man who always took precautions. "And the gallery was closed by the time I knew about this trip. I wasn't even sure you worked here."

"Sure enough to chance finding me here tonight, though," Tori commented.

"I was more or less heading in this direction anyway," he said again, then laughed at himself. "Are you glad I did?"

"Yes," she answered simply and gave a shy, hesitant smile. "But why did you?"

Serge wasn't used to having his actions questioned so closely. He stood up and stretched his long frame. He was

restless from all the enforced inactivity he'd had to endure—two cross-country flights in two days. High above
the clouds, he'd spent a lot of time thinking about her. It
had surprised him that she'd been so much on his mind.
He wasn't the sort of man who dwelt on women.

"I'd like to take you out to dinner tonight," he replied,
again in a gruff, rather impatient tone. "What do you
say?"

It wasn't the most graciously stated invitation she'd ever
received, but she couldn't remember when she'd wanted to
accept one more. "I say okay."

He tried not to show how pleased he was. "Even though
we haven't been properly introduced?" It still irked him
that she'd refused to tell him her name in the park.

His sarcasm didn't slip by her. She was well aware that
he thought her too stiff and proper, despite the kiss they'd
shared. She decided it would be fun to play up to this
impression he had of her for a little while longer.

"If you pass my inspection during dinner, I'll do you the
honor of relating my name," she joked. "Just be careful
to pick up the right fork."

He put on a puzzled expression. "Fork? What's a
fork?"

She laughed. She was beginning to like him, which was
a big step beyond her immediate physical attraction to him.
That attraction was a little frightening to her, but his simple humor was comforting. "You could tell me your name,
though," she allowed.

He tried to look affronted but couldn't keep the smile
out of his slanting eyes. "Don't rush me, lady. You've got
to pass inspection, too. A man can't be too careful nowa-
days. Last thing I need is some strange woman hounding
me day and night."

Tori arched her eyebrows. "We are not amused," she said in what she considered a fairly good imitation of old Queen Victoria. "But speaking of hounds, how is your darling Duke? Preying on creatures much smaller than himself, no doubt."

Serge ignored the slur. "Duke's fine, and thank you so much for inquiring." He glanced under the desk. "I see that Mr. Jiggs is as brave as ever. Duke would have shred that guy's purple shirt into ribbons."

"How very civilized of him." Tori replied dryly. She cajoled little Jiggs out from under her desk with a dog biscuit and picked him up. "Jiggs is better than brave: he's loving. I don't expect any more than that."

"You don't? From anyone?"

Tori gave Serge a quizzical look. "I was only talking about my pet. It gets a lot more complicated with people."

"Yeah, especially with women," Serge remarked.

Tori heard the disdain in his voice and didn't care for it one bit. A moment ago she'd thought she liked him, but now she wasn't so sure. But then he flashed his boyish, smile at her, and she couldn't help herself from smiling back.

"Come on," he said. "Let's share a fine dinner together. I promise I'll use a fork instead of my fingers."

"You're on, mister."

She put down Jiggs and after making sure he had fresh water, his chew bone and a night-light to keep him company, she turned on the alarm system and left the gallery with the man she knew nothing about.

But her own personal alarm system was also turned on. She wanted to go very slowly with this man. She wanted to take it one careful step at a time. A little backtracking was in order, to begin with. They'd skipped way ahead of themselves with that first kiss. Knowing how easily he could make her respond to him, Tori was now on guard for his next move. This time he wouldn't catch her by surprise. This time she'd be ready. Ready to accept or reject him? She didn't have the answer to that one yet.

Dusk had fallen. Serge took her by the arm and led her to his car, parked a block away. It was foreign and looked expensive but not ostentatious, a gray sedan gleaming silver under the street lamp. When she slid into the passenger seat Tori breathed in the potent scent of leather, then discovered a pink-tinged rose waiting for her there. She picked it up and inhaled the more delicate fragrance.

"Your cheeks," Serge said, getting in on the other side and turning on the motor.

"What?" She brought her hand to her face.

"That rose. I brought it for you because it's the exact shade of your cheeks when you blush."

He knew women liked corny little gestures like that. Corny as it was, though, it was a sincere one on his part. Rushing out of Logan airport, trying to make up his mind whether or not to track her down at Back Bay Gallery, he'd spotted this particular rose bunched into a container with less perfect ones at a flower stall. The color and texture of the petals did in fact remind him of her complexion after he'd kissed her. It had been the deciding factor that inspired him to go to the gallery.

Tori immediately forgot her prejudice against roses. He'd made this particular one very special to her. She thanked him for it and leaned back into the butter-soft leather seat as they sped off. She didn't ask him where they were going. What did it matter? It was spring, it was Saturday night, and the man beside her was exactly the one she wanted to be there. She hadn't experienced such exhilaration in a very long time. She felt more like seventeen than twenty-seven. She wanted to unpin her hair and shake it loose. She wanted to unbuckle her seat belt and slide across the expanse of leather until her body pressed against his. She did neither.

But she did study his blunt profile through the veil of her lowered lashes. He looked more like a banker than a jock to her now, handsome in a much more conventional way than he had in the Public Garden. His thick dark hair was combed neatly back from his broad brow, and she missed the rumpled look of it. He smelled of shirt starch and lime after-shave instead of sweat and sun. Passing headlights made the simple gold cuff links at his wrists glitter. The jogger she'd been thinking about all day wouldn't have owned a pair of cuff links! She'd imagined him far less civilized. Yet he and this man were one and the same. Beware of wolves in Brooks Brothers clothing, she warned herself.

They headed west, to an area of the city with which Tori was unfamiliar. He turned his car into a side alley and shut off the motor. It was a dark and isolated place to park.

"This is it," he announced. He smiled at her. His strong white teeth glittered in the darkness.

"This is what?" she asked warily. She sat very still, not moving a muscle but unable to prevent her heart from pounding.

Serge could sense how tense she'd suddenly become. Was it possible that she was afraid of him? It disturbed him to think she could be. He wanted her trust, not her fear. He wanted her total compliance. More than that, he wanted her joyful abandon when they finally made love. He'd had a taste of it already when he'd kissed her in the Public Garden and it had whetted his appetite for her. But he wasn't going to rush things. Not again. Somehow, since that first kiss, it had become too important to him.

He reached toward her but only touched her face with one fingertip, sliding it down the petal-soft plane of her cheek to the firmness of her chin. "This is where we get out," he said.

And that's exactly what he did, leaving her sitting alone in the dark as he went around the car to open her door. Tori wasn't sure what she felt more—disappointment or relief. She'd expected him to kiss her. Her dry lips had even parted automatically in anticipation. At the same time her mind was warning her to hold back with him. Unexpected passion in a public park was one thing. But things could get way out of hand in the isolated privacy of his luxurious car. She wasn't sure she was ready for that. Not quite yet, anyway. Luckily or unluckily, he hadn't given her the opportunity to find out if she was.

He took her hand, giving it a friendly squeeze, and they walked out of the alley and down a side street. They stopped in front of a doorway that was painted bright red. A small sign above it proclaimed the place to be Café Mother Russia.

"Ever eaten here?" Serge asked.

"No, never." She'd heard of the restaurant before but rarely dined at places that specialized in ethnic cuisine.

"Then you're in for a treat," Serge promised her. "The first time for anything is always special."

He opened the door, glossy as a candy apple, and Tori walked in, feeling a little like Alice stepping into Wonderland. The unpretentious entrance to the restaurant gave little hint of the old-world splendor within.

Crystal chandeliers floated high above, basking everything beneath them in a golden glow. The walls were draped in gold brocade. The banquettes along them were covered in plush crimson velvet. There were candles on all the round tables draped in white linen; and small cut-glass

vases holding carnations. A fine collection of antique sa-
movars was displayed on an elaborately carved sideboard
in back. The place was busy. The sound of silver clinking
against china, soft laughter and the murmur of intimate
conversation floated Tori's way, along with the heady
aroma of rich food. Tori's stomach began to growl quite
rudely, reminding her that the only thing in it so far that
day had been an English muffin with jam at breakfast.

A pretty young hostess dressed in a white peasant blouse
and gaily printed dirndl skirt greeted them. "What an
honor to have you here this evening, sir," she said.

Tori wondered if she said the same to all the male guests
who entered. But she didn't think so. The look the hostess
was giving her companion was a bit too chummy.

To confirm this, he ruffled her short chestnut hair. An
intimate gesture. Tori experienced a quick jab of jealousy, entirely unexpected. How could she possibly be
jealous over a man when she didn't even know his name
yet?

"Have you saved me a table, Neda?" he asked.

She winked her vivid blue eye. "What would Mother
Russia say if I hadn't? Fifty lashes with her tongue at
least!"

They chuckled together at this private joke and then
Neda showed them to their table at the back. It was the
most private one in the restaurant. She pulled it out to allow Tori to slide across the velvet banquette behind it.
Serge followed her, sitting close enough to press his leg
against hers. Tori very subtly moved her thigh a few inches
away from his—at least she thought she was being subtle
about it.

"Alex will serve you tonight," the hostess informed
them. Apparently this, too, was cause for mirth because

they laughed again while Tori placed the heavy napkin on her lap, not getting the joke.

Alex made his appearance soon enough, and he didn't look especially funny to Tori. He was dressed as any proper waiter should be, black suit and bow tie, white shirt. And he was very handsome; younger than the man sitting beside her, but just as well-built and tall. His hair was dark and thick. His eyes were ice blue, too. The only funny thing about him, Tori thought, was that he and her companion could almost be brothers. But that idea was quickly dispelled when he addressed them so formally.

"We feel truly blessed with your presence here tonight," he said. "I want to thank you. Neda wants to thank you. And most of all Mother Russia wants to thank you."

"Thanks, Alex," Serge said flatly. "Now cut the act short and bring us some champagne."

"Your wish is my command, sir," he said, bowing as he backed away.

"You're certainly a valued customer here," Tori couldn't help but remark. She didn't add that she thought he'd behaved much too abruptly to a waiter so eager to please.

"This place is almost like home to me," Serge told her. He placed his long arm along the edge of the upholstered seat behind her and his eyes roamed her face. "Just as I thought," he concluded. "Your skin soaks up candlelight and then reflects it back even better. Pale women like you look so right in candlelight. At times I think you come from another century."

Tori laughed at that. "They say I'm the image of my great-great-aunt, but I don't take that as much of a compliment. Not only was I named after her, but I had the misfortune of inheriting the same long nose."

"You have an absolutely perfect nose," Serge declared. Taking in her strong profile as she sat beside him, he forgot that he'd considered her nose more than a trifle too long when they'd first met. Now he didn't wish to shorten it by one millimeter or change anything about her appearance. "What was your very-great-aunt's name, by the way?"

"If I told you that, then you'd know mine. We weren't going to exchange names until after this dinner interview, remember?" She liked that part of the game they were playing. It kept them in suspense about the conclusion of the evening.

"Oh, come on," Serge urged. He knew how *he* wanted to conclude the evening. "It's awkward to keep addressing you as Lady Green Eyes."

"I suppose," she agreed. "I don't know why you call me that anyway. My eyes aren't green; they're hazel."

His arm left the banquette and rested lightly around her shoulders. "They're green when you look at me."

She turned to gaze into his face, as if it were a mirror. What she saw reflected back was a smile of admiration.

"My name is Victoria," she told him. At this point it seemed silly not to. His arm felt so right around her.

"It suits you," he said, nodding his approval. "Very proper and old-fashioned."

"But I'm not like that at all," she protested. "I'm a very modern, liberated woman." She truly believed she was. "My friends all call me Tori," she added.

"Tori," he repeated as if tasting it on his tongue. The flavor of it seemed to please him. "Tori," he said again, this time a whisper close to her ear.

His mere breath on her skin made her shiver. She covered it up by shrugging off his arm, which he returned to the edge of the banquette. "What do people call you?" she asked him.

He chuckled. "That depends. But my name is Serge." He stressed the foreign pronunciation.

"I've never met anyone named that before."

"Of course you haven't. I'm one of a kind," he said more or less in jest. "I intend to prove that to you soon enough."

As she lifted her sleek eyebrows in response to his boast Alex returned with champagne in an iced silver bucket. He bowed again, this time even lower, and presented the bottle to Serge so he could examine the label.

Serge nodded. "Mother Russia is pulling out all the stops tonight, I see."

"It's to show her approval." Alex deftly uncorked the bottle and poured the pale effervescence into two tulip-shaped glasses. "All of us here at this humble restaurant approve of your lovely dinner companion, sir."

He left them before Tori could thank him. Not that she understood why a waiter or anyone in this hardly humble restaurant should declare their approval of her—as if she were a bottle of wine or something. Feeling self-conscious, she placed the pink rose she'd carried in with her on the table.

"Why do I get the feeling I'm under inspection here?" she asked Serge.

"Oh, don't pay any attention to Alex." He raised his glass to her.

She picked up hers in response. "What shall we toast?"

"How about your namesake, Aunt Victoria," he suggested.

She liked that and clicked her delicate glass against his. She took a swallow of champagne. It tickled all the way down her throat. "Poor Aunt Victoria," she sighed. "She died of a broken heart, you know."

"Did she?" He couldn't have cared less. He was much more interested in the way Tori's full bottom lip brushed against the rim of the wineglass when she drank.

"Ah, yes." Tori sighed. The champagne went immediately from her empty stomach to her head. "She fell madly in love with her Italian music teacher. He promised to marry her but instead found himself a much wealthier wife. Not a Bostonian, but a nouveau riche New Yorker." Tori wasn't aware of the disdain in her voice; she was simply retelling a family story as it had been told to her.

Her provincial snobbism amused Serge, but he kept his smile at bay. He liked the sound of her voice, as clear as the ring of the crystal glasses, and he wanted to keep her talking. "So she died young, this great-aunt of yours?"

"Actually, she lived well into her eighties."

This time he couldn't keep his smile from curving up. "Her broken heart wasn't terminal, then?"

"In a way it was. I mean it did ruin her life. The day the music teacher left she went up to her bedroom and never came out again."

"Never?"

Tori shook her head emphatically. "Not ever. A special servant had to be hired to take up her food and..." Tori paused. "And empty out her chamber pot and such. None of the others would do it. They thought she was being much too dramatic. But if it was an act, it lasted her entire life. She was carried out on a stretcher and died in the hospital an hour later."

"How pitiful," Serge remarked.

"I find it highly romantic," Tori contradicted.

"Sounds more like hurt pride than a broken heart to me. This aunt of yours must have been a stubborn old fool."

"I imagine her as being very sensitive and fragile," Tori objected.

Serge poured them more champagne. "Do you? Would you give up on men because one love affair turned sour, Tori?"

She shifted uncomfortably. "Things were different in those days," she said, directing the conversation back to the long-ago past. "Victoria's reputation was tarnished, as they used to say. No man from her own set would marry her after that."

"So she preferred living in isolation to marrying beneath her station?" Serge's tone was sardonic. "Then I was right. It was foolish pride that ruined her life."

His know-it-all attitude irritated Tori. It was *her* ancestor they were talking about, not his. "Maybe she didn't want another man in her life. Her affair with the music teacher could have convinced her that passion wasn't all it was cracked up to be."

"You think she found the act of making love such a disappointment?"

Tori shrugged. "Who knows? It could have bored her to tears."

Considering this, Serge toyed with the rose he'd given Tori, which lay between them on the table. "If that's true, I hope you didn't inherit that trait from her, too," he said, caressing the delicate bud. "Do you find sex boring?"

She watched as he stroked the soft petals with his long, strong fingers. She felt the pressure of his thigh against her again but didn't move away this time. She imagined the hard solid muscles of his legs beneath the pin-striped trousers. "I was talking about the other Victoria, not myself," she reminded him.

She hoped he wouldn't pursue the subject, and he didn't have a chance to. Attentive Alex returned to serve them the first course—shimmering blocks of gelatin topped with whipped cream.

"We start with dessert?" Tori asked him, surprised.

"No, ma'am. It's the specialty of the house," Alex began to explain. "It's called *kholodetz*, which is—"

"If she doesn't care for it, I'll order her something else," Serge interrupted, waving the waiter away.

Tori plunged her spoon into the strange dish and tasted it. An unexpected jolt of horseradish caused tears to spring to her eyes. "Interesting," she managed to say. She boldly took another bite. This time she was prepared for the zing of horseradish in the cream. The gelatin, textured with meat, had a tangy, piquant flavor. "It's really very good," she said. "What exactly is it?"

Serge smiled. "Pickled calves' feet."

"Oh." Tori carefully put down her spoon. But then she gave a little shrug, picked it up again, and polished off the rest with obvious pleasure. "What's next?" she asked her dinner companion. "Marinated monkey toes?"

Serge laughed at that. His laugh was really more a deep low chuckle, and Tori was beginning to grow very fond of the sound of it. "We Russians aren't quite that exotic."

Tori smiled her sweet smile. "Too bad. I'm game for anything this evening. I feel very daring and adventuresome." Was that herself talking or the champagne? she wondered.

"I'll remind you of that later," he promised her softly.

The main course was *blini* with red caviar and sour cream. Serge showed Tori how to soak the feather-light buckwheat pancakes in melted butter and then wrap them around the sour cream and glossy amber salmon roe. She'd never tasted anything so delicious.

"I think I've consumed more calories than I usually do in a week," she said after Alex removed the empty plates and carried them away.

"You can afford them," Serge told her, his eyes skimming her slender frame. He wondered now why he'd considered her too thin at first sight. She was elegantly built. Like a clipper ship, he thought. Or a gazelle. He kept these images to himself, though. He wasn't one for overly elaborate compliments.

Tori rested her back against the plush banquette, contentment easing through her. Satiated with rich food and champagne, she was totally relaxed and unguarded. When Serge took up the rose again and brushed the tip of it down the long expanse of her neck, she closed her eyes. The sensation was sweetly thrilling, and she couldn't help but imagine his lips following the same sensuous trail.

"We could have dessert at my place," Serge whispered.

Tori's clear, wide eyes flew open. She didn't want to go back to his place. Not quite yet, anyway. "I'd prefer just a cup of coffee here, if you don't mind," she said a little sharply.

If he did, he didn't show it. He ordered them a pot of coffee and settled back, prepared to sit there with her for as long as she wanted. He was an impatient man by nature but had trained himself long ago to bide his time when going after something he really wanted.

"Do you have any other eccentric relatives besides your Aunt Victoria?" he asked Tori to make idle conversation and put her at ease again.

"Generations of them! But I'd rather hear about some of yours." He was still a complete mystery to her, she realized. She didn't know much more about him than when they'd first met, except for his first name and that he drank his coffee black.

"Sorry, but I don't have any charming little stories about spoiled relatives who required special servants to indulge their silly whims," he said. He noted her frown and also the sarcasm in his own voice. He toned it down. "I really don't know that much about my ancestors. But they were probably serfs before the Russian revolution. There's nothing fancy about my heritage. Most of my relatives work in factories back in the Soviet Union. And when we first came to America, my parents started out as a chauffeur and cook."

Tori found this information fascinating, as she did everything about him. "How old were you when you came to this country?"

"Almost ten." He smiled to himself, remembering. "I fell in love with baseball immediately. I had a passion for it and would listen to all the Red Sox games on the radio that first summer here. Lost my accent completely by trying to imitate the sports announcers."

Tori poured out more strong rich coffee for both of them. "Was it hard for you to adjust?" She tried to picture him as a shy little boy, unsure of himself. She couldn't.

"Not really. Kids take new experiences in stride. Once I started school here I did fine. But that first summer was kind of tough. I had nobody to play with but the son of the people my parents worked for. He was a spoiled brat and took an instant dislike to me. Made fun of the way I talked, the way I dressed. Everything."

Tori's heart fluttered in sympathy. "Children can be cruel."

"I was no saint myself," Serge admitted. "We were always getting into fights, and it caused a lot of friction between his parents and mine. In the end they got fired because of me." He took a sip of coffee. It tasted bitter to him.

"That doesn't sound fair." Tori shifted closer to Serge, automatically siding with him.

"I felt rotten about it for a long time. The last straw was when I hit the little wimp with a baseball and gave him a black eye. Ironically, we were getting along fairly well at the time, and it was a complete accident. But his mother reacted hysterically and threw my parents and me out of her house."

It was like a page right out of Dickens, Tori thought. She imagined his poor mother in a *babushka*, his father in peasant garb, little Serge in rags, with snow falling upon them all. "But where did you go? What did you do?"

"We managed," Serge replied succinctly.

Tori shook her elegant head. "That family your parents worked for must have been awful."

"They weren't all bad, I suppose," Serge allowed graciously. "Just spoiled and shallow. The mother was silly. The father was weak. They had another child, too. The homeliest little baby girl I'd ever seen. But she could barely talk at the time and may have turned out all right. The son, though, grew up to be an even bigger jerk. I ran across him again years later at Harvard."

Tori was having a little difficulty moving her image of a shivering little Serge in rags to the ivy-covered campus of Harvard. Langford men had attended that university for generations.

Serge observed the puzzlement on her face. "I attended on a scholarship," he explained. "My father always told me that this was the land of opportunity, and I was smart enough to believe him."

"Yes, it seems you were smart enough all right," Tori proclaimed. Her cheeks tinged pink in a rush of pride. For him. For America. For Harvard. If there was a flag handy, she would have waved it. Instead she picked up the pink rose and brought it to her cheek. "I'm glad your story has a happy ending, Serge." Saying his name for the first time sent a little thrill up and down her spine. "Luckily your first experience in this country with that dreadful family your parents worked for didn't embitter you."

"Let's just say it didn't cramp my style." It had taken him a long time to get over the guilt of his parents being fired because of him. And at times he still felt burdened by resentment.

He wondered why he'd even brought up the subject with the woman sitting beside him. His fingertips were vibrant with desire to touch her skin. He watched as she unconsciously brought the rose to her lips so that the petals just grazed them. He had the impulse to snatch away the damn flower and cover her mouth with his.

The last time he'd tried that, it had worked. He wasn't about to forget how she'd reacted to his kiss in the Public Garden. But this place was even more public. Eyes more or less the same color as his and just as sharp were observing them. He'd been foolish to bring her to this particular restaurant if what he wanted was intimate privacy. But she was a woman a man liked to show off to the people he cared about. There was a dignity about her, a special sense of self that made Serge proud to be with her.

He spotted a tiny silver-haired lady in black silk and pearls heading toward their table from across the room. Her journey was slow and meandering as she stopped at other tables and chatted with diners. But Serge knew what her goal was and that nothing would stop her from eventually reaching it. There was no way he was going to escape from this restaurant without her getting a closer look at his dinner companion.

"I think I should warn you, Tori. Mother Russia is approaching," he muttered.

"You mean the proprietor of this wonderful place? Why, I'd love to meet her."

"She also happens to be my mother. Make sure you tell her what a perfect gentleman I am." In playful contradiction he caressed her knee under the table.

But he stood up promptly when his mother arrived and leaned down to kiss her on both cheeks. "The *blini* were heaven, Mama."

She straightened his tie. "The closest you'll get to heaven anyway, darling." Her voice had a lilting European accent. "Don't you know it's a sin to avoid your poor family?"

"I'm sorry, but I've been so busy lately. I flew in from California earlier this evening."

"My son, the jet-setter," she said, unimpressed. "And where are your manners, Serge? Did you lose them during your travels, or are you going to introduce me to your friend?"

He suddenly realized that he still didn't know Tori's last name. She realized at the same moment and extended her hand without missing a beat. "How do you do? I'm Victoria Langford."

The older woman's bright blue eyes widened in surprise. She took Tori's hand in both of her soft little ones and squeezed it warmly. "Of course. I see the resemblance now. You have your mother's gentle eyes. Little baby Victoria! I taught you a lullaby in Russian when you were just learning to talk. You were so clever!"

Tori was totally confused, and when she glanced toward Serge for enlightenment she saw a shocked look on his face.

"But this is too wonderful," his mother bubbled. "You cut your baby teeth on my black bread, and now here you are, all grown-up, eating in my restaurant." She turned to her son. "What a delightful surprise, Serge."

"It sure is," he mumbled. He had a strong desire to crawl under the table but remained standing, feeling an awkward fool. He wondered how he could possibly save himself in Tori's eyes, but his mother went on to seal his fate.

"You were much too young to remember us, darling," she told Tori. "But my husband and I worked for your parents many years ago. It was our first employment in America and we were very grateful. This calls for a toast. Tell Alex to bring more champagne, Serge. And have Neda join us, too." She beamed back at Tori. "My other two children. Both born in this country," she explained proudly.

Serge quickly took in Tori's face and saw a dawning in it. Her hazel eyes didn't look so gentle to him as they bored into his, shooting out lasers of green rage. "We can't stay a minute longer, Mama," he said in a tight voice.

"Of course you can," Mrs. Zhdanov insisted.

"I'm so sorry but we can't," Tori said, standing up, too. She forced a polite smile. "It was a fabulous meal. One I'll never forget. Thank you."

"Well, if you must go, you must," the older woman conceded. "Perhaps we can get together over tea someday soon. I want to hear all about your family."

"That would be nice," Tori said, meaning it. She liked Serge's mother very much. But she was sure they would never get together, since she had no intention of ever seeing Serge again.

She allowed him to take her arm and guide her out of the restaurant. Before she left she thanked his brother Alex for waiting on them with such elaborate attention, and she also expressed her thanks to the hostess, his sister Neda. But once outside, alone with Serge, she let her anger break through her veneer of politeness, and she yanked her arm from his grip.

"Goodbye. I'll take a taxi home," she said through clenched teeth as she hurried up the street, away from him.

Except he wouldn't let her get away from him and kept pace. "Listen, I'm terribly, terribly sorry, Tori. I would never have said what I did about your family if I'd known you were a Langford."

"Then I would have never known how much you despised them. My mother was *not* shallow. My father was *not* weak. And my brother is *not* a jerk. Lies! All vicious lies!" She left out his description of her as the homeliest baby he'd ever seen, but that hurt, too. She was near tears but much too furious to cry.

He wasn't about to retract what he'd said because he'd spoken the truth as he'd known it. And as bad as he felt about hurting her feelings so unknowingly, he was also having a little difficulty overcoming his prejudice against her for being a Langford. But the fact remained that he was still attracted to her; and that he liked her. He wasn't going to let her go storming off into the night and out of his life.

"Let me drive you home," he said. "Please," he added. It was a word he rarely used.

"Get lost," she replied. She'd never said that to anyone before. She stopped at the corner and watched the traffic go by, hoping to spot a cab.

He waited in silence with her, a stubborn set to his strong Slavic face. He noticed that she was shivering in the cool night air, perhaps with rage, and he took off his suit jacket and draped it over her shoulders. She wrenched it off and tossed it onto the pavement. It was such a strong gesture of rejection that it surprised them both. She saw the stunned look of hurt in his face and was about to apologize. But then she remembered how much he'd hurt her. When she ran across the street toward a taxi stopped at a red light, he made no attempt to detain her.

He picked up his custom-tailored jacket, brushed it off, slung it over his shoulder and marched to his car. The hell with her, he thought. She was a Langford, all right—spoiled and superior and disdainful. If he never saw her again it would be too soon.

He drove back to his apartment on automatic pilot. At least that's where he'd intended to go. But somehow he ended up back on Newbury Street. A taxi was waiting in front of Back Bay Gallery. He figured she was inside, picking up her dumb little pooch before going home. He parked behind the cab, gave the driver fifty bucks to beat it, and waited for her to come out. He had absolutely no idea how he was going to patch things up with her or why he wanted to so much.

Chapter Four

Tori waited in the shadows of the gallery for Jiggs to respond to her call. It usually took him a matter of seconds to hurry to her and leap into her arms. But he was apparently deep in sleep and hadn't heard her.

"Mr. Jiggs!" Tori called again. "Wake up and come here. The taxi meter's running." As if that mattered to him, she thought.

She began to be concerned when he still didn't respond. As she headed to her back office to get the reluctant spaniel, she bumped into a Plexiglas pedestal in the gloom of the showroom and just managed to catch the sculpture displayed on it before it crashed to the floor. She swore under her breath, still bristling from her encounter with Serge Zhdanov. Spiteful man!—to talk about her family that way! She'd actually begun to like him, too. Tori shook her head over her lack of good judgment concerning him as she entered her office.

Jiggs wasn't curled up asleep in his wicker basket as she'd expected. She hurriedly looked around—under the desk, behind the file cabinet, then under the desk again because there was nowhere else to look. It wasn't like Mr. Jiggs to play hide-and-seek with her. He usually greeted her with boundless enthusiasm the moment she came back into his life. Tori began to sense that something was terribly wrong.

And then she saw it—a note propped up in Jigg's bed. It had escaped her notice before. She snatched it up and the harsh, ugly scrawl blurred in front of her eyes. She took a deep breath to calm herself. But her mind seemed to have frozen up in fear and she had to read the note twice before it finally sank in: her little spaniel had been dognapped.

Tori grabbed onto the edge of the desk to steady herself. Her heart was pounding, a cold sweat encased her, and there was a thunderous hammering in her head. She was sure that she was going to pass out, but miraculously she didn't. She'd never felt so completely alone in her life. The note had warned her not to notify the police. The instructions were to go home and wait for a call. Tori felt she had no choice but to do exactly that.

Already in a state of shock, she got another when she went out the front door of the gallery. Serge Zhdanov was leaning against the side of his Mercedes, arms folded, waiting for her. Her taxi was gone.

For one mad instant Tori thought that he was somehow responsible for her dog's disappearance. But of course that was impossible. They'd been together all evening. And as much as she wanted to dislike Serge for his slander against her family, Tori sensed that he wasn't the sort of man to play cruel jokes.

He gave her a tentative smile and his white teeth flashed under the glow of the street lamp. "Seems I've gotten into the bad habit of following you around, lady," he said in his calm, gravelly voice. Then he noticed how distraught she looked. Her face was chalk white; her glazed eyes expressed horror. "Hell, I can't be that disgusting, Tori. Can't you forget what I said about your family?"

"It's my dog," she managed to get out.

"Hey, I didn't say a word against the pooch all evening, as I recall. Go back in and get him. I'll take you both home."

Tori ran down the brick gallery steps to Serge and clutched his arm as if for strength. "Jiggs is gone! Here, read this!" She shoved the crumpled note under his nose.

"Jiggs ran away and left you a note?" Maybe she really was a bit eccentric, Serge thought. Hadn't she mentioned that it ran in her blue-blooded family?

Tori gripped his arm even harder, her fingers digging into the hard muscle beneath the cloth. "This isn't a joke, Serge. You're the only one I can turn to now."

When Serge heard the desperation in her voice, his smile faded. He held the note under the light of the street lamp and read it.

"But this is crazy," he said. "We've got to call the police immediately."

"No!" Tori cried. Her expression was frantic. "I can't risk it. The note says that—" She stifled a sob, horrified at the thought of Jiggs being tossed into the Charles River.

Serge took her into his arms for the second time that night. "Okay, okay, we won't call the cops," he promised. He didn't think that the Boston Police Department would drop everything to investigate a dog theft anyway. No, he would have to handle this. "Tell me, Tori. Do you have any enemies? Anyone who would do this to you out of spite?''

She pressed her cheek against his solid chest. ''Not that I know of.''

''What about some rejected lover?'' Serge persisted. ''Or maybe a jealous one? Or one who took the relationship more seriously than you did?''

Tori looked up at Serge. ''Good Lord, you make me sound like Heartbreak Hannah! I don't lead men on, Serge. And the history of my love life is a lot briefer than that list of suspects you just rattled off.''

Serge was not unhappy to hear it. ''We'll forget motives for a while. Was anything else taken besides the dog? And how'd the thief get in? Was it forced entry?''

Tori pressed her fingertips to her spinning head. ''Stop shooting all these questions at me. All I noticed was that Jiggs was gone.''

''Come on,'' he said, taking her by the arm. ''Let's return to the scene of the crime and investigate. Maybe the perpetrator left some clues.'' He'd always wanted the opportunity to use such phrases and considered this the perfect one.

Tori tossed him a reproachful look. ''Do you think this is fun and games, Mr. Zhdanov? Or that you're Sherlock Holmes?''

He saw the pain in her face, pain he was adding to with his flip attitude, and experienced a deep, immediate regret. ''Sorry, Tori. I got carried away. I do want to help you, though. Will you let me?''

It was past midnight, and Tori looked up and down the street. Not a soul was in sight. ''Do I have any choice? You're the only one around. Even my taxi's disappeared.''

''Thanks for the vote of confidence,'' Serge muttered.

They went back inside the gallery, and while Tori took a quick inventory of the art on display, finding nothing missing, Serge tried to discover how the thief got in without setting off the alarm system. Walking down the long hall, he spotted something shiny on the floor and picked it up. It was only a foil gum wrapper, which Serge absently put in his pocket.

He was in her office, checking out the window there, when Tori joined him. "All the windows are wired to the alarm," she said. "Gordon designed the system. It's foolproof."

"Not if a fool designed it, it isn't," Serge commented dryly.

"I happen to have a very high regard for my brother, and I'd prefer that you keep remarks of that sort to yourself, Mr. Zhdanov," Tori told him in a high voice.

Melodic as it usually was, her voice grated on him at that moment because she was using it to defend Gordon, whom Serge had absolutely no regard for. He was about to come back with another sarcastic remark, but discovered that he didn't have to. In fact what he'd discovered was that the window connectors were faulty. He pointed this out to Tori with a certain degree of satisfaction.

She examined the evidence briefly. "Well, that doesn't mean the design of the system was faulty," she insisted. "Only the installation, with which Gordon had nothing to do."

She would come to her brother's defense no matter what, Serge realized. It had most likely become an ingrained habit with her since he was sure Gordon needed a lot of defending.

"It doesn't really matter where the blame lies," Serge said in his most generous manner. "This is how the thief got in to snatch Jiggs, and that, little lady, is the bottom line. Now what?''

''The instructions were to wait at home for a call,'' Tori replied in a shaky voice.

''Mind if I take you home and wait with you?''

Mind? The last thing Tori wanted was to be alone at a time like this. And despite her reservations about the man, Serge Zhdanov was the person she most wanted by her side right now. There was something about his physical presence that gave her a sense of safety—of security. False as it might be, it was still comforting.

''I'd very much appreciate it,'' she replied, her hazel-green eyes welling with gratitude.

Serge touched her face in a brief, tender caress, his fingertips stroking her cheek. ''Don't worry. I'll see this through with you, honey.''

Although Tori didn't usually care for such endearments from men she barely knew, Serge's low, deep voice was so comforting that she had the sensation of sweet, thick honey melting deep within her when he said the word.

Tea! Serge shook his head over Tori's impulse to brew a pot of it during such a crisis. But she'd claimed it would help her relax and had gone off to the kitchen. Not a tea lover himself, Serge could have a suggested a few better ways to get Tori's mind off her problems. But he hadn't. He was determined not to take advantage of the situation or to take advantage of her. At the same time, he wanted her more than ever. Decency and desire warred within him.

He roamed around the large front parlor as he waited for Tori to return. If the circumstances had been more pleasant, it would have amused Serge to be a guest in the house where his parents had once been servants. He'd never been allowed in the front parlor as a boy. His mother had forbidden it, no doubt on instructions from the aloof Mrs. Langford. Mrs. Zhdanov had warned her son that any one of the antiques in the room was worth more than his parents made in a year. That hadn't seemed right to the boy. He concluded that either his parents were terribly underpaid, or all the old stuff in the room was vastly overrated.

Serge remembered the room as cluttered but elegant. Now it seemed rather bare to him. And a little shabby. The wallpaper, patterned in fleurs-de-lis, was faded, and the swags of gold silk above the tall windows looked tired. There were cracks in the high ceiling and even a few rust stains from faulty plumbing above. Much of the furniture was gone, and so were all the fancy bibelots Serge had been cautioned not to touch as a boy. It appeared that the Langfords had fallen upon hard times.

On the drive to the house from Newbury Street, Tori had told Serge about her parents' fatal boating accident fourteen years ago. He wondered why she continued to live in this drafty old house with her brother. She'd mentioned that Gordon was off on a vacation somewhere. Serge was relieved that he wouldn't have to put up with his company.

He walked over to the far wall and studied the collection of portraits hanging there—a gaggle of Langford ancestors, he surmised, taking in their rigid poses and stiff upper lips. He winked at one especially dour old lady in a high-necked black dress.

"Hey, baby. Wanna have a good time?" he asked the hatchet-faced image.

"I doubt she'll take you up on the offer," Tori said, laughing as she entered the room with a tea tray. "That's poor Aunt Victoria, the one I told you about at dinner."

She glanced around the room for a place to set down the tray. Then she remembered that Gordon had sold the tea table to an antique dealer a few weeks before, so she put the tray down on the worn Oriental rug in front of the fireplace. The dealer had expressed great interest in the rug, too, and he and Gordon were still negotiating over it.

Serge was still studying the portrait. "You may have her name, but you don't look a bit like her," he stated firmly. "She has small eyes and no chin!"

"The nose," Tori explained, tapping her own with her index finger. "The indelible imprint of generations of Langford women. Oddly enough, none of the men seemed to be cursed with it. My father had a short nose. And so does Gordon."

Serge crossed the room to her and gave her a hug. "You were blessed, not cursed with that elegant proboscis, my little chickadee," he said in a fairly bad imitation of W.C. Fields. He kissed the tip of it.

Fully intending to laugh, Tori began to cry instead. "Poor Jiggs," she choked out. "We've never spent the night apart. He must be terrified."

Sighing, Serge pressed her closer against him. Unable to think of anything comforting to say at the moment, he rocked her back and forth in his arms. He had doubts that she'd ever see her fluffy little mutt again, but that was the last thing he was going to tell her. He offered her his handkerchief.

It was of the finest linen, Tori noticed as she dried her eyes with it. "It doesn't make any sense that anyone would steal Mr. Jiggs," she sniffed.

"Why not for ransom?" Serge asked. "Dognappers have always preyed on the rich."

"I'm hardly rich," Tori told him. "Gordon and I barely manage to maintain this house. And our father had to struggle to keep up appearances because Grandfather lost a great deal in the stock-market crash. There hasn't been much money in the Langford family for years.''

Serge had already guessed that, figuring that they'd been selling off all the antiques just to make ends meet. ''Whoever stole your dog may not know that,'' he pointed out. ''We'll just have to sit tight and wait for the call to find out what the creep wants.'' He took off his jacket and loosened his striped silk tie. ''It may be a long night, honey.''

Tori picked up the jacket he'd casually thrown on the faded brocade sofa and folded it neatly so it wouldn't get wrinkled. She took pleasure in doing this for him. ''Let's have the tea before it gets cold,'' she suggested, gesturing toward the tray she'd placed on the rug.

''Ah, picnic-style,'' he said, tossing two sofa cushions on the rug. He plopped down on one and patted the other. ''Just place that cute little behind of yours right here, my lady.''

She couldn't help but smile and joined him on the floor, her long legs folded sideways and properly under the skirt of her blue knit dress. ''I'd be going mad with worry by now if you weren't here, Serge. Why doesn't Jiggs's abductor call!''

''He will, he will,'' Serge assured her softly, reaching for her hand. ''Your fingers are as cold as icicles,'' he observed, bringing her hand to his mouth and blowing on it.

Her slender fingers curled under the warmth of his breath. ''It's always chilly in the front parlor,'' she said as casually as she could while his sweet breath blew straight to her heart.

''I know how to warm you up, honey,'' he told her in his low gruff voice.

"Yes, I'm sure you do, Serge," she agreed. "But this isn't the time or place. I can't concentrate on anything but that expected phone call." He should realize that without my telling him, she thought with disappointment.

"Then it's the perfect time and place for a cozy fire," Serge told her. "It'll relax you."

Tori reddened, knowing that he'd led her on deliberately just to tease her. But then she laughed, her tension abating. "Yes, of course. That's what I thought you meant."

There were logs already in place in the hearth of the marble fireplace, and Serge had no trouble getting it started. Tori noticed that the flickering glow brought out golden highlights in his dark chestnut hair. She found this fascinating, but managed to remember her duties as hostess.

"How do you like your tea, Serge?" she asked, raising the pear-shaped silver teapot.

In fact Serge didn't like tea at all. He picked up his cup and saucer reluctantly. The white bone china was so translucent that it took on a rosy luster in the firelight. So did Tori's porcelain skin, Serge observed. She had the sort of complexion that seemed absolutely poreless. It amazed him how she continued to grow more and more beautiful right before his eyes. Was she actually casting a spell on him? Maybe some of her long-ago relatives had been witches, and she'd inherited their power along with that distinctive nose of hers.

"How do you take your tea?" Tori asked again, wondering where his thoughts had wandered. "Cream or lemon?"

"Oh, I don't care."

Tori put down the silver pot without pouring. "You don't care for tea very much, do you? Would you prefer some sherry?"

Serge made a wry face. "Only over tea, lady. I don't suppose you have any brandy around?"

"Yes, of course. I'll get it for you."

Serge placed his big hand on her slender shoulder. "No, don't get up. Just tell me where it is, and I'll get it myself."

"In my father's study." Tori felt a sad little tug at her heart. "Well, it's Gordon's study now."

"I remember where it is," Serge said. "I'll be back in a minute."

Serge went down the long, dim hall that led to the back of the big house and paused before a heavy oak door. He had the impulse to knock before opening it. "You must never, ever bother Mr. Langford," he remembered his mother enjoining him. "He's a very private gentleman, a history scholar."

Well, the sad truth was that there'd be no disturbing Mr. Langford anymore, Serge thought, throwing open the study door. He pulled the metal chain of the Tiffany lamp on the library table. The book-lined room took on a dusky illumination.

It hadn't changed much since he was a boy, Serge noted with pleasure. He'd always been most fond of this room and would sneak into it when Mr. Langford was away to read the books, and to observe the trappings of a real Boston gentleman. Mr. Langford's pipes were still on the smoking table, collecting dust. The old etching of sailboats still decorated the oak-paneled walls. And the leather wing chair was still positioned near the fireplace. The winecolored leather was worn and cracked with age.

Serge glanced around the room, recalling how impressed he'd once been of it. It, too, seemed rather shabby to him now. But still impressive. Tori's father had been a vague sort of man, always lost in his own thoughts. What Serge had taken as weakness as a boy he could now understand as intellectual preoccupation. The world around Mr. Langford had probably been less interesting to him than the historic events in his head.

There was a photograph of him on the bulky slant-top desk, sucking on his pipe, looking as distracted as Serge remembered him. "I'm back, sir," he said aloud to it. "I've come back for your daughter. I'm determined to have her."

Feeling a bit foolish after stating this to a photograph, Serge picked up the cut-glass brandy decanter and two crystal glasses from the library table.

Tori was gazing deeply into the fire when Serge came back to the parlor. Her smile was wan, her eyes glistening with contained tears when she looked up at him. "I was just thinking how nice it would be to have Jiggs curled asleep in my lap right now," she said.

"He'll be back," Serge promised softly, and because he'd stated it he resolved to do any and everything in his power to make it come true. After placing the brandy and glasses on the marble mantelshelf, he rejoined her on the floor, moving his cushion much closer to hers. "In the meantime, why don't you come curl yourself in *my* lap, honey."

"I'm not a little girl in need of comforting, Serge," she replied, despite her aching need for it right then—or perhaps because of it.

He put his big strong arm around her anyway. "Come on, rest your head on my shoulder," he urged.

She did, rather tentatively at first, but then she relaxed under his soothing strokes up and down her back. Tori couldn't remember the last time she'd been cuddled and held like that. Then Serge began humming a tune, his deep baritone vibrating into the ear she had pressed against his chest.

"I know that song," she murmured, eyes half closed.

"I doubt it," he said. "It's a Russian lullaby."

The words came back to Tori in a rush of childhood memories, and she sang them.

Serge was a little taken aback. "Well, the accent is a bit off. But you got the lyrics right, more or less," he admitted. "Don't tell me you were Catherine the Great in another life."

"Your mother taught me that song when I was a baby," Tori explained to him. "What do the words mean? I've always wondered."

Serge laughed, and the deep sound of that vibrated in her ear, too. "It's just nonsense," he said. "About a wolf who gets lonely in the tundra and goes to a village to find a mate."

"And does he succeed?" Tori wanted to know.

"No. Everyone there is much too civilized for him. Or rather, he's not civilized enough. The townspeople end up driving him out by stoning him, doing great damage to his pride."

Tori was disappointed. "I always assumed that it was such a cheerful little song."

Serge patted her back. "Don't worry, honey. There's a happy ending. Alone and miserable on the tundra again, the wolf lets out a plangent howl. And lo and behold, a she-wolf responds! They seek each other out and live happily ever after."

"Lovely," Tori said with a sigh. "I suppose the song's message is that you have to openly express your need for love in order to find it. If he hadn't howled, she wouldn't have responded."

"Maybe." Serge's voice held doubt in it. "I always thought the moral was to stay in your own territory to avoid being hurt and humiliated."

"That's a totally unromantic interpretation," Tori objected.

Serge shrugged. "I'm not a romantic. I'm a realist. Besides, a simple peasant ditty isn't meant to be deeply analyzed. It amazes me that you actually remember it, Tori."

"That's about all I do remember of that time you and your parents were here. I don't remember you at all, Serge."

"That's because I completely avoided you," he admitted. "Ten-year-old boys don't go out of their way to seek the company of blubbering baby girls, you know."

"Especially exceedingly homely ones," Tori reminded him.

He pressed her head closer to his chest before she could raise it. "How was I to know you'd grow up to be such a beauty? Or maybe my memory is wrong and you were always this beautiful, Miss Langford."

His compliment appeased her somewhat. "I think your memory is more off concerning my parents. They were gentle people, Serge. They would never intentionally hurt anyone."

"How can a boy judge adults?" Serge asked, more or less conceding. The past was over and done with, her parents were gone, and he saw no sense in hurting Tori.

"And my brother Gordon," Tori pressed on. "You remember him all wrong, too."

That was a bit too much for Serge. He wasn't going to back down on his opinion of Gordon Langford. "I got to know your brother as an adult. We were on the same crew team at Harvard. And I'm not going to change my mind about him no matter how attractive his sister is."

"But he's not a jerk," Tori insisted.

Serge sighed. "Listen, Tori. I don't like your brother, and he doesn't like me. Let's just drop the subject, okay?"

She sat up straight and faced him. "No, it's not okay. I'm sure you can't give me one good reason for disliking Gordon."

She'd taken on that haughty tone of hers, the one Serge found so irritating. "I could give you a hundred reasons," he told her. "For starters, he's a snob without any reason to feel superior. Being a Langford doesn't make him any less an idiot."

Blood rose to Tori's cheeks. "Gordon happens to be a genius."

Serge didn't hold back his derisive laugh. "The only genius Gordon has is for avoiding work. I bet you support him, Tori."

His guess was close enough to the truth to make her flinch. It had been a long time since Gordon had contributed to the household expenses. One of the reasons Tori still lived with him was because she feared he couldn't manage without her support and would be too proud to take money from her if she moved out.

The house had been passed down to him, the male heir, in the Langford tradition, and Tori had inherited enough money to start the gallery. As far as they were both concerned, what was his was hers and vice versa. Not that she and Gordon had ever really discussed finances; it was a subject they avoided, making Tori even more reluctant to discuss it with an outsider.

"That's absolutely none of your business," she told Serge.

He nodded. "You're right. None of this is my business. I certainly had no intention of getting involved with the Langford family again."

"Then leave!" Tori suggested hotly.

Serge almost took her up on it. But his temper cooled when he saw the apprehension in her hazel-green eyes. "You can't get rid of me that easily," he told her gruffly, not budging.

Relief coursed through her. "That's the last thing I want to do," she told him, touching his hand lightly. How warm and solid it felt beneath hers. "I'm sorry I was so sharp, Serge. I had no right to be. I asked for your opinion of my brother, and you gave it to me. I appreciate your honesty even though I don't agree with you."

Spoken like a true lady, Serge thought. "There's one more thing I have to say. And you're not going to either appreciate or agree with it, Tori."

"What is it?" She tensed.

"I think your brother had something to do with your dog's disappearance."

"No! That's impossible. Gordon would never do anything to hurt me."

"Maybe not intentionally. But I think he's gotten himself into some kind of trouble." Serge rested his big hands on her shoulders and looked her straight in the eye. "Who was that sleazy character in your office tonight, Tori? He was there looking for Gordon, wasn't he?"

Tori turned away from his incisive ice-blue glaze. "I can't discuss that with you."

He gave her an impatient little shake before releasing her. "You're going to have to learn to trust me, honey. I'm the only friend you've got right now."

"Are you my friend, Serge? Or my brother's enemy?"

Before he could reply, the phone rang.

Chapter Five

Tori and Serge ran out to the foyer where the shrilling telephone sat on a wobbly Sheraton table. Serge reached it first.

"Don't you dare pick it up," Tori enjoined. "I have to handle this."

Never able to pass up a dare, Serge did pick up the receiver, but he handed it to Tori without speaking into it. She grabbed it from him impatiently.

"Langford residence," she said, her voice high with tension.

"Hey, baby. How ya doin? I got your little dog here with me."

Tori's throat closed, and she was unable to speak for a moment. There was no mistaking that oily voice: it was Purple Shirt. He snapped his gum as he waited for her response.

She swallowed hard. "Please don't hurt him," she begged.

"Hurt the little fuzz ball? I wouldn't do that," he replied, as if deeply offended by such a suggestion. "Not unless I have to, anyway."

"Why did you do this? What do you want?" she cried. She was on the edge of losing control.

"You don't have to shout. My hearing's twenty-twenty," Purple Shirt replied. "I want you to tell me where your brother is, that's all."

Tears of frustration sprang to Tori's eyes. "I told you I don't *know* where he is. You've got to believe me."

"I don't gotta do nothin'. You know that your fuzz ball shed all over my shirt? That's very irritating. I could lose patience any minute now."

Tori gripped the receiver tighter, trying to keep a hold on her own sanity. "You want money, don't you?"

"Bingo! I want what Gordie owes me, and I want it fast. If he won't choke it up, then you better, sis. Or else I choke your little beastie."

Tori swayed but Serge was right behind her and gripped her shoulders to steady her. "I'll give you all the money I have," she told Purple Shirt.

"Hey, you're missing the point." He took on an offended tone again. "I only want what's due me, sis. What your brother borrowed and never bothered to pay back. If he wanted charity, he shoulda gone to the Salvation Army. I got a business to run. I got my own debts to pay out. I got my reputation at sta—"

"How much?" Tori shouted. Her knuckles turned white as she strangled the receiver, wishing with all her heart it was Purple Shirt's throat.

"It's so *rude* to interrupt, baby doll." He sighed over her lack of manners. "Like I was saying, I got my reputation at stake here. I got bets to cover Monday. I can't have my customers going around saying Ulger skunked them, can I?" His voice was a grating whine.

She would have to humor him, she realized, and directed all her energy into being patient. "No, you can't have that, Mr. Vulgar," she replied politely.

"The name is Ulger. And it's my first name. You think I'm stupid enough to tell you my last, sis? I'll tell you who's stupid. Your brother's stoo-o-pid." He drawled it out. "If he just showed up like he was suppose to with the ten grand he owes, I wouldn't have fur all over my clothes now. You think I wanted to borrow your dog, girlie? No way! I'm a cat person, myself."

"My brother owes you ten thousand dollars?"

Ulger sniffed. "That's the interest he owes me anyway. And that's how much it's going to cost you to see your little fuzz ball again."

Tori turned to Serge, her face stricken. Hearing her end of the conversation, he understood the situation. "Stall," he whispered. "But promise him the money."

Finding the strength she needed in Serge's steely blue eyes, Tori quickly pulled herself together. "I don't have that kind of money lying around the house," she told Ulger. "I'll withdraw it from my bank account Monday morning."

"You got till then, sis. I'll be in touch to arrange an exchange. But if I don't get the money Monday, your dog ain't never gonna wag his tail again." With that he hung up.

Tori replaced the receiver with a trembling hand and pressed her back against the wall for support. She began sliding down it as her legs gave out on her.

Serge caught her by the waist before she sank to the floor. "Are you going to faint?" he asked in a worried tone.

She shook her head, but she wasn't really sure. She'd never fainted before in her life. Everything around her was spinning, and she clung to Serge to keep her balance.

Not knowing what else to do, he acted instinctively and kissed her blood-drained lips, as if his warmth could make the color return to them. Tori responded without thinking, deepening the kiss with an urgent demand. She didn't want to think. She wanted to lose herself in mindless sensation. She wanted to take all Serge could give her at this moment. Her lips devoured his, and her frigid fear began to melt in the heat of their embrace.

But it was wrong to use Serge like a drug to blot out reality, her conscience warned. He deserved better than that. She stopped clinging to him and pulled away, determined to stand on her own two feet.

"I'm all right now," she said, not quite meeting his eyes.

It took a great deal of effort, but Serge reined in the desire she'd sent racing through him. He was still determined not to take advantage of the situation. He'd claim her later, when the time was right. His only satisfaction now was that the color had returned to her lips and face. Indeed, she looked slightly flushed.

"Would you like some brandy?" he asked, gently taking her arm and leading her back to the parlor.

"No, thank you. I need to keep a clear head now." She reminded herself that she'd almost lost it completely a moment ago. She was grateful Serge hadn't protested when she'd abruptly withdrawn from their embrace. He really was a gentleman, she thought. Perhaps the first true one she'd ever known. Aside from her father and brother, that is.

They sat together on the sagging Chippendale sofa. Serge shifted uncomfortably. Did it still have its original stuffing of horsehair? he wondered. "Did you recognize the caller's voice?" he asked.

She nodded. "You were right. It was the man in the purple shirt. He told me his first name was Ulger."

"I was right about Gordon's involvement in this, too, wasn't I?" Serge pressed.

Tori sighed and nodded again. It was futile to keep back anything from Serge now that he'd overheard so much. Besides, she was more and more inclined to trust him. "Ulger claims Gordon owes him money, but I don't see how that's possible. My brother wouldn't deal with a person like that."

"Maybe he was forced to. It could be a gambling debt. It could even be drugs. Or this Ulger creep could be blackmailing Gordon." Serge was of the opinion that an idiot like Gordon could have gotten himself into all kinds of messes.

Apparently Tori didn't hold this same opinion because her strong Langford chin shot up defensively. "My brother would never do anything illicit. He doesn't gamble, and he certainly doesn't use drugs. He rarely even drinks. And as far as blackmail is concerned, why, that's absurd! Gordon has always led an exemplary life."

Serge ran a hand through his thick hair impatiently. "Maybe we should set up a shrine for Saint Gordon."

Tori already had—in her heart. She would always be thankful to her brother for taking care of her after they lost their parents. "Your sarcasm isn't helping the situation one little bit," she told Serge.

"You're right," he conceded. "Let's get down to the nitty-gritty of the problem. Do you have the money to pay the dognapper or not?"

Tori shook her head. "I was bluffing about that. But I'm sure I could raise it with enough time."

"Didn't you agree to pay this Ulger by Monday morning?"

"What else could I do?" The grandfather clock in the foyer chimed twice, as if to remind her that it was already Sunday and time was running out. Panic flickered in Tori's eyes as she looked at Serge.

"Don't worry about the money. I'll give it to you," he said brusquely.

"Are you serious?" Tori was completely taken aback. "But we hardly know each other."

That was true enough, and Serge asked himself if he'd suddenly lost his head. He didn't go around offering large sums of money to women because he happened to like the way their eyes changed color. But he'd never met one whose did until Tori.

He got up and walked to the mantel, where he'd left the brandy decanter. So maybe he *had* lost his head, he thought, pouring himself a shot. "Yeah, I'm serious," he told Tori. "I'll give you ten thousand dollars as soon as the banks open Monday." He swallowed the brandy.

"I'll only accept it as a loan," Tori insisted.

"Hell, no." He shrugged. "I was thinking of making a big donation to some animal shelter anyway."

Tori stood up and folded her arms across her chest. "I'm not some charity case you write off on your tax return," she informed Serge stiffly. "I won't take a handout from you."

Serge didn't want to waste time arguing about it. "Okay, okay, a loan," he agreed impatiently. "But there's one condition."

"Which is?" Tori became uneasy.

"Let's try to find your dog before Ulger's deadline. Let's do our best to outsmart the little creep."

"It's a deal," Tori agreed heartily, offering her hand. "There's nothing I'd like better."

Serge pressed her small hand between his large ones, pleased by her spunky attitude. "The first thing we have to do is track down Gordon. He's the key to the whole puzzle."

"I'm afraid that's impossible," Tori said. "His plans were so vague. All he told me was that he'd be in Vermont until Monday or Tuesday."

"Then we'll have to search through his personal papers," Serge said matter-of-factly.

"I beg your pardon?"

"You know . . . letters, address books, diaries, anything where he'd write down Ulger's last name or number."

Tori extracted her hand from Serge's grip. "Certainly not! I would never intrude on Gordon's privacy or, worse, allow a stranger to."

Serge's eyes frosted over. "Pardon such an offensive suggestion, lady. Outsiders like me don't know any better." His gravelly voice was heavy with sarcasm.

Tori paled under his cold gaze, sensing she'd injured him deeply. "Forgive me, Serge. Of course you're right. We have no choice but to look through Gordon's papers for a clue. Let's start with the desk in the study."

"No, you look. I'll stay here. I wouldn't dream of intruding." Serge remained rigid and aloof.

Tori was going to beg his forgiveness once more but thought better of it. It would only make matters worse, she decided. "Very well," she agreed. "Make yourself at home while I go see what I can find."

She left him alone in the bleak front parlor again. Who could make himself at home in this cheerless formal atmosphere? Serge wondered. He would always be a stranger in this house—an outsider, an alien. And what the hell was he doing here in the first place? He'd never intended on getting involved with the Langford family again. Nothing was preventing him from walking out the front door, he reminded himself. Absolutely nothing.

Tori returned to the parlor a few minutes later, clutching Gordon's leather-bound appointment book against her chest. Serge wasn't in the room and his absence jolted her as hard as a kick in the stomach. She sank down into the sofa and gazed forlornly at the dying embers of the fire. She really couldn't find it in her heart to be angry with Serge for deserting her, especially after she'd so stupidly hurt his feelings.

Feeling desolate and weary beyond measure, Tori leaned her head against the back of the sofa. She turned her cheek so that it touched Serge's jacket and closed her eyes. They flew open an instant later. Since Serge's jacket was still here, that meant he most likely was, too. Tori leaped up from the sofa, heart racing, and went looking for him.

She found him in the pantry, searching the shelves. "Don't you have any coffee in this place?" he asked, glancing toward her with a frown.

His face had never looked more handsome to her. "There's a jar of instant behind the tea tins," she managed to say.

"Instant," he grumbled. "It'll have to do, I suppose." But he looked very out of sorts about it.

She couldn't help herself. She flung herself at him and hugged him with all her might. The scent of his lime aftershave and starched shirt blended with the pantry aromas of spices and herbs. This is what heaven must smell like, Tori decided as tears of relief sprang to her eyes.

"I thought you'd gone," she told him in a breathless voice.

"Gone where?" He was puzzled for a moment. He was also surprised at the strength of her arms around him. She wasn't as delicate as she looked. "You mean you thought I'd walked out on you? No way, lady." He wasn't about to tell her how close he'd come to doing just that.

All Tori wanted to do at that moment was to melt into his solid frame and lose herself in him entirely. But she couldn't allow herself such an indulgence while Jiggs was still in jeopardy. She released her hold on him.

"Look what I found," she said, opening her brother's appointment book. "Gordon made a notation to go to a place called The Friendly Florist at three o'clock, Saturday. But he took off the day before. Maybe he wanted to avoid that appointment."

Serge couldn't help but laugh. "I don't know, honey. The Friendly Florist doesn't sound too ominous."

Tori sniffed. "It seems very suspicious to me. I think we should go there and check it out."

"At two-thirty Sunday morning!" Serge's frowning expression made it clear that he wasn't too inclined to follow her suggestion.

Tori turned to put the kettle on. "Do you have any better ideas?" she asked him.

He came up behind Tori and put his arms around her waist. "I sure do," he murmured in her ear, producing a quivering within her. "But they have nothing to do with the problem at hand, so I'll keep them to myself for the time being."

Concentrating more on his words than on what she was doing, Tori turned up the flame too high and quickly lowered it. "I still can't believe that my brother is involved with someone like this Ulger person."

"You'd be surprised how easily a slime like that can ooze his way into people's lives," Serge told her. "I had a friend with a weakness for the horses. A good family man by the name of Waldo. Trouble was, Waldo couldn't stop gambling. Got himself into deep debt with a bookie. He was forced to sell his house to pay it off."

The kettle began to shrill, and Tori took it off the burner. "I'm quite positive that Gordon isn't a gambler, though."

"Yeah, that's what poor Waldo's wife used to say." Serge spooned some instant coffee into his cup.

Tori poured hot water over the granules. "Did she?" There was a note of doubt in her voice now. "Well, maybe it wouldn't hurt to call Waldo and ask him if he knows a bookie named Ulger."

"That's exactly what I intend to do," Serge stated. He took a sip of coffee and wrinkled his blunt nose. "But I'm sure Waldo's going to appreciate a call at this time of night even less than I appreciate instant coffee." He glanced around the kitchen. "Where's the phone?"

"We only have the one out in the foyer," Tori told him.

"You're kidding? One phone in a house this size?" Serge left the kitchen shaking his head. He'd forgotten how frugal these old Boston Brahmin families could be.

Tori sat at the wooden kitchen table and leafed through Gordon's appointment book for more clues. She noticed Ginger's name listed often during the winter months, sometimes with a heart drawn around it or exclamation points after it. How sad, Tori thought, that things hadn't worked out for the two of them. As unsuitable as Gordon and Ginger appeared to be, she sensed that they could have been good for each other.

Tori glanced up hopefully when Serge returned. "Any luck tracing Ulger?" she asked.

"I think we hit pay dirt," he said, straddling the Shaker chair next to hers. It squeaked under his muscular frame. "After Waldo cursed me out for waking him up, he told me about a loan shark named Ugly."

Tori's eyes lit up. "The perfect nickname for Ulger! Did your contact supply a last name?"

"My contact?" Serge grinned at her. "You're really getting into this, aren't you? Waldo didn't know his last name, though. These characters usually avoid relating them.

"How are we going to locate him then?" Tori's face fell.

But Serge's grin remained wide and steady. "I do believe we already have. Before he hung up on me Waldo mentioned that Ugly uses a flower shop as his front."

"The Friendly Florist! So my suggestion to go there wasn't so silly, after all."

"It was brilliant, and you're an adorable sleuth." Serge picked up her hand and kissed it. "But I'm going to take it from here, honey. Waldo gave me the address, and I'll check it out right now."

"I'm going with you," Tori declared.

"No, you're not," Serge replied just as adamantly. "You're staying here, where it's safe."

Tori's eyes flashed green. "I can take care of myself. I'll be a help, not a hindrance."

"Oh, yeah? You got a black belt in karate?"

She ignored his sarcasm. "Listen, if Jiggs is being kept at that flower shop, we stand a better chance of rescuing him together." It seemed so obvious and logical to her.

Serge willed himself to be patient with her. Firm but patient. "Let's not waste precious time arguing, honey. Just give me a kiss for good luck, okay?"

Taking in his wide, stubborn face, it was clear to Tori that this man would not listen to reason. She let out a soft little sigh, as if in submission, and leaned across the table to give him the sweetest kiss possible.

He enjoyed it thoroughly. "Now, that's more like it," he said.

"Finish your coffee," she suggested amiably. "I'll go get your jacket for you."

"Thanks," he agreed, approving of her compliant attitude and the way her hips swayed as she walked out of the kitchen.

He sipped his coffee, musing over how sweet she could be, when he heard a honking horn. It sounded very much like his car horn. He slammed down his cup. It *was* his horn, dammit.

His car was parked out front where he'd left it, but the motor was turned on. He yanked open the door and glared at Tori, who was sitting in the driver's seat.

"Cute trick," he said through clenched teeth. "Now get out, Tori."

Ignoring his order, she smiled winsomely. "The keys were in your jacket pocket. Get in. I'll drive."

"Like hell you will."

The undercurrent of controlled rage in his voice excited more than intimidated her. "You might as well admit defeat, Serge. I'm coming with you, and that's that."

"Stubbornness is not a very attractive trait in a female," he informed her, his jaw set.

"You think it is in a man?" She fiddled with the gearshift.

Serge let out a sight of resignation. "All right, Tori. You might as well come with me. But slide over and let me do the driving."

She gladly complied. She didn't know where they were going, anyway. All that mattered to her was that she was going with him.

The city streets were deserted as they headed toward the Fenway area. Except for the full moon, it seemed they were the only ones out in the wee hours of the morning. Tori's blood was racing with the sense of adventure and the thrill of having Serge be a part of it. She'd always known that life beyond the boundaries she'd set for herself could be unpredictable and dangerous. What she hadn't realized was how quickly she'd take to it. She reached over and squeezed Serge's knee. It didn't even occur to her how uncharacteristic this gesture was.

It surprised Serge, though—but only for an instant. He was getting used to her being full of surprises. "Keep your hand there," he told her. Again he was surprised when she actually did.

"Where is this flower shop, anyway?" she asked him, her voice filled with excitement.

"A few more blocks." He slowed his car down. "Our chances of finding Jiggs there are slight, you know." He could tell she was high with hope, and he didn't want her to crash-land with disappointment.

"Don't be a pessimist," she reprimanded, lightly pinching his thigh.

"You're making certain parts of me very optimistic right now," he replied.

She did take her hand away then. "It makes perfect sense to me that Ulger would leave Jiggs in his shop for the night."

Serge didn't reply. They would find out soon enough. He turned down a side street and doused the car lights. The buildings were run-down, some unoccupied. There was no sign advertising a florist's shop, and this shabby area seemed an unlikely location for one. But the tattered awning over the door of one shop caught his interest. The number corresponded with the one Waldo had given him.

"That must be the place," he told Tori and then parked a short distance away from it. He didn't want to make their visit too obvious, in case Ugly was inside.

Arm in arm, Serge and Tori strolled up the empty street and paused in front of the flower shop to casually look at the window display. Not that there was much to look at— an extremely unpleasant collection of cacti, a dusty philodendron, and a tawdry arrangement of plastic flowers comprised the display.

"Jiggs is in there," Tori whispered to Serge. "I can feel it."

"Sure you can." Serge wasn't a big believer in female intuition.

"He's in there!" Tori insisted. "I can practically hear his little heart pounding with fear, poor thing."

"You don't hear the pounding of Ugly's heart, by any chance? I'd like to know if he's in there, too." Since Tori didn't seem inclined to answer his question, Serge began knocking on the door and window. He had more faith in actions than in nebulous feelings.

Tori pressed her ear against the shop window. "I can hear Jiggs barking in there, Serge!"

"Right. Like you heard his heartbeat."

She waved her hand to hush him. "That's Mr. Jiggs's bark all right. I'd stake my life on it."

Just so she didn't expect him to stake *his* life on it, Serge reflected. Feeling a bit foolish, he squashed his own ear against the pane. He heard something, too. It could have been a dog's bark.

"We'll have to break in and get him out," Tori said.

Her voice was as soft as always, but Serge had come to recognize that determined set to her face. Her sharp Langford chin was thrust out. Despite this, he still attempted to reason with her.

"Honey, we can't just break into a flower shop," he said in his most reasonable voice. "It's against the law, you know. Plants have rights, too."

She didn't crack even the smallest smile. Instead, she gave Serge a reproachful look. "You mean you're not going to do anything to save my dog?"

Her eyes glowed in the moonlight as she looked up at him. They were filled with disappointment. Serge gave in to her once more.

"I've got a flashlight in the trunk. I guess it won't hurt to take a look around back." And look was all they were going to do, he promised himself.

But Serge's sense of adventure got the better of him when his flashlight illuminated an open basement window at the rear. The boy in him sprang to life. How could he possibly pass up such an invitation?

He handed Tori the flashlight. "Beam me down, Scotty."

It was her turn to have misgivings. "Do you really think you should climb through?"

"This is no time to think, Tori. That would ruin everything. Men don't stop and think before rushing to the aid of beautiful women in distress. It just isn't done that way."

Without further ado, he saluted and climbed through the window. Before Tori could warn him that it might be a big drop to the bottom, she heard him land with such a thud that she was surprised the entire building didn't shake. Her heart was in her throat when she knelt on the ground and shone the flashlight into the basement.

"Are you all right, Serge?"

He was back on his feet immediately, brushing off the seat of his pin-striped pants. He smiled up at her.

"Why shouldn't I be all right, Tori? This is such a wonderful idea you had. I couldn't think of a better way to spend a Saturday night. Dinner, a dognapping, then breaking and entering."

She figured he had every right to sarcasm now. "I know this is a terrible inconvenience, Serge. I'm really very sorry."

An inconvenience? They could get arrested at any moment, his entire career could be destroyed, he was risking life and limb for this woman he barely knew, and she was apologizing for "inconveniencing" him. He threw back his head and roared with laughter. The absurdity of the situation delighted him. He hadn't behaved so foolishly since he was a teenager, before ambition had caught him by the throat and he'd become driven to succeed.

His boisterous laughter made Tori hope his brain hadn't been rattled by his fall. "Is there any sign of Jiggs down there?" she asked, to remind him of his mission.

"It's pitch-black. Stop shining that damn flashlight in my face and toss it down to me."

She followed his instructions, and he darted the thin stream of light into the corners of the basement. It was crowded with boxes and junk, but no little floppy-eared dog could be seen cringing in the shadows. "He must be upstairs," Serge told her. "If he's in this place at all, that is."

"Of course he is. I heard his bark."

Serge wasn't as sure about that as she was. "He's not barking now."

"Try calling him," Tori suggested.

It was a sensible enough suggestion, but Serge hesitated. As far as he was concerned, dogs should be given names like Buster, or Rover, or Duke. Certainly not Mr. Jiggs. Steeling himself he shouted the spaniel's name at the top of his lungs.

A timid but definite bark emanated from above. "That's Jiggsy for sure," Tori confirmed from the window.

Serge headed up the rickety basement stairs, ready to burst through the door and save her little darling. His hand on the knob, he hesitated. It occurred to him that he wasn't about to do the wisest thing he'd ever done. Who knew what danger lurked behind that closed door? No risk, no gain, he reminded himself. That philosophy had rarely let him down in business.

Still, he opened the door very cautiously, and the beam of his flashlight proceeded him into the flower shop. He half expected the clinging tendrils of some man-eating plant to reach out and grab him.

What Serge didn't expect was for the little spaniel to attack him. But all of a sudden he heard a snarl from the shadows and felt a sharp pain in his leg. He looked down to see Tori's "darling" gripping onto his trousers like a miniature version of Jaws.

Chapter Six

You poor dear,'' Tori said softly, examining Serge's injured leg in the upstairs bathroom of the Langford house.

"It's only a flesh wound," he declared stoically. Perched on the rim of the big marble tub, he was enjoying the attention. Tori opened the medicine cabinet and took out a brown bottle. "I'm so sorry about this, Serge. I'm sure Jiggs is, too."

Serge glanced at the culprit, who was peeking into the bathroom from the hallway. The big-eyed spaniel didn't look very remorseful to him. In fact, he was wagging his tail as he gazed up at Tori. All Jiggs seemed to care about was that he was reunited with his adored mistress.

Both Tori and Jiggs had wept with joy all the way back from The Friendly Florist as Serge drove in stony silence, his leg bleeding. He'd been sorely tempted to grab the stupid little mutt from Tori's lap and toss him out the car window without slowing down. But if he'd done that, he wouldn't be enjoying Tori's sweet attentions right now.

"What is that stuff?" he asked, eyeing the brown bottle with suspicion.

"Hydrogen peroxide. Don't worry, darling. It won't sting."

Busy soaking a cotton ball with the disinfectant, Tori hadn't noticed the endearment slip off her tongue. But Serge had.

"Please roll up your pant leg higher," she instructed.

"Why don't I simply take off my pants?" he suggested, grinning up at her.

"That's hardly necessary," she replied in a cool, prim voice. Her touch, though, was loving and gentle as she dabbed the shallow wound with the cotton ball. "Thank goodness it's not a deep cut," she said with great relief.

"It's not a cut, it's a dog bite," Serge was quick to remind her. "You should get a muzzle for that mutt of yours."

"Jiggs would never hurt anyone," Tori said, quickly plastering over evidence to the contrary with a Band-Aid. "Not intentionally," she added. "He was frightened and confused when you walked into the flower shop."

"Always making excuses, aren't you, Tori?" Serge rolled down the leg of his torn, ruined pants and stood up. "First you refuse to blame your brother for getting us involved with this Ugly creep. Now you defend your idiot dog for attacking me while I'm trying to rescue him. Don't get me wrong. I admire loyalty. But you carry it too far, honey."

Tori wasn't about to quarrel with the man who had saved her precious dog. Instead she gave him a wide, glowing smile. "You were very brave and wonderful, you

know.'' Her eyes blazed green with admiration and gratitude.

Serge stifled the inclination to shuffle his feet and say
''Shucks.'' But he did let out an embarrassed little laugh.
''Hell, it was no big deal.''

''No big deal? Why, you risked life and limb! Of course
Jiggs can't appreciate that. But I certainly do.'' And she
did, with all her heart.

''Last of the knights in shining armor, that's me,'' Serge
said, never modest for too long.

Tori nodded her head solemnly in agreement. ''I
thought they were an extinct breed until now.''

He wished she'd stop looking at him as if were a saint or
something. He broke their gaze and turned his attention to
the huge marble tub.

It was almost deep enough to float in. And certainly big
enough to accommodate two comfortably, if one of the
two was a slender female, he thought.

''My grandfather had it made to his specifications,''
Tori said, noting Serge's interest. ''He was a large man like
you.''

''I bet he and your grandma had some splashing good
times in it together?'' Serge's boyish smile split his lips.

Tori was both shocked and amused. ''I doubt it!'' She
giggled at the very idea of it, remembering the dour, conservative old man. ''Grandfather Langford was a very
proper gentleman of the old school.''

''Well, he couldn't have been proper all the time or you
wouldn't be here, now, would you?''

''I'm sure he and Grandmother thought it their duty to
produce progeny,'' she replied stiffly. ''But I certainly
doubt they splashed around naked together in this tub!''
She couldn't help but giggle again, though. It was too absurd.

"Then they missed a lot of fun, didn't they, Tori? Making love should be a pleasure, not an obligation, right?"

He pinned her with those piercing blue eyes of his, waiting for an answer. The laughter died on her lips because she had no answer. She certainly believed in the principle of enjoying the act of love, but in fact she hadn't enjoyed it much at all during those brief, fumbling times when she was engaged. Of course she'd been very young then, completely inexperienced. But it had been such a disappointment that she was almost relieved when her fiancé had called off their marriage.

She forced herself to look away from Serge. "Why are we standing here in the middle of the bathroom? It's much more comfortable downstairs in the parlor."

"I'm perfectly comfortable up here," Serge said, ignoring her nervousness. "Why don't you show me your room, Tori? No, better yet, let me find it on my own. I'll just follow the scent of lilacs."

He turned and headed down the long, dim hall. Like a wolf on the prowl, she thought. And she had let in this dangerous creature quite willingly. What to do now? she wondered.

She followed him and was surprised when he went directly to her closed bedroom door, after passing by a few others. He turned the glass knob and opened it, then walked right in without hesitating.

"So this is where Victoria Langford spends her nights," he mused aloud.

Moonlight beamed through the gauzy lace curtains and illuminated everything in a hazy, subtle glow. Her bed, especially, seemed to soak up the moonbeams because the embroidered comforter was white, as was the intricately worked crocheted canopy hanging from the four high posts. The kind of bed a princess would sleep in, Serge thought, not especially surprised.

"Shall I turn on a light to better satisfy your curiosity?" Tori asked sharply. He'd invaded her inner sanctum without so much as asking her leave, and as he scrutinized her bedroom she felt that a secret part of herself was on display, too. She decided that he might as well take a good look. She had nothing to hide.

"No, we don't need more light right now," he told her. He turned to her slowly and captured her chin with his fingertips, tilting it up. "It seems right that the first time we make love your body should be bathed in moonlight, Tori."

She opened her mouth to object to his presumption, but his lips smothered her protest. She allowed this liberty as she had the first time he'd kissed her in the Garden.

No, she didn't so much allow it as find herself helpless to resist it. She would have pushed away any other man, but she delighted in this one's audacity. It thrilled her that he should have such power over her whenever he touched her. It frightened her, too. She'd never felt such a compelling physical attraction to a man before.

Their kiss deepened, and she melted against him. Desire, sweet and thick, flowed through her. It was a delicious sensation, one she wanted to prolong forever. He released her mouth and slid his lips up and down her long neck, indulging in little nips and kisses that burned a trail along her throat. "My sweet Tori," he whispered, and his hot breath against her ear made her shiver.

Dizzy with delight, she clasped her hands around his neck to keep her balance and pressed closer against him. She adored the feel of his big, solid body. He ran his hand down the curve of her spine, then massaged the sensitive small of her back. Every muscle in her body relaxed. She barely noticed when he pulled down the zipper of her dress with his other hand, but then his strokes and caresses became even more arousing through the thin layer of her silk slip.

"Let me help you take this off," he offered, slowly pushing the dress down past her shoulders and breasts and waist. When it fell to the floor, he gave her his hand and helped her to step out of it.

It happened so smoothly, so easily, that it wasn't until Tori felt the cool air on her skin that she fully realized she was undressed. She looked down at herself. Her creamy silk slip shimmered in the moonlight.

"Now you help me with my shirt," Serge said.

She did her best to remain calm and collected. She didn't want him to know how apprehensive she was. But her hands were trembling as she fumbled with his shirt buttons.

"I'm not very good at this," she apologized softly, referring to much more than the simple act of unbuttoning a man's shirt.

He realized then how nervous she was. She looked so vulnerable in her pearly slip, and his heart went out to her. He promised himself to break through her reserve slowly and not to rush her in any way. He'd waited this long, and he could take his time now. He'd sensed from the beginning that she was different from the women he'd known in the past, and he was determined to treat her with special care.

He captured her hands and kissed the cold fingertips. He led her to an old-fashioned dressing table in the corner of the large bedroom. "Sit down and let me unpin your hair," he said.

It was a request she hadn't expected, and she gave out a little laugh. "If you'd like," she consented, then perched on the cushioned bench. Her reflection in the gilt-framed mirror looked pale in the moonlight streaming through the tall windows. Her eyes, she thought, looked so much larger than usual.

Serge began to slowly extract the long hairpins holding her intricately coiled chignon in place. They clicked against the tabletop as he tossed them down. One pin snagged in her hair, and he apologized. "I've never done this for a woman before," he said.

Most likely the only thing he *hadn't* done, Tori thought uneasily. As self-possessed as she was in most areas of her life, she was unsure of herself when it came to intimacy and was afraid of disappointing him. She was sure he'd had far more experience. She'd never quite overcome her shyness and inhibitions. Compared to most women her age, she felt as old-fashioned as the elegant dressing table she sat before.

"I'd never buckled a woman's shoe before yours, either," Serge continued. "You're teaching me a whole new way to make love, Tori."

A self-disparaging smile touched her lips. "I doubt I could teach you anything new. Don't expect too much from me."

A few more pins clattered on the table before he spoke again. "You're a puzzle to me, Tori. When we kiss there's so much heat between us that my head spins. Yet you seem so unsure of yourself now. Don't you enjoy making love?"

She hesitated for only a moment. "No," she answered honestly. "I never really have. But I've learned to accept my inability to respond. There are more important things in life."

Serge bent down and placed a lingering kiss on her neck. "Not tonight, there aren't," he whispered in her ear.

He removed the last few pins, and her glossy brown hair cascaded down to her waist. He combed his fingers through the slippery length of it, then spread the tawny locks over her white shoulders like a cloak.

"How lovely you are, Tori."

"Not really."

"Yes, really." He slid down the straps of her slip to reveal the lacy bra beneath and traced the scalloped edges of it with his fingertips. Then he undid it to reveal her small, full breasts, smooth as alabaster. "Look for yourself. The mirror doesn't lie."

Her half-naked reflection embarrassed her, and she turned her head away. But Serge gently twisted her face to the mirror again. Complying with his silent demand, she sat as still as a statue and watched as his big, tanned hands cupped her pale breasts from beneath. The soft weight of them filled his palms.

"See how perfect they are," he said. The tips of his thumbs slowly circled around and around the pink nipples until they budded to life.

The obvious excitement his caress produced made Tori blush all over, but she didn't tell him to stop. And she couldn't tear her eyes from the mirror as he continued to fondle and knead her soft flesh. Fascinated, she watched through half-closed eyes, luxuriating in the sensations he was producing deep within her. Minutes could have passed. Or hours.

He was too tall to be completely reflected in the mirror as he stood behind her, and Tori longed to see his face. She leaned back against him and could feel the hard pressure of his arousal against her bare skin, along with the cold metal of his belt buckle and the cloth of his trousers. It thrilled her.

Then he knelt down before her, and his blunt, handsome profile became part of the mirrored fantasy she was observing. She gasped when he took the rosy tip of her breast to his mouth. The sight of their intimacy framed in gilt enthralled her. It was almost as if she were dreaming, yet her body was wide-awake and throbbing.

His tongue flicked from one breast to the other, producing magical effects upon her. She saw her own hand, so white against the darkness of his hair, press his head against her softness. Accepting her silent invitation, he sucked the sweetness of her swollen buds. Passion flowed through her.

When Tori met her own eyes in the mirror, though, she was shocked. Deep pools of desire, they weren't her eyes at all. The woman she saw reflected was a stranger, her lips parted and voluptuous, her expression sensuous and yielding. No, this wasn't Victoria Langford at all, and the metamorphosis frightened her a little. She stiffened.

Serge lifted his face to look up at hers. "Do you want me to stop?"

He might as well have asked her if she wanted to stop breathing, to stop being alive with sensation. She shook her head silently, unable to speak.

That wasn't enough for him. "If you don't want this as much as I do, it won't be good for either of us," he said. He didn't want to take from her. He wanted her to give of herself.

"I've never wanted a man so much," she replied simply.

He nodded, satisfied. "Good. And we're just beginning."

In one quick movement he stood and plucked her up from the bench as if she weighed less than a feather. He carried her to her bed and when he placed her down on it, she had a floating sensation, as if she were drifting away to a place she'd never been before.

Her silky underthings seemed to drift away, too. As Serge slowly stripped her he covered each inch of flesh he exposed with kisses. He was stunned by her naked beauty. Her pale body was luminous in the moonlight, celestial as the moon itself. Her long hair spread across the pillows, silky streamers against the white. She stared up at him with wide, trusting eyes, and although it was too dark to make out their color at that moment, Serge was sure they were as green as the most precious emeralds.

He stood before her, and in the aura of her shimmering feminine beauty he suddenly felt himself too big, too muscular, and more than a little awkward. He took off his vest, then fumbled with the same shirt buttons she had fumbled with earlier. Her eyes were like magnets pulling at him.

"You make me self-conscious," he told her. It was a hard thing for him to admit. He'd never before had trouble undressing in the presence of a woman. But those eyes of hers!

She found his sudden shyness endearing. And comforting. "Would you prefer me to look away?"

"No," he said. "I never want you to turn away from me, Tori."

And so she watched, not at all surprised at the perfectly shaped body he revealed to her. She'd already admired it from afar in the Garden as he'd run across her line of vision. It had never occurred to her then, sitting on a park bench watching a stranger, that it would come to this.

There was no hiding his excitement and desire for her as he stood naked by her bed. "May I join you?" he asked, flashing his white teeth, grinning his wolfish smile. She slid her sleek body across the white comforter to make room for him. "Don't worry, Tori," he murmured, taking his place beside her. "I won't rush you."

And during the long, heady hours that followed, Serge proved to her that he was a man of his word. His knowing caresses amazed and dazed her as he slowly explored every detail of her body. She couldn't help but respond in kind and touched him as she'd never touched a man before. The texture of his skin and muscles delighted her. She exalted in his maleness, discovering in him a new world of pleasure.

In the glow of her moonlit bedroom they came to know each other intimately as they traveled on a long, leisurely journey toward a final consummation. When they finally arrived at that special, inevitable moment when their bodies joined, Tori realized how far Serge had taken her.

Yet he took her still further, beyond her imagination and expectation, and the power of her response exploded within her. She cried out with relief and joy. She would never underestimate the act of love again.

Serge was awakened by a strange sensation early the next morning; there was a heavy weight on his chest. Slowly raising his lids, he came eyeball-to-eyeball with Mr. Jiggs, who was perched on top of him. The dog began to lick his face with friendly abandon.

Although he would have much preferred Tori's sweet kisses, Serge didn't push the little dog away. It was about time he and Jiggs came to terms. Smiling, Serge turned to Tori, but her side of the bed was empty.

He could hear water running and surmised she was drawing a bath in the big marble tub down the hall. He sighed with remembered pleasure. She'd satisfied him completely the night before, and it gave him a welling sense of pride to know that he'd pleased her just as much. Still waters run deep, he thought. He'd discovered her passionate nature beneath her veneer of reserve.

He wasn't surprised. He'd sensed it from the beginning. That's why he hadn't been able to get her out of his mind since they'd met in the Garden.

His sharp blue eyes roamed around her bedroom, taking in every detail. A collection of antique fans was displayed on one floral-papered wall. Photographs of family, framed in silver, crowded a dresser top. There was a tufted chaise longue upholstered in faded mauve silk in one corner of the room, and Serge could easily imagine a delicate lady from another era reclining upon it. The decor of the room vaguely irritated him as he viewed it in the bright morning light—he was a man more concerned with the future than the past.

He shifted impatiently as he waited for Tori to return to him. Remembering the soft smoothness of her lilac-fragrant skin, he wanted to make love to her again. Right away.

He heard a vague splashing in the distance and pictured her slender white body immersed in warm water. It was an image that made him restless, and pushing Jiggs aside, he got out of bed. Pacing the room, he caught a glimpse of his naked body in the gilt-framed dressing-table mirror and let out a laugh. His muscled limbs and hairy chest looked so alien in this delicate, feminine setting. It made him wonder, for just a moment, if he could ever fit into Victoria Langford's private world. There was nothing in the room that was modern. The furnishings and decor were from centuries past.

He moved to the long, lace-framed window and gazed out. The window faced the enclosed back courtyard, and Serge noticed the blooming magnolia tree in the middle of it. The beauty of the luxuriant pink blossoms captivated him. He was sure that they were as soft to the touch as Tori's flesh. A notion both romantic and a bit absurd suddenly inspired him. Completely disregarding the fact that he was stark naked, he quickly headed down the hall and back stairway and out the kitchen door.

Tori pressed the back of her long neck against the cool marble of the deep tub's rim and closed her eyes. She smiled.

As the bathwater caressed her, she was recalling Serge's caresses during their long, blissful night together. She'd left him sleeping so peacefully in her bed, the lace-edged sheet incongruous against the springy, dark hair of his chest. No man had ever slept in her white canopied bed before.

How sweet his face had seemed to her in repose. Awake, his piercing light eyes could be so intimidating. No matter how much they'd shared together recently, she was still a little wary of him. She'd tiptoed out of the bedroom to be alone, away from his masculine force for a little while. But now, her limbs relaxed in the warm water, she felt a tug of desire to be with him again—to begin the lovemaking all over again; again and again. She'd never thought she would want a man so much, so badly.

She heard a sudden splash in the bathwater, followed quickly by a few more. Her eyes sprang open and the first thing she saw was lush magnolia blossoms floating all around her. And then she saw Serge standing naked above her, his boyish, lopsided grin stretched across his wide, handsome face.

"I thought you'd like some company," he said. He was pleased with his gesture. The flowers brushed against Tori's pale, pink-tipped breasts.

Caught by surprise, she laughed and captured a floating blossom in her wet palm. "You're crazy," she told him.

"Yes, I am," he readily admitted. "Crazy about you." His glinting eyes took in her pale lovely body encased in clear water, and it was the most enchanting sight he'd ever seen.

He didn't wait for a formal invitation. He joined her in the tub without a moment's hesitation. His big body made the water slosh over the edge and onto the black-and-white tiled floor, and Tori laughed again.

"I've never bathed with a man before."

Serge fully intended to do more than just bathe with her. His erotic imagination had been captured by the big tub the moment he'd set eyes on it the night before. And he'd been right in his estimation. It was a perfect fit for a man and a woman together; this man and this woman, in particular.

A part of Tori resented his intrusion into her privacy. But a deeper part of her delighted in it. He was rude and bold and sexy. She'd never known a man like him.

"Do you expect me to wash your back?" she asked him.

"Don't dwell on my back," he replied with a teasing smile. They were face-to-face in the tub, knees touching.

She picked up her bar of lilac-scented soap and rubbed it against his muscular chest very slowly. She could see his arousal grow underwater and delighted in her power to excite him. Sweet-smelling suds caught in his mat of chest hair.

He grabbed the bar from her. "My turn," he said.

He slid the soap over her small, perfectly shaped breasts, then under and around them until they were completely slippery.

"Quick little seals," he said when he tried to capture them in his palms and they escaped from his grasp.

She blushed all over, turning a rosy pink in the warm water. But she didn't stop him from gliding his hands everywhere. His touch saturated every pore of her.

"Let's go back to bed and make love again," she whispered. For her it was a bold request, and she was delighted that she could make it.

But he refused it. "No, we'll make love right here."

"In the *tub*?" Her laugh came out high-pitched, excited.

"Move on top of me," he urged in his deep, gravelly voice.

She complied, easily shifting her position. The water made her feel weightless. She floated above Serge's big long body for a moment, as if lost in space, but then he grasped her slender waist and pulled her down to him. He entered and possessed her with magical ease, filling her completely. Tori's eyelids fluttered with ecstasy, then closed. The bath became an ocean of pleasure as she rode each high wave of his powerful thrusts.

Serge watched her, pleased with what he saw. Her long hair streamed down and clung to her breasts, and she looked like a mermaid, a Siren. But she was all woman, and he gloried in being melded to her under the soothing water. He took his time. They had forever. An eternity. She was the buoy, he was the anchor, and they drifted through an endless sea of sensuality together.

When it was over, when they were both numbed by the pleasure they'd given each other, they stepped out of the bath and dried each other with soft towels. They spent more time in this afterplay than necessary, still delighting in each other's bodies as the water drained from the tub.

Tori pressed her cheek against Serge's damp chest, now scented with her lilac soap. "Each time we make love it gets better," she said.

"Then imagine what we have to look forward to."

She smiled, and his chest hair tickled her lips. It made her feel good to hear him allude to a future together, no matter how vaguely. She knew with every nerve ending in her body that she was completely committed to him physically. Her emotions, though, were in a state of chaos. He'd smashed into her calm, well-ordered world with such force that her head was spinning.

They went back to her bedroom and dressed without talking much. Serge had left his clothes in a heap at the foot of the bed the night before, and he was sure that Jiggs had slept on them. It irritated him to dress in wrinkled clothes. He rubbed his hand across his face. That, too irritated him. He needed a shave.

He eyed Tori critically. To his surprise, she'd put on a denim shirt and jean. She certainly had the perfect figure for body-molding jeans, but Serge didn't like them on her.

"I prefer you in a dress," he told her.

Her sleek eyebrows went up and so did her hackles. "I've never needed a man to tell me what to wear before."

He hated it when she used that cool, superior tone with him. "You don't seem to mind needing me in other ways, honey."

She turned away from him and stared out her bedroom window. She saw nothing but red rage, though. Of course, she'd known from their first encounter in the Garden that he was a male chauvinist. Yet, she'd still been attracted to him. "Need and enjoy are two different things," she pointed out to him.

Serge stood in the middle of her room, not knowing how to reply. He hadn't intended to start a quarrel. The problem was that their emotions were too close to the surface right then. He moved behind her and began stroking her back. He felt the melting of her anger beneath her thin cotton shirt.

"You can wear whatever you like, Tori," he allowed, cupping her breast.

But she brushed his hand away. "This used to be Aunt Victoria's room," she said. "I often imagine her gazing out the window, unable to leave this self-imposed prison. Her need for a certain man ruined her life."

"Because she let it," Serge replied a bit impatiently. He didn't want to talk about any of her illustrious ancestors now. "Maybe I should be leaving. I don't want to outstay my welcome."

She turned to him then and placed her hand on his arm. "Please don't, Serge. I don't know why we're suddenly rubbing each other the wrong way, but I don't want you to leave in a bad mood."

"You're the one in a bad—" He caught himself and grinned at her. "We're both out of sorts. It could be hunger. It seems the last time I ate was a week or so ago."

"It was only last night," she reminded him, smiling.

"A lot's happened since then."

"Now, that's an understatement if I ever heard one! Let's go downstairs and rustle up some breakfast."

And rustle they did. The Langford larder was hardly well stocked. Serge found some stale white bread in the pantry. Tori discovered four eggs in the refrigerator.

"What do you people live on? Air?" Serge asked.

Tori shrugged. "My brother usually dines out. Neither of us has a big appetite. Food doesn't interest me that much."

Serge recalled that she'd practically said the same about making love the night before. He smiled to himself. He'd certainly changed her mind about *that*.

"Why do you suddenly look like the cat that just swallowed the canary?" Tori asked him.

"I was thinking about us making love," he admitted.

She didn't mind his self-satisfied grin. She allowed that he had a right to it. "You make me feel treasured when we do," she told him.

Her frank admission pleased him immensely. "That's because you are a treasure," he said, a catch in his gruff voice. Then he changed to the teasing tone he was more comfortable with. "But I'm beginning to realize that you lack one essential skill that most men expect from a woman."

Her sharp chin shot up, as if to counter a blow. "What skill is that, pray tell?"

"The ability to cook. Admit it, Tori. You can't."

"Oh, that." Her slight shrug demonstrated how little it mattered to her. "I can boil water," she offered. "Which means I can boil eggs. How would you like yours? Hard or soft?"

"I'd prefer an omelet," he said. "And you're in luck, lady. You've found yourself a man who knows his way around a kitchen." He began opening cupboards and drawers. "You must have a skillet around here someplace."

Tori found it for him and handed it over. "I didn't know that macho men could cook."

"Honey, they can do anything." He tossed the pan into the air. It somersaulted and he caught it by the handle again. "Especially this one. I used to be a short-order cook in my parents' diner. That was long before Mama ran her fancy restaurant."

"And what do you do now?" she asked him.

"I never did tell you, did I?" He turned away and found a bowl in the cupboard. He cracked two eggs into it, using one hand. "For all you know I could be a common criminal like Ugly."

Tori watched him whisk the eggs with a fork. The sleeves of his wrinkled white cotton shirt were rolled up, revealing his tanned, powerful forearms. Even without his tie and jacket, scrambling eggs, he looked like a man used to giving orders rather than taking them.

"Oh, no," she said. "You could never be a *common* criminal, Serge. Maybe the leader of the pack, though."

He grinned his wolfish smile. "I don't know whether to be flattered or insulted. Do you really picture me as an underworld boss?"

"I've pictured you as so many things," she said. "Now you're probably going to tell me you're a stodgy State Street banker."

"Close but no cigar," he replied. "Actually, some people would say I'm a cross between a banker and a loan shark." He opened the refrigerator and took out a stick of butter.

"Really?" Tori said a bit uneasily. "Is what you do...legitimate?"

The butter sizzled in the pan. "What if I said no. Would you send me away, Tori?" His vivid blue eyes locked with hers.

His question made her catch her breath. "Stop teasing me, Serge," she demanded, hoping with all her heart that he was.

"Okay, I will. I head a firm called Hub Venture Capital. Strictly on the up-and-up." He poured the eggs into the skillet. "I provide seed money to companies just starting up and help manage their growth. It's investing at its most speculative, but it has a tremendous upside potential."

Tori was greatly relieved. And also a little disappointed. "I imagined you in a more dangerous profession."

Serge folded the omelet and laughed. "Believe me, being a venture capitalist is risky business. That's why I do it."

"In a way we do the same sort of thing," Tori told him. "I provide a showcase for artists just starting out and help manage their careers."

"So we have more in common than I thought," Serge said, sliding the perfect golden omelet onto a plate.

"It's the excitement of discovering new talent that interests me, not the profits," she added.

"Then again, maybe we don't. I'm in it for the profit, honey, and make no bones about it."

She sensed the danger lurking in him again, even as he handed her the food he'd cooked with such casual expertise. He did everything that way, including making love, she thought.

She wondered how seriously she should take him, how seriously he took *her*. Had she made a mistake getting so suddenly and completely involved with him? His voice, his touch could be so warm, but his eyes could be so cold. She knew one thing for sure: when it came to business deals, Serge Zhdanov would always have the upper hand. She hoped he wasn't as calculating when it came to love.

He was starting on the second omelet when the front doorbell chimed. "Were you expecting guests?" he asked, frowning at the interruption as he broke open two more eggs.

Tori also resented this intrusion of the outside world. "No, I have no idea who it could be," she told him.

"Don't answer it, then," he advised.

"All right, I won't," she agreed, hoping Serge would stay for the rest of the day.

"Why don't we go back upstairs after breakfast?" he asked softly, as if reading her mind.

As she was nodding in agreement the doorbell chimed again, and then she heard her name being called.

"Are you home, Victoria? I forgot my key!"

It was her brother Gordon.

Chapter Seven

Tori left Serge in the kitchen to go to open the front door for her brother. "You're back early," she commented, forcing a smile.

Gordon placed his worn but elegant leather suitcase on the threadbare Persian hall rug and gave Tori a kiss on the cheek. "Did I return at a bad time? You seem a little perturbed."

"Not at all!" she objected. "This is *your* home, after all."

"Our home," Gordon corrected. Jiggs pranced into the foyer to greet him, and Gordon bent down to pet the dog, turning his attention from Tori. "Did you miss me, boy? Anything exciting happen while I was away?"

If only Jiggs could talk! Tori thought. She cleared her throat. "Actually, a lot's happened. And I have a guest here for brunch." She thought that more discreet than referring to the meal as breakfast. Besides, it was close to noon.

Gordon stood up, frowning. "A guest? Not Ginger O'Neil, I hope. I'm in no mood to put up with her nonsense."

"Not Ginger." Tori observed that her brother looked more disappointed than relieved. "It is someone you know, though. I'm sure you must remember Serge Zhdanov."

Gordon's gray eyes widened. "Are you joking?" A tense little smile stretched his lips. "How could you have met up with someone like that, Victoria?"

She ignored his disparaging tone. "We met in the park the other day while I was walking Jiggs."

"And you invited him here?" He seemed aghast that she could do such an unseemly thing. "I don't want that man in my house, Victoria."

"You just said it was 'our house,' Gordon. And he's my guest. I expect you to be civil with him." Her brother's vehement disapproval put her a little off balance.

"I certainly will not be," he stated firmly.

"Keep your voice down," she whispered harshly. "He'll hear you."

"I don't give a damn if he does or not. Where is he?"

Tori couldn't remember ever seeing her brother so ungracious. "In the kitchen," she replied.

"At least he knows his place." Gordon flicked back a strand of his sandy hair. "You may not recall this, Victoria, but his parents used to be servants here."

"Times change, Langford," a low, even voice broke in.

Tori and Gordon turned quickly to see Serge standing at the end of the hall, his arms casually folded across his chest. He was smiling his dangerous wolf smile. The two men stared at each other a long moment. Neither offered the other his hand.

"I doubt you've changed," Gordon finally said. "You were always barging in where you weren't wanted, Zhdanov."

"Gordon!" Tori cried, shocked by his rudeness.

But Serge didn't so much as blink. "And you were always a bit of a horse's ass, Gordo," he commented coolly.

Now Tori was shocked by Serge's rudeness. "You're both behaving like ill-mannered children," she said.

Both men ignored her.

"I want you to leave immediately, Zhdanov," Gordon commanded in an imperious tone. "You do remember where the back door is, don't you?"

"I remember a lot about my time here—most of it unpleasant." He gave Gordon his direct, piercing look. "And I certainly wouldn't be here now if it weren't for your sister."

"Leave my sister out of this!"

"She's the only one I'll listen to. Would you like me to go, Tori?" His icy gaze turned in her direction.

She hesitated. She couldn't understand what was going on between the two men. "What I'd like is for the two of you to shake hands and be friends."

Gordon put his hands in the pockets of his gray flannel pants. "That's impossible, Victoria."

Serge merely shrugged when she looked at him. "Your brother and I have a mutual disregard for each other."

Tori wanted to tell them both to grow up. "I'll make some tea," she suggested lamely. Neither man seemed particularly cheered by her suggestion.

"If you don't tell Zhdanov to go, then I'll be forced to leave my own house," Gordon said to her. There was a pleading in his mild gray eyes.

His ultimatum gave her little choice, Tori thought with a sinking heart. The last thing she was prepared for was a showdown with her brother. She could never turn against him. And no matter how senseless she found his threat to leave, there was no way she could oblige him to go through with it. She gave Serge a desperate look, hoping he would understand.

It appeared that he immediately did. He nodded to her sharply, marched to the parlor to get his suit jacket, and left by the front door without a word.

Gordon sighed with relief. "I hope that's the last we've seen of Serge Zhdanov."

Tori silently prayed that it wasn't. "What did he do to make you dislike him so much, Gordon?" She stiffened, prepared to hear the worst about the man she'd taken to her heart and her bed.

"It's not one specific thing he did. It's a cumulative dislike. To put it simply, he's not our kind, Victoria."

She was stunned by his flimsy reply. "That's not a good enough answer," she told him angrily. "I deserve a better explanation than that from you."

"The point is, little sister, that you deserve better than the likes of him." Gordon looked at her with unusual severity. "I don't want you getting involved with that interloper."

"It seems I already am." She brushed past her brother. "Excuse me, Gordon."

"Where are you going?" he demanded.

She paused at the door to throw him a challenging look over her shoulder. "After Serge Zhdanov, of course! To apologize for your rude behavior and my tolerance of it. I should never have let him walk out like that."

Tori hurried out and spotted Serge a good distance away, heading for his car parked at the end of the narrow cobblestoned street. She called out to him, but he didn't seem to hear her. Before she could catch up to him, he got into his car and drove off. Flushed and out of breath from running, Tori watched the gray Mercedes disappear around the corner. A heavy desolation descended upon her. What if he had heard her call his name and hadn't turned around on purpose?

"Home sweet home, huh, pal?" Serge asked his husky when they entered his top-floor condominium. Duke was panting with happiness and excitement. He stayed with a neighbor when Serge traveled.

Duke had no way of knowing, of course, that Serge had come back to Boston the night before. But Serge still felt the need to make amends and broiled a little steak for the husky—medium rare, just the way Duke liked it. Duke merely sniffed it, then walked out of the gleaming modern kitchen without touching it, head low, tail dragging.

Serge was more than a little concerned with this reaction. It wasn't like Duke to pass up a good steak. Maybe the dog was in a sulk because he'd gone off on a business trip, Serge thought. Fine. They could sulk together. Serge didn't have much of an appetite himself. He got himself an imported dark beer from the refrigerator and drank it straight from the bottle as he headed for the vast living room.

He gazed down at the city from his floor-to-ceiling expanse of windows. His penthouse topped a modern high rise in the very heart of Boston. Viewing the flat rooftops below made Serge feel he had the world at his feet.

He took another swig of the brew and considered his accomplishments since obtaining his Harvard MBA. He was proud that he'd built a highly lucrative business on sheer talent and brazen nerve. He'd found his niche in an area of investments considered too risky for more conservative, established firms. He'd found the race toward success exciting, intense and thoroughly rewarding.

So why should he feel vaguely discontented now? he asked himself. That women drifted in and out of his life like sweet but fading dreams had never bothered him much before. Yet now he worried about the elusiveness of his own feelings. Some men simply weren't inclined to have deep, permanent relationships. Maybe he was one of them.

Yeah, he was meant to be a loner, he thought with resignation. The memories of what he and Tori Langford had shared would eventually disappear like all the others. At least he hoped so. It was clear to him that they weren't going to see each other again. He'd seen it in her eyes as she stood beside her brother, hoping he'd go away. So he had. For good.

"So long, lady," he said aloud, raising his beer bottle. He was sure she'd be relieved if she knew that he'd never bother her again. Once her snobby brother had come back into the picture, she'd seen how poorly Serge Zhdanov fit into it. What did they have in common except for the fact that his parents used to be servants to hers?

The phone rang and Serge remained by the window as his answering machine turned on. He listened as a clear, light voice projected across the room.

"Hello, it's me." A small, nervous laugh. "Tori Langford, that is. Are you there, Serge?" She waited a moment. "I guess not. Would you call me back when you get in? It's impossible for me to carry on a conversation with your machine." That awkward laugh again. "Please call me back," she added with more force. Then she hung up.

Serge crossed the room and replayed the message. He replayed it three times. "Let's go for a walk, Duke," he finally said. He would have to think long and hard about returning her call.

"Who were you just talking to?" Gordon asked, returning downstairs after unpacking his suitcase.

"A machine," Tori reported sadly.

Her brother waited for her to say more, and when she didn't he sighed deeply. "Don't you have more self-respect than to chase after a man like Serge Zhdanov, Victoria?"

"It's my life, Gordon." She went into the parlor, and he followed her there.

"Zhdanov shouldn't be part of it," he persisted. "He's got a vendetta against our family—at least, against me."

"I can't believe that, Gordon." She plopped down on the sagging sofa, exhausted. "Not after the way he helped me out last night."

"Last night?" Gordon stood over her, eyes narrowed. "Don't tell me he spent the night here with you?"

"All right. I won't tell you. It's none of your business, anyway," she replied wearily. "I'm not your baby sister anymore. I'm an adult and can make my own decisions."

Gordon pulled at his sandy hair. "You'll always be my little sister," he told her adamantly. "I know you're a grown woman now, with your own successful business, but in many ways you're still terribly naive. Especially where men are concerned. Didn't I try to warn you once before about that gigolo you almost married?"

"That was years ago. And it has nothing to do with this situation whatsoever. The reason Serge came home with me last night was because—"

"I don't want to hear it!" Gordon shouted. He took a deep breath to calm himself. "Please listen to me, Victoria. I know Zhdanov better than you do. He was a year behind me at Harvard. He was so jealous of me, so hateful. Being a poor scholarship student, he had this enormous chip on his shoulder. He knew that he didn't fit in, that he didn't really *belong* there."

Tori gave her brother a cool look. "Perhaps it was you, not Serge, who thought that." For a brief instant she almost disliked Gordon. But then all she felt was concern for him. "The past doesn't matter right now," she told him. "You're in some kind of trouble, and that's what we have to work out."

Gordon began pacing in front of the fireplace. "Trouble?" he repeated, as if it were a new word.

"Level with me," Tori demanded.

Relief crossed his face when the phone began to ring. "I'll get it," he said.

Tori jumped up from the sofa. "No, I will," she insisted, sure that it was Serge returning her call.

Her heart floated in her chest like a bobbing balloon as she hurried to the foyer. She picked up the receiver on the third ring. When she said hello the voice on the other end hissed laughter into her ear and her heart turned to lead. Even before he spoke, Tori knew it was Ulger, not Serge.

"Cute trick you played on me, baby, stealing your own dog back last night. Gotta hand it to you. You outsmarted me."

Who couldn't? Tori almost retorted. But she held her tongue. She sensed that no matter how stupid he was, Ugly was a dangerous character. The fact that he *was* stupid most likely made him more so. She didn't want to antagonize him.

"I'm thankful you didn't harm Jiggs," she told him, her voice strained.

"I kinda wish I did now," he replied. There wasn't the least trace of humor left in his oily voice. "No more games, doll. Let me speak to Gordon."

"I told you he was away on a trip." Tori instinctively wanted to protect her brother for as long as she could from this creature.

"Don't lie to me, sis. I'm having your house watched now, and I know he's back. If he tries to run away again he'll get as far as the nearest hospital."

"There's no need for threats," Tori told him, her stomach turning queasy. "You'll get the money Gordon owes you. I promise."

"I want all of it," Ulger stressed. "I'm sick of dealing with you Langfords. I want fifty grand by tomorrow night, and I wipe the slate clean."

"Fifty?" Tori could barely squeeze sound through her tightening throat. "You said he owed you ten!"

"That was interest, baby. Interest. But now I want to wash my hands of the whole deal. It's been nothing but aggravation."

"You're asking the impossible," Tori cried. "We can't possibly raise that much money by—"

"Hey, what's money compared to health?" Ulger interrupted to ask in a bland, conversational tone. "How's your brother's health, by the way? Has he broken any bones lately?"

Tori went rigid with fear. "You wouldn't dare harm Gordon!" she challenged. "I'll call the police."

"Not me!" Ugly protested, all innocence. "No one's been able to pin nothin' like that on *me*. I always got an airtight alibi. It's my friends who like to break things—like furniture, and windows. And, oh yeah, arms and legs. Take my advice, baby. Don't call in the cops. Gordon will get more than hurt if you do. Get my drift?"

"Yes." Her voice came out small and hopeless.

"Good girl. Gordon better bring the cash to the flower shop tomorrow night. You don't want he should end up in a wheelchair for the rest of his life, do ya?"

Ugly didn't wait for a reply, and the click that followed reverberated in Tori's ear. She returned to the parlor, pale and shaken, her large hazel eyes filled with misgiving. Gordon turned from the window on the other side of the room and took in her obvious agitation.

"You were talking to Zhdanov, weren't you? That's why you're so upset. He's not worth it, Victoria."

Tori shook her throbbing head. "That wasn't Serge. It was a man called Ugly. I believe you've done business with him."

Gordon blanched. "That lowlife had the gall to call my home?" He seemed more concerned with the impropriety of it than anything else.

Tori's patience snapped. "Dammit, Gordon, tell me what the hell is going on!"

"You needn't use profanity," he said huffily.

She'd never spoken to her big brother like that before. And now she wanted to grab him by the neck and throttle him. She clenched her fists to calm herself and took a deep breath. "Is it true that you owe this loan shark fifty thousand dollars?"

He nodded sharply. "It's none of your concern, though, dear. I can handle it. Ugly had no business bothering you about it."

"He's done more than just bother me, Gordon. He stole Jiggs last night."

Her brother gave her a disbelieving look, then glanced at the little spaniel curled up asleep on the sofa. "It appears that Mr. Jiggs found his way back to the comforts of home."

"Because Serge broke into The Friendly Florist and saved him!" Tori shouted. She decided to skip over the details of that episode and get to the heart of the matter. Gordon's inability to come to terms with the situation was rubbing Tori's nerves raw. "You're the one who's in danger now, Gordon," she told him, a quiver in her voice. "If Ugly doesn't have all the money you owe by tomorrow night, he'll hire some thugs to *hurt* you."

The color drained from Gordon's face, but he forced a smile. "What nonsense. He's bluffing."

Tori flung out her hands in frustration and despair. "Wake up and face reality, brother! You're in deep trouble. And don't think you can run away from it again. Ugly is having the house watched."

Gordon sank down on the sofa and stared at Tori with glazed gray eyes. It appeared she'd finally gotten through to him. "What am I going to do now?" he asked hopelessly.

He looked so helpless to her. She realized then that their roles were now reversed. Gordon had taken care of her when she was young, but now she would have to somehow take care of him. Her back straightened with resolve. She would find a solution.

"Get a bank loan," she said. "This house is worth a lot. You can put it up as collateral."

Gordon passed his hand across his pallid face. "I've tried that already. Months ago, before I got involved with Ugly. They treated me like a pariah. Me! A Langford. Our family name meant nothing to them. All they cared about was how I could repay the loan without any steady income or salary. They refused to consider the potential of my latest project, Victoria. Yet the only reason I needed the money was to continue work on it."

Tori almost felt relief. So that's why Gordon was in such debt. It wasn't gambling, or drugs. But was his obsession with this latest invention just as destructive? she worried.

"Oh, Gordon," she cried. "How could you have done such a stupid thing as borrow money from a loan shark? Why didn't you simply *sell* our house if you were so desperate?"

Her brother's eyes filled with disbelief and horror. "How could you even suggest such a thing? This house represents our heritage, Victoria. It stands for everything that we are. It would be like selling my soul."

"Maybe it's time you let go of the past, dear," Tori told him gently. "It's the life you have ahead of you that matters." She didn't press him further about selling the house, though. It was too late for that. Ugly's deadline loomed heavy and immediate. "Aunt Olive!" Tori suddenly cried.

Gordon moaned. "She wouldn't give me a penny."

"But she's our only living relative. It's worth a try."

Gordon drew back his hunched shoulders and sat up straight and rigid. "I won't do it, Victoria. I won't go begging to that awful old woman."

Tori knew her brother well enough to see that there was no arguing with him. Men and their stupid pride, she thought with more sadness than anger.

"Then I will, Gordon," she said.

She marched out of the parlor and went upstairs to change from her jeans to a demure gray dress. A supplicant's proper attire, she thought, pinning up her long hair. It was still a little damp. The memory of how it had gotten wet suddenly exploded in her mind, full force. Had it only been a few hours ago that Serge Zhdanov had joined her in the bathtub? She felt such a sudden deep longing for him that tears sprang to her eyes. She blinked them away—blinked away all thoughts of him. He was gone, and she had no time for regrets now. All that mattered at the moment was that her brother was in danger. Tori rushed out to take on the dreadful Aunt Olive.

Late-afternoon light slanted though Serge's condominium windows when he and Duke returned home from their walk. Serge had avoided the Public Garden, giving himself the excuse that it would be too crowded on such a balmy Sunday. He'd strolled along the Charles River instead, admiring the sleek racing shells skidding across the water. They reminded him of his glory days on the varsity crew team in college.

Which in turn reminded him of Gordon Langford, who'd been on the same team. They were more subtle about their dislike for each other in college than they'd been as boys, but it was just as strong. Serge had purposely chosen crew as his sport to outshine Gordon, who was captain of the team and had the key position of stroke. By junior year Serge had taken both honors away from Gordon. Looking back from the vantage point of maturity and success, Serge realized that a certain amount of spite had motivated him then. But Gordon had managed to get back at him years later, when Serge had applied for membership to a private rowing club. Gordon, a longstanding member, had blackballed him. Serge was sure of it.

But what did it all matter now? Serge asked himself wearily. Those old grudges seemed so unimportant in the light of Tori's eyes. He recalled how she'd sided with her brother earlier that day. Maybe she hadn't kicked him out in so many words, but she hadn't needed words; her look had been eloquent enough. He would always be an outsider as far as the Langfords were concerned. So what? he thought, shrugging. He'd never wanted any part of their stuffy world. Far better for Tori to become part of *his* world—if they had any chance of a future together, that is. Since her brother had made his appearance, Serge had doubts about that.

Serge filled Duke's bowl with fresh water and watched him lap it up. He'd never seen Duke so thirsty. After slurping up two bowls of water, the husky flopped belly down on the cool kitchen floor, still panting from the exertion of the walk. Serge was surprised that the mild exercise had exhausted him so much. He told himself that it was the sudden change to warm weather that was causing Duke's fatigue. Serge wasn't going to admit that his trusty pal for over fourteen years was getting old.

He turned on his stereo, opened another dark beer and settled in his Eames chair to watch the sun set. His thoughts skidded back to Tori. Last night, in her old-fashioned moonlit bedroom, he'd thought of her as a princess held captive by her own heritage. And he had wanted to help her escape.

But what if she didn't want to escape? What if she were perfectly content to live her exclusive, limited life in that mausoleum she called a home? Except for an unexpected and compelling physical attraction, they really had so little in common, Serge decided. What he couldn't decide was whether or not to return her call.

She'd hurt him that afternoon, quite deeply, when she'd given him that pleading look to go. Why hadn't she stood up to her brother? Why hadn't she insisted that he stay? Had what they'd shared together meant nothing to her in the end?

But of course, it had. He knew that much. Serge had never given or received so much satisfaction while making love. Of course, he would call her back, he thought, smiling to himself for having doubted it. He couldn't let her slip out of his life so easily. They would have to play out what they'd started together.

But the hurt still remained—a dull ache in his gut. For the sake of his injured pride, Serge decided not to contact Tori right away. He'd chased after her enough. It was her turn.

Chapter Eight

Tori's spirits were low when she returned home from her Aunt Olive's mansion in Brookline. She didn't look forward to telling her brother that the old lady had refused to lend the money. She went to the kitchen to put on the kettle for tea and could hear Gordon puttering about in his workshop below. Aunt Olive had accused him of being a worthless dreamer. Much like his father, she'd proclaimed.

What a bitter old lady, Tori thought sadly. As she stood waiting for the kettle to boil her slender shoulders sagged. She still couldn't believe that Aunt Olive had turned her back on them, even after she'd explained how urgent the situation was. She heard Gordon coming up the basement stairs and straightened her slumped shoulders. But her posture and brave smile didn't fool him.

"I told you it was a waste of time to ask Aunt Olive for a loan, Victoria." His expression and attitude were resigned. "Was she as nasty as ever?"

"As lonely as ever," Tori replied. "At least she has her cats, though. I counted at least ten of them roaming about her house."

"All she deserves for company is cats," Gordon declared. "She's an impossible old witch. I don't know why you tried to keep up a relationship with her all these years."

"Because she's our mother's sister, that's why," Tori told him softly. "Yet so unlike Mother." She gave a little shiver. "How Olive terrified me when I was a child!"

"And it terrified me to think of you being raised by such a cold woman," Gordon said. "That's why I fought so hard to become your guardian. Sometimes I wonder if I acted in your best interest, Victoria."

Tori frowned. "What do you mean?"

"She's a very wealthy woman. If you'd become her ward you might have been designated her heir."

Tori waved away that possibility. "Who cares about that? Let her leave all her money to her cats! I would have been so miserable living with her, Gordon. I'll always be grateful to you for saving me from that fate."

He patted her shoulder. "I never wanted or expected your gratitude." The kettle began to boil, and he turned away to take it off the flame. "Besides, in the end I failed you completely, didn't I?"

"No, that's not true," Tori objected. "You've been a wonderful brother."

"Hah! I can barely keep a roof over our heads. Seems I didn't inherit the Langford touch for making money."

"Neither did Father," Tori reminded him. "But we still adored him. And I'm no longer your responsibility anyway, Gordon. It's up to me to support myself."

"You do. The trouble is that you support your older brother, too."

"Why shouldn't I contribute to the household expenses? You paid all mine for years."

Gordon's expression remained bleak as he stared at her. "I'll never forgive myself for running off to Vermont and leaving you alone," he said. "But it never crossed my mind that Ugly would bother you, Victoria. You must believe me!"

Tori took her brother's hand and squeezed it. "Of course, I believe you. But you should have realized that Ugly is from a different world than we are, Gordon. He plays by different rules. If you don't pay him, he'll surely hurt you."

Her brother forced out a weak laugh. "Like I said before, Victoria, that insignificant worm is bluffing." The note of bravado in his voice rang false. "When I meet with him tomorrow evening, I'll give him a few thousand. I called that antique dealer I've been selling to, and he agreed to pay me cash for the silver candelabra. That should satisfy Ugly for a while. I'll get a lot more for the Persian rug in the parlor as soon as the dealer finds a buyer. I'll explain all that to Ugly. He'll understand he has to be patient to get his money."

"But he won't understand!" Tori cried, fearing that Gordon would never understand the danger he was in, either. "Ulger has it in for you now. He wants the entire amount you owe him."

"He's just trying to frighten you to get to me," Gordon insisted.

"He stole Jiggs!"

"A sick joke, that's all. He didn't actually harm the dog, did he?"

"He might have if Serge hadn't rescued him."

"Zhdanov, the big hero." Gordon snorted to show his disgust. "Don't be deceived, Victoria. He knew it was all a big game and was only playing along to impress you."

"That's not the way it happened at all. You weren't there, Gordon. You don't know."

"I know Zhdanov, though. For a lot longer than you have. He's capable of doing anything to get what he wants. How many times do I have to tell you that, Victoria?"

"Once was sufficient," she replied coolly. "I refuse to discuss him with you anymore. Besides, we're getting off-track. You've got to pay Ulger off tomorrow night."

"If I could, I would," Gordon replied in a weary voice. "But since I can't, I'm not going to worry about it. *Che sarà, sarà.*" With a gallant wave of his hand, he left the kitchen and went back to his basement workroom.

Tori could hear the patter of rain against her bedroom window when she awoke the next morning. She'd resolved during the night to save her brother since he wasn't going to make the least effort to save himself.

She reviewed all possibilities once again before getting up. There were no other relatives to approach now that Aunt Olive had turned her down. The close friends Tori had were mostly struggling artists to whom *she* lent money on occasion. Gallery sales had been good during the past few months, but the cash flow was still a mere trickle. Like most art dealers, Tori had informal extended-payment arrangements with her clients. She'd considered applying for a bank loan on the basis of gallery sales projections, but that would take too long. No, there was only one real possibility, and she didn't like it any better than she had all during the long, restless night.

If only she could stay in bed and listen to the rain instead of facing the problems that awaited her, she thought longingly. But heaving a deep sigh, she threw off the covers. Face them she must. She couldn't hide in her bedroom all her life the way her namesake had. Or even all morning.

Tori selected a pale lemon suit to wear, hoping the sunny color would improve her frame of mind. She automatically reached for the silk blouse she usually wore with it, then hung it back in her closet. Why not be a little daring for once? she asked herself. But after studying herself in the mirror, she decided that the V of the blazer dipped a little too daringly for comfort. She compromised by closing the plunging neckline a little higher with a cameo brooch. The brooch had been in the family for generations, and many of the Langford ladies were wearing it in their portraits.

Staring at herself in the gilt-framed oval mirror, Tori remembered too much in too fast a rush. She would never be able to look into that mirror again without seeing Serge's dark-haired reflection as it had looked in the silvery moonlight.

She'd waited for his call all night. She'd prayed for it. She'd even sat beside the telephone for a long while, as if her presence would coax it to ring. But nothing had worked. Serge didn't call her back.

If only he had, how much easier this morning would be, Tori thought. But nothing had ever come easily for her, she reminded herself. How foolish for her to expect her life to change now. She adjusted the cameo brooch ever so slightly, hoping it would bring her some sorely needed luck.

"There's a very persistent young lady outside, Serge," his secretary Sonya Poliky announced as she stomped into his office. "One of those hoity-toity society types. I told her that she couldn't possibly see you without an appointment, but she insists."

Serge glanced up from the prospectus he was perusing. "What's her name, Sonya?"

"Victoria Langtree. Or something like that."

"Close enough." Serge smiled. So Lady Green Eyes had decided to pursue him after all. Good for her! "Show her in, Sonya."

Mrs. Poliky sniffed and checked the timepiece dangling from a velvet rope around her neck. It was a stopwatch. She took great pride in arranging Serge's schedule down to the very second. "You don't have time. We're expecting those Japanese investors. I can put Ms. Junior League off. Most likely she's here to ask you to donate to some charity or other."

Serge's smile didn't waver. He was used to Mrs. Poliky trying to tell him how to run his business. She was his mother's cousin and had been with him from the very beginning. And she was right. The scheduled meeting was very important to Serge. It had to do with a complicated electronics venture he'd been putting together for months. But if he refused to see Tori now, he'd be lowering his chances of ever seeing her again, he decided. He hadn't expected her to come in person to apologize to him. That took a lot more guts than another phone call.

"Don't keep the lady waiting," he told Mrs. Poliky. "When our visitors from Tokyo show up, offer them tea."

Mrs. Poliky's eyes narrowed with disapproval. "Oh, really, Serge! They won't appreciate tea bags in hot water. And they won't appreciate cooling their heels after traveling halfway across the world to see you. Let me tell this Ms. Langtree to come back some other time.''

"Show her *in*," Serge repeated, this time without a smile.

Mumbling something in Russian that Serge didn't quite catch, Mrs. Poliky stomped out as irately as she'd stomped in.

Tori looked up expectantly when Serge's secretary returned to the reception area where she'd been ordered to wait. She realized now that she should have made an appointment. She had realized it even before Mrs. Poliky had made it so very clear to her that Mr. Zhdanov was an exceedingly busy man. Hub Venture Capital was located in one of Boston's recently erected mirror-glassed towers, and the firm's office suite was impressive. As risky as Serge claimed his occupation to be, he was apparently very successful at it.

"He says he'll see you right now, Ms. Langtree."

Tori jumped up from the sleek leather-and-chrome chair she'd been perched on, sensing that when Serge's secretary said *now* she meant this very instant and no later. Intimidated by Mrs. Poliky's glowering countenance, Tori didn't correct her about mistaking her name. It had taken all her gumption to insist on seeing Serge in the first place.

When Tori entered his inner sanctum Serge stood up. "You look just like a daffodil," he said.

His comment took Tori aback, and then she looked down at her yellow suit and laughed self-consciously. She wished she'd worn her sensible navy blue one instead. That would have been much more businesslike. She touched her cameo, as if for luck.

Serge couldn't believe what had just popped out of his mouth. A daffodil? How corny could he get? But she really did remind him of one, with that graceful, long neck of hers. "Have a seat," he offered a little brusquely.

Tori settled herself in the chair in front of his massive, streamlined desk. Briefcase on her lap, she crossed her legs, then recrossed them. Observing this nervous poetry in motion, Serge sat down again himself to get a better view. He wasn't thinking about silly daffodils anymore; he was remembering the last time they'd made love.

Say something! Tori commanded herself, but the jolt of seeing Serge again had made her suddenly speechless. She'd almost gotten used to his virile presence during the many hours she'd spent in his company over the weekend, had actually felt easy and comfortable with him at times. Now his effect on her was as potent and disquieting as the first time they'd met in the Public Garden. What was it about this man that made her head spin so fast that all thoughts flew out of it? She was sure that he could hear her heart pounding. The sound of it filled her ears and must have filled the entire room. "I realize how busy you are," she finally managed to say. "I won't take up too much of your time."

How cool and aloof she was, Serge thought. She was acting as if they were strangers who'd shared nothing at all together except polite conversation. But if she felt that way, then what was she doing here? "Take up as much time as you'd like," he replied with the same strained civility as she'd used.

It was obvious to her that he meant just the opposite. She should never have come. They hadn't parted on good terms, he'd never returned her phone call, and he probably never expected or wanted to see her again. She tried to push all that out of her mind, telling herself that the purpose of her visit had nothing to do with personal feelings. And she almost believed this to be true.

She cleared her throat. "Serge, I might as well get directly to the point."

He leaned back in his swivel chair, ready to hear the apology that he assumed she'd come in person to give him. He was sure things would warm up between them once she got it out of the way. He gave her an encouraging nod.

"Well, figures speak louder than words." She snapped open her briefcase. "I worked up a rough financial report on Back Bay Gallery for you. I can supply more details if you need them." She pulled out some papers and placed them on his desk. "But as you'll see from this income statement, sales have doubled this year. And my projection for next year is—"

"Hold it," Serge interrupted. "You've come here to discuss your art gallery with me?" He raised his thick dark eyebrows, and his vivid blue eyes regarded her sharply. "Why?"

"Actually, I've come to discuss a business loan."

"I see." And he did, very clearly. Like everybody else who came to his office, all she wanted from him was money.

"How much?" he asked flatly.

"Fifty thousand dollars."

Serge gave out a harsh laugh. "You think a night with you was worth *that* much, Ms. Langford?"

Tori shot up from her seat, and the open briefcase tumbled to the floor, spilling out its contents. "How could you say something so cruel?"

"It was easy." Serge felt no remorse whatsoever. "You kick me out of your house one day, and then have the nerve to come here asking for money the next. What kind of chump do you take me for?"

"My mistake was taking you for a gentleman."

Serge laughed again. "I never claimed to be one."

Tori bent down and began collecting all the scattered papers and stuffing them into her briefcase. Gentleman or not, Serge came around his big desk to help her. "Why don't you go to a bank if you need a loan?" he muttered.

"Because I need the money by tonight. Do you think I would have come here if I weren't desperate?" She snatched back the papers he was holding, threw them into her briefcase and slammed it shut. "But it's obvious that I made a terrible mistake. Goodbye, Mr. Zhdanov. Sorry to have wasted even a moment of your precious time."

He blocked the doorway with his large, solid frame before she reached it.

"How desperate are you, exactly?"

She raised her firm Langford chin. "Not enough to beg from you, if that's what you mean. I came here with a legitimate business offer. There was no need for you to insult me like that."

"So now you want money *and* an apology?" Serge reached out and tilted her chin even higher with his fingertip until she was looking directly into his eyes. "You've got a lot to learn about business, honey. To get what you want, you've got to take a lot, too. And never, ever let the other guy know you're desperate."

She twisted her face from his light touch, but her eyes remained riveted to his. "Thanks for the belated advice."

"So what's your offer, Tori? What do I get in exchange for that amount of money? Surely you don't expect me to simply hand it over out of the goodness of my heart?"

"Hardly!" There was nothing in his tough, lean face that would lead her to believe he even had a heart. He was a stranger to her now, not the man she'd given herself to so completely. "You'll get your money back, plus interest, within a year."

Considering this, he fingered the cameo brooch holding her jacket together. "Now tell me why you want it so badly."

"It's for Gordon," she admitted outright.

Serge released his hold on the cameo. "That's what I guessed. Your brother always comes first with you, doesn't he? You're only here for his sake."

"He's in big trouble, Serge! Ugly will have him hurt if he doesn't pay off his entire debt by this evening."

Serge appeared completely unmoved by the tremor in her voice. "Why the hell should I help out your brother? He's never done anything for me."

Tori flinched inwardly at the bluntness of his refusal. "If you want me to beg, then that's what I'll do. Please, Serge. Lend me this money." Her face was pale with the effort of pleading.

A spark of triumph gleamed in his chilling blue eyes, but he shook his head slowly. "You came to the wrong place, lady. I don't make money lending it out. I invest it in businesses that have growth potential. You say sales in that gallery of yours have doubled this year?"

Tori took a step back from him. "I'm not looking for a partner," she said warily.

"No, but you're looking for fifty thousand dollars. I'd be willing to give you that for a sixty-percent share in your business."

She reacted as if he'd just slapped her. The color rushed to her cheeks, and her eyes blazed green. "That's ludicrous! I've devoted my life to Back Bay Gallery these past five years. You can't expect me to agree to that!"

"I guess I can't expect anything from you, Tori," he replied softly. His tone changed. "Okay. I'll settle for a fifty-percent share."

"Do you realize how unfair that is?" Tori crossed the room and slammed her briefcase on top of his desk. She shuffled through the disarrayed papers in it until she found what she was searching for. She shook it in front of Serge's impassive face. "Take a look at these figures. An equal partnership is worth three times what you're offering."

"I believe you," he said without so much as glancing down at the sheet. "But you're in no position to haggle."

"And you're no better than Ulger," she told him.

Her insult made no dent in his cool demeanor. He simply shrugged. "I'm offering you exactly what you need, lady. No more or less. That's about as fair as life gets. Take it or leave it."

"I'll never let you be my partner!" She headed for the door again, and this time he didn't try to stop her from leaving. She paused, gripping the doorknob so tightly that pain shot up her arm. When she turned back to Serge he was settled behind his desk, watching her. "You win," she said, tears of frustration stinging her eyes. "I have no choice but to accept your terms."

Serge merely nodded, demonstrating no pleasure in his victory. He scribbled a note and handed it to her. "My lawyer's address. He'll have a contract ready for you to sign this afternoon, and a check you can cash immediately."

"Very well." Tori left without offering her thanks or her hand.

Not that Serge had expected either. The moment she was gone he began to regret driving such a hard bargain with her. He wasn't the least bit interested in her art gallery. He'd really been bargaining for some control over her, he admitted to himself.

And that's exactly what he'd gotten. He settled back in his deep leather chair a bit uneasily. Funny, but he'd never wanted control over a woman before. Was he just being vindictive because Tori was a Langford? Or did he resent how deeply she'd gotten under his skin?

Serge shifted uncomfortably. Motives like that left little room for self-respect. And self-respect was what mattered most to him—more than money or power or perhaps even love. He had a reputation for being shrewd and hard-driving. It was a reputation he'd fostered. But no one he'd ever done business with could ever have accused him of being underhanded or even unreasonable—no one until Victoria Langford.

Of course she didn't realize that entrepreneurs came from all over to seek out his aid in their new ventures. Serge was more than a financier. He took an active role in the development and management of start-up companies and was proud of his success rate. Everybody profited in the end. And with the benefit of his business savvy, so would Tori. Reminding himself of this salved Serge's conscience. In fact he began to feel almost saintly as he considered how much he could help her with her little art business. If she continued to resent his part ownership in her gallery, he could always release her from the deal. He wasn't an ogre, after all. He really did have her best interests at heart. And to top it off, he was saving her brother's scrawny neck, wasn't he?

Fifty thousand dollars was a lot of money to owe a loan shark, especially a small-time hood like Ugly, who could get real mean if he got desperate for it. Tori had been right to be so concerned. The dognapping had just been a little mind-game Ugly had been playing. But if Gordon owed that much... Serge shook his head. Gordon had really made a mess of things this time.

Growing up in a tough city neighborhood, Serge had dealt with sleazy characters like Ugly before. At heart they were chicken and always backed away from a showdown. Then they would wait for the chance to catch you from behind. The secret of survival, Serge had learned, was to never give them that chance.

But what did people like the Langfords know about survival? A big nothing, that's what, Serge thought. He drummed his fingers against the desktop and came to a decision. He would have to pay a little visit to the Friendly Florist that day. A *friendly* visit. He wasn't going to twist Ugly's arm or anything. Not if he didn't have to, that is. No, he was just going to make it clear to the little creep that it was Zhdanov's money paying off Gordon's debt. And it was Zhdanov he'd have to answer to if any harm ever came to any member of the Langford family, including the little spaniel.

Chapter Nine

"Are you going to tell me why you've been so depressed lately, Tori?" Ginger asked. She was perched on a stool behind the gallery counter, nibbling on Godiva chocolates. "Or am I going to have to pry it out of you?"

Tori continued to gaze out the large showroom window overlooking Newbury Street. She counted three black umbrellas, one gaily striped, and one proclaiming the bearer to be a supporter of public television. It had been raining nonstop for four days, since Monday morning. Business was slow.

"It's the weather," she replied. "What a miserable spring it's turning out to be. Poor Jiggs is going stir-crazy without his morning walks in the Garden."

"Are you depressed, too, Jiggs?" Ginger asked the little dog, who was regarding each bite of candy she took with intense desire. She gave him a piece. "Well, at least blue-eyed wolves can't attack you in here. Right, Tori?"

"Yes, we can be grateful for that I suppose," she answered.

Then she saw Serge charging across the street, heading straight toward the gallery. Adrenaline shot through her, and her immediate impulse was to flee. But she held her ground. "Looks like we have a customer, Ginger," she reported in a deceptively mild tone.

"A live one?" Ginger looked toward the door just as Serge walked in. "Oh, yes, indeed." She beamed with appreciation at the sight of him.

Serge's galvanizing presence seemed to fill every inch of the gallery's air space the moment he entered. He brought in the fresh smell of rain. His beige trench coat was damp, and he ran his hand through his thick dark hair, flicking off droplets. His light, bright eyes went directly toward Tori, who remained standing by the window, as still as one of the sculptures on display—except her hammering heart, that is.

"Good afternoon, Ms. Langford."

She barely nodded a greeting. "What brings you here, Mr. Zhdanov?"

"Just checking up on my investment," he replied breezily.

"I assumed that you'd be a silent partner," she said, her expression so stiff that her lips barely moved.

"Oh, no. I believe in staying totally involved in all my affairs. I'm a hands-on sort of guy." He noticed that she was wearing her exquisite cameo brooch again, pinned to the lapel of her white gabardine shirtdress, and he reached out to touch it.

This time Tori brushed his hand away. "And I'm a *hands-off* sort of gal," she told him.

"Really?" He grinned. "You could have fooled me, lady." His grin was as wide as a schoolboy's.

Tori found his gloat more than a little offensive. "You're the one who fooled me in the end, Mr. Zhdanov. Of course, I've had little experience with your type."

"You make up for your lack of experience by being a fast learner, though, if I remember correctly," Serge reminded her. He was picturing her exactly the way she had looked, pale skin flushed, in a bathtub filled with magnolia blossoms.

And as if she could read his mind, Tori blushed that same delicate shade of pink. "You should have made an appointment before barging in here."

"Why? Isn't this gallery open to the public?" Since Tori remained silent, Serge turned to the pretty little blonde behind the counter, who was leaning forward, straining to hear their conversation. "It's okay if I look around, isn't it, miss?"

"Of course it is!" Ginger assured him enthusiastically. "Back Bay Gallery welcomes browsers."

She was taking Serge in with the same intensity with which Jiggs had watched her eat chocolates. Pretty soon she's going to start drooling, Tori thought sarcastically. Then she recalled that she, too, had gawked at Serge the first time she'd seen him running in the Garden. She forgave Ginger instantly.

"Why don't you show the gentle—" Tori stopped herself deliberately. "Why don't you show this man around, Ginger," she suggested.

Ginger almost bounded over the counter. "I'd be thrilled to," she replied, taking the long way around it. She still managed to be at Serge's side in a second flat. "Let me hang up that wet coat of yours first," she offered.

"Why, thank you, that's very kind," Serge replied, slipping it off. "*You* certainly know how to make someone feel welcome, miss."

"Call me Ginger," she urged, beaming up at him. "What's your name?"

He told her, then took her plump, soft little hand. "It's a pleasure to meet you, Ginger." And Serge meant it. He'd always liked curvaceous little blondes with easy smiles and cute snub noses just begging to be kissed.

"The pleasure's all mine, Serge," she replied, batting her baby blues.

Tori couldn't stand their banter a moment longer. "I'll be in my office," she informed her assistant crisply. She didn't bother to say anything to Serge before she left the showroom.

Alone in her small office, Tori breathed a sigh of relief. She found it absolutely suffocating to be in the presence of Serge Zhdanov now. She could never forgive him for what he'd done to her. He'd deliberately and coldheartedly taken half of the only thing she cared about—her gallery. That she had cared so much about *him* made it all the worse. But that, at least, was over and done with. She would never allow Serge to come so close to capturing her heart again. And to think she'd actually believed that she was falling in love with him at the time!

Tori shook her head weakly over her own stupidity. Sex was one thing. Love was a different matter entirely. She resolved never to get the two mixed up again. It was far wiser to stay away from either inclination, she decided. Less than a week ago, minding her own business as she walked her dog in the park, she'd been relatively content with life—until she'd spotted Serge Zhdanov. Then everything had changed . . . for the worse.

"Oh, Jiggsy," she moaned aloud. "If only I hadn't let you run free that day."

Tori glanced around her office, suddenly realizing that her constant companion hadn't followed her into it. She opened the door and called softly down the long, narrow hall. There was no response. She paused before entering the showroom. She could hear Serge and Ginger laughing together, having a wonderful time. She peeked in to see Jiggs in Serge's arms. Unreasonable as she knew it to be, a burning sense of betrayal scorched her heart. Serge, the enemy in her camp, had won over her dog and best friend! At the same time Tori was thankful that it was her dog in Serge's arms and not Ginger. Totally confused by her clashing emotions, Tori tiptoed back into her office, hoping she could sort them out. But confusion still reigned when, a short time later, there was a tap on her door.

Tori was standing by the little half-raised window, breathing in the scent of rain on the tarred alleyway. "Come in," she called, hoping it was Ginger, while at the same time hoping it wasn't.

Serge entered, Jiggs trotting in right behind him. "This crazy dog of yours has become very attached to me," he announced.

Tori gave them both a cold look. "Dogs aren't very good judges of character," she remarked dryly.

"Yes, they are. They're more discriminating than people," Serge contradicted.

"If that's the case, Jiggs was right about you in the first place. I should have paid more attention when he bit you."

"I liked your initial reaction to me a hell of a lot better," Serge told her in his husky, low voice, moving in closer.

Tori's office was too small for her to keep much of a distance between them. She extended her arm. Her palm pushed against hard muscle beneath his white cotton business shirt. "Stay away from me," she said.

He didn't back off. "I have. For three and a half days. I figured that would give you enough time to cool down."

"You figured wrong." Between clenched teeth, her tone was seething. "Why are you here bothering me? I already signed my name in blood on those hateful papers giving you half my business." That was a bit of an exaggeration. She'd used his lawyer's sterling-silver pen to sign them.

Serge raised the thick dark eyebrows hooding his icy eyes. "You got what you wanted in return, didn't you?"

"I got the money I needed, if that's what you mean."

"Then what are you bellyaching about?"

"You do have a charming way of putting things, don't you?" She threw him a condescending look. "Do you expect me to *thank* you for making that deal with me?"

"Yeah." He pressed his chest against her palm. "I think a simple thank-you is in order."

"Hah! Then you'll die of old age waiting for it."

With as little effort as it took him to blink, he grabbed her wrist and pushed back her forearm. He got as close to her as he wanted to then, only a hairbreadth away. "I don't like to wait for anything," he warned. "If you keep pushing me away, I'll stop coming back."

"Is that a threat? I hope it's a promise. I don't want you to come back, Serge. You've ruined anything we ever had together." Her throat tightened as she stated this, and she almost choked on the words.

"No, I haven't. You still want me." Grabbing her by the waist, he tugged her to him, none too gently, until their bodies melded.

She could feel the heat of him through his business suit—and the heat of her own desire as she pressed against him. His lips crushed down on hers, demanding a response. She gave him what he wanted, unable to hold back. It angered her to be so weak, so powerless in his arms. How could she let him take from her like this? How could she still want him so much? But the taste and touch of him was as exhilarating as always, too exhilarating to shut out. Self-control was nearly impossible now that she knew what further ecstasy his kiss could lead to. *Nearly* impossible. She would not allow herself to give in to him. As much as her body was throbbing for him, her mind was set against him. She tore her hungry lips from his.

"No!" she cried out. "It's over between us."

"Liar," he whispered. But he released her immediately. He'd fully expected her to object. What he hadn't expected was how easily, how quickly they could arouse each other. No, that part of their relationship hadn't changed at all. And she knew it as well as he did.

"It would go against my principles to make love with a man who robbed me blind," she told him, head high, eyes unwavering as they locked with his.

Serge groaned. "I really hate it when you use that superior tone with me. Didn't you go against those high principles of yours when you asked the man you recently made love with for money?"

"You were the last person I wanted to ask," she replied softly. "But you were also the only one I could turn to. So I did what I had to do to help my brother." A certain sadness crept into her voice. "I never wanted to take advantage of you, Serge. And I didn't expect you to take such advantage of me. I guess you really don't know a person until you're forced to do business with him.''

He glared at her indignantly. "Listen, lady. People line up outside my office to *beg* me to go into partnership with them. And do you know why?'' Obviously she didn't, so he didn't wait for a reply. "Because they know that Serge Zhdanov has the magic touch, that's why.''

Tori knew that well enough on a more intimate level but wasn't about to tell him so. "Like Midas, you mean?'' she asked coolly.

Serge ignored her sarcasm. "Exactly. I turn every business I touch into gold. We're talking millions, Tori, not thousands. Your little art gallery is hardly worth my time or effort.''

She pressed her palms together. "Then give it back to me,'' she requested.

His slanting blue eyes narrowed. "Maybe I will—eventually. But first I'm going to prove to you that I did you a big favor by buying into it.'' He shrugged. "Who knows. I'll probably make you rich. I'm in the habit of doing that for my partners.''

"I'm managing just fine on my own,'' she objected. "The last thing I want or need is your interference.''

He completely ignored her protest. "First things first. Let me take a look at your books.'' He rubbed his hands together, eager to get started. "Turning around this business is going to be child's play.''

"My gallery isn't a new *toy* you just purchased. I don't want it turned around. I want it left alone. I want you to butt out of my business, Zhdanov!'' She threw open her office door and waited beside it for him to leave.

Serge *tsk*ed his tongue. "Rudeness doesn't suit you, Tori, but you'll be gushing with gratitude soon enough." He immediately made himself comfortable behind her delicate Hepplewhite desk—as comfortable as possible, anyway. He shifted his large frame in the graceful shield-back chair. He could barely fit his long legs in the desk kneehole. He began to open drawers and pull out files.

Tori watched him, eyes blazing green. "Are you deaf? Didn't you hear what I just said?"

He glanced up as if surprised that she was still hanging around. "Didn't you read the contract you signed, lady? I'm half owner of this enterprise now. I think that gives me the right to look over the finances, doesn't it?"

Tori wanted to scream. Better yet, she wanted to grab hold of that silk tie he was wearing and strangle him. Instead she stamped her foot—an ineffectual gesture that made her feel ridiculous. "You can't just barge in here and take over like this."

"Sure, I can," he replied easily.

"This office isn't big enough for the two of us."

He nodded in agreement. "You must have *something* you could do out in the showroom, Tori. I noticed that some of the picture frames needed dusting."

Tori didn't even slam the door when she exited. Such demonstrations of pique weren't her style. She wouldn't let Serge Zhdanov turn her into a screaming fishwife, either. No, cool dignity was the best policy when dealing with him, she told herself. In the end he would get bored of this little game he was taunting her with, and she would see the last of him. Happy as this last thought should have been, it did little to comfort her.

"Where's the hunk?" Ginger asked when Tori entered the showroom.

Tori rolled her eyes. "He's really not *that* attractive, Ginger. Especially after you get to know him."

"Come off it, sweetie!" Ginger gave her a knowing smile. "Your cool princess act can't fool me. You've got it bad for that guy. The minute he walked in you started vibrating."

"He's strictly a business associate," Tori said distinctly. "Nothing more." As far as she was concerned, that's the way things would stay between them. She preferred to keep what they'd shared in the past to herself.

"What kind of associate?" Ginger wanted to know. "Somehow he doesn't strike me as the artsy type. He told me that all the paintings would probably look better hanging upside down. Or facing the wall. But he was joking... I think."

Tori smiled tightly. "His taste probably runs to toreadors painted on black velvet. But for better or worse, he's my partner now, Ginger. I sold him fifty percent of my business."

Her friend's round eyes rounded even more. "Whatever possessed you to do that, Tori?"

She smoothed her hand over her sleek chignon. "I had a bit of a cash-flow problem."

Ginger folded her arms across her ample chest. She wasn't buying it. "But you've always had that problem and struggled through it. Why sell out now, when you're finally showing a profit? It doesn't make sense to me. Especially with the big gallery show coming up. That's going to produce a lot of publicity and sales.

"There's no guarantee that it will. What if it's a total flop?"

"Oh, Tori, that doesn't sound like you at all. You're not leveling with me." Ginger's full, rosy face took on a hurt expression.

Tori looked away from her, feeling terrible. Ginger was not only a good friend, but a trusted employee who'd stuck it out with her through thick and thin. And now she was keeping back so much from her. She didn't think she had the right to tell Ginger the whole truth, though. Langfords were always discreet about family problems, and Gordon's debt was his private affair. He'd never forgive her if she told Ginger, of all people, about it. It was bad enough that she'd been forced to confide in Serge Zhdanov, his old enemy. Tori shuddered to think how her brother would react if he found out it was Serge's money that got him off the hook with Ugly.

Ginger studied her long nails during the uncomfortable silence that followed, as if deeply contemplating the wisdom of painting them a different shade. But when she spoke it was apparent that she'd been reflecting on a more serious matter. "I think I understand what's going on here," she said. "You needed money to get Gordon out of debt, didn't you, Tori?"

"You know about that?" Tori was both shocked and relieved that she did. She'd been longing to confide in her all week.

"I've known about it for months," Ginger confessed, "I was the one who introduced Ugly to Gordon."

Tori's mouth flew open. "You set my brother up with a loan shark?"

"Not intentionally!" Ginger protested. "I met Ugly at a big party Gordon and I went to. He told me he was a bookie, and I thought it would amuse Gordon to chat with him. Hah! Once they got to talking, your brother told Ugly how much he needed money to buy materials for this project he was working on. Ugly offered him a loan."

"Oh, Ginger, why didn't you tell me all this sooner?"

Ginger pulled at her fluffy halo of hair. "I promised Gordon that I wouldn't. You had your own business worries. Besides, Gordon didn't want his little sister to know how desperate he was to keep financially afloat."

"Yet he shared his problems with you," Tori pointed out softly.

Ginger sighed. "For a while there, Gordon and I had no secrets. We were like *that*." She crossed her first two fingers together tightly, revealing more to Tori with that little gesture than she ever had before. "But we argued constantly. About Ulger...about other things." She brushed at the sleeve of her hot-pink sweater, as if brushing away the past. "Anyway, Gordon convinced me that it would be unnecessary to bother you about his debt because everything would work out in the end."

"How on earth did Gordon think that he could ever repay it?" Tori asked, her voice high with exasperation.

"His latest project is sure to be a success once he gets it off the ground," Ginger replied with a great deal of conviction.

Tori shook her head. Her own faith in Gordon was quickly diminishing. "If you believe that, then you must still be in love with him."

"I never said that I was *ever* in love with him," Ginger objected in an uncharacteristically sharp tone. "Let's get back to Serge. He's your partner now because he gave you the cash to pay off Ugly, right?"

Tori nodded and clutched at her friend's arm. "But Gordon must never know that, Ginger. Promise me you won't tell him. He thinks the money came from a bank loan."

"Why shouldn't he know the truth?"

"He hates Serge. Serge hates him. It goes back a long way. I don't understand it completely. But please promise me."

"All right," Ginger agreed reluctantly, her round face pinched with misgiving. "But it'll all come out in the end. These things always do."

"Talking about me?"

Both women looked up, startled, to see Serge's tall frame in the doorway, holding Jiggs.

Tori took the toy spaniel from his arms. He hadn't bought a fifty-percent share in Jiggs's affections, after all.

"I was just apprising Ginger of our business arrangement, Mr. Zhdanov," she said stiffly.

"Did Ms. Langford tell you how I took advantage of her?" he asked Ginger, giving her a smile and a wink.

"No. But I can't say I'd mind you taking advantage of me someday, Serge," Ginger replied, using her most sensuous tone of voice. She winked back.

It was a little too much for Tori—this easy camaraderie the two of them had instantaneously settled into. To say nothing of Jiggs's complete about-face. The dog was restless in her arms, apparently preferring to be held by Serge.

Tapping her foot impatiently, Tori listened to Ginger and Serge flirt for a while.

"Your name suits you, Ginger," Serge was saying. "I bet you could spice up any man's life."

Giggles bubbled up Ginger's throat. "I've been known to do just that. Not that I want to brag or anything." Eyes lowered, she studied her long nails modestly.

"Whoever you're involved with now certainly must feel like bragging about it."

Ginger's rosy color got rosier. "There was someone special for a time, but I'm back to playing the field. A rolling stone has a lot more fun than a mossy one, right?"

Serge threw back his head and laughed. "I couldn't have put it better myself, Ginger."

Enough! Tori wanted to scream. "It's closing time," she said instead, glancing at her watch. Actually it was ten minutes short of that. "Why don't you and Mr. Zhdanov continue your deep conversation over a drink or something, Ginger? I'll close up shop." She hoped her suggestion had come out light and friendly and uncaring despite her being set on edge.

"That's a great idea," Ginger enthused, looking from Tori to Serge. "But why don't you join us, Tori?"

"Please do, Ms. Langford," Serge said smoothly. "As Ginger here might say, two's a crowd, but three's company."

Tori didn't crack even the smallest sign of a smile. "But I'm sure you mean just the opposite, Mr. Zhdanov."

"Oh, come on, Tori. It'll be fun," Ginger urged. "Maybe we can get Serge to spring for a bottle of champagne."

"Excellent suggestion." Serge gave her an approving glance. Then he turned an icy gaze on Tori. "We'll toast our new partnership."

"I have other plans for this evening," she said curtly. And so she did. She had planned to finish reading *Pride and Prejudice*. Not that she didn't know how it ended; she had read it many times before. It was one of her favorites.

Ginger made a few more attempts at persuading her to join them, but Tori remained politely adamant. Giving up with a shrug, Ginger went off to get her raincoat and Serge's, hanging in the back hallway. The moment she was gone, Tori lit into him.

"I thought that even you would be above such blatant and immature tactics," she told him in a harsh whisper.

"I beg your pardon?" he asked in a loud, injured tone.

She gestured for him to lower it. "This little game you're playing with Ginger: you're using her to get back at me."

"Is it getting to you?" His wolfish smile flashed bright.

"No!" she protested loudly. Then she lowered her voice to a sizzling whisper again. "There's nothing between us now. Nothing! But don't you dare hurt my friend to be spiteful. For all her bravado, Ginger is basically very naive and trusting. And I like her too much to let her get hurt by someone like you."

"I like her, too," Serge replied. "But if you're so concerned about her, why'd you suggest we go off and have drinks together?"

Tori didn't quite know why she *had* done that. Her immediate impulse at the moment had been to simply get them both out of her sight. "I figured that once she got to know you better, she'd see through you. I know I certainly did."

"Why, I almost feel naked under your disapproving gaze, Ms. Langford."

"Don't flatter yourself into thinking that's how I'm picturing you, Mr. Zhdanov."

"Would your expression be just as disapproving if you were?" He moved in closer.

She stood her ground. "It's your *character* that I find lacking, not your physique."

"I'll tell you what I find lacking in you, lady."

She arched her eyebrows and pretended nonchalance. "Do tell."

"Your ability to keep good accounts. Your bookkeeping is a crime, Tori!"

"I'm sure I know more about keeping books than you do about art."

"So smug." He lightly tapped her sharp chin with his forefinger. "I'll tell you what. If you let me show you how to set up proper account records, I'll let you give me an art education. Maybe then we can come close to being on the same wavelength."

"I doubt we ever will be, but it's worth a try," she agreed reluctantly. "Have you ever visited the Museum of Fine Arts?"

"I'd be willing to let you give me a tour," he allowed.

"You'll probably be bored to death."

"Well, that's one way to get rid of me as your partner," he joked.

As they made arrangements to meet at the museum the next morning, Ginger returned with Serge's raincoat over her arm. "Where shall we go for a drink?" she asked him.

"I think the Ritz Bar," he said, shuffling his big frame into it.

"Oooh," Ginger cooed. "I dearly love a classy man."

"Sure you won't change your mind and join us, Ms. Langford?" he asked politely.

But once Tori's mind was made up, it remained so. "Thank you, but no. As I mentioned, I do have other plans this evening."

"Well, have a good time. I know we will!" Ginger said in parting as Serge ushered her out the door, his long arm around her waist.

To make matters worse, Jiggs started trotting along in their wake, perfectly willing to join their little party and leave his mistress behind. Tori called him back sharply, and Jiggs stopped short in his tracks. He came back to her reluctantly, white plume tail drooping.

"So you were going to desert me, too, weren't you, little fellow?" Tori asked, a lump in her throat as she patted him, feeling very sorry for herself, indeed.

Tori was in bed reading later that evening, when Gordon tapped on her door. She told him to come in, surprised at such a rare visit from him.

He glanced around. "Nothing's changed much since Great-Aunt Victoria's time here, I see," he observed.

"I had the room repapered last winter," Tori told her brother.

He examined the roses and lilies on the wall intently. So intently that Tori put down her book and examined him in the same manner. "You didn't come here to look at my new wallpaper, did you, Gordon?"

He gave out his hesitant little laugh and looked back at her. "No, of course not. I don't mean to intrude, Victoria."

"But you're not. Have a seat," she said, gesturing toward the velvet chaise longue in the corner.

He accepted her invitation and perched on the edge of it, looking very awkward, as any man would. It was a plush, curving piece of furniture designed especially for a woman.

Uncomfortable, he stood up again. "I guess this could wait till morning."

Tori wasn't about to let him politely retreat. "Apparently it can't wait, or you wouldn't be here now, Gordon. What is it? Not more trouble with Ugly?"

"No, thank God." Gordon brushed his hand across is high forehead. "Ugly hasn't bothered me since I paid him off. A day doesn't go by when I don't thank you for that bank loan, Victoria."

His gratitude made her uncomfortable because it amplified the guilt she felt over lying to him about it. "Is that all you came to tell me?"

"Not exactly. I thought you'd be interested to know who I saw at the Ritz Bar this evening."

Tori arched a sleek eyebrow, knowing what was coming next.

"Serge Zhdanov," Gordon said harshly. "With your little friend Ginger O'Neil." He said her name more slowly, stretching out each vowel as if it were a sad chant.

Since this wasn't news to Tori, she could pretend complete indifference. "So?"

Disappointed by her mild reaction, Gordon frowned. "Don't you find that the least bit upsetting? I assumed you still cared for Zhdanov despite my objections."

"I changed my mind about him." Tori smoothed the bed covers over her lap. "But not because of anything you said, Gordon."

"At least you came to your senses." The relief on Gordon's face only lasted a second. Anxiety quickly replaced it. "But how did Ginger meet him?"

"At the gallery," Tori replied, unable to lie to him again. She held her breath, waiting for Gordon to guess that it was Serge who gave her the fifty thousand and now had a business interest in her gallery.

But Gordon had reached conclusions of another sort. "It doesn't take that little flirt long to pick up a new man. I could never trust Ginger."

Tori reached up and touched her brother's arm. "Perhaps if you'd trusted your own feelings for her, everything else would have worked out."

Gordon's pale, even-featured face softened. "I doubt that, Victoria. Ginger has probably given her heart away so many times that she's totally mislaid it."

Tori shook her head. "You're wrong about that. She's the most sincere person I know. Once Ginger commits herself, it'll be for good."

Gordon went back to studying the wallpaper. "She told me that herself once, but I found it so difficult to believe."

"Your loss," Tori murmured with a sinking heart. All she wanted was for her brother to be happy.

"My gain," he corrected. "Luckily I saw right through that little Kewpie doll before it was too late—as you did that Russian peasant."

"Yes, aren't we fortunate to be so discerning," Tori replied, her voice heavy with sarcasm. "It's so comforting to be exclusive and all alone, isn't it, Gordon? Think of what we can look forward to! We'll be clattering around this empty shell of a house like two ghosts in our old age. Maybe we'll start collecting cats like dear Aunt Olive."

Gordon waved away such a dreary image. "You're talking nonsense, Victoria. You're an intelligent and attractive young lady, and you'll find someone suitable one day soon. Someone whose background, tastes and values match yours."

How utterly boring, she thought. "What about you, Gordon? Don't you ever intend to marry?"

"Kewpie dolls don't make good wives, I'm afraid." He laughed as if he'd made a joke, then frowned as if he'd realized the joke was on him. "No, my work keeps me very busy. My projects require all my time. But I look forward to being an indulgent uncle to your charming children some day."

"Only if you approve of my choice of husband, that is," Tori added sharply.

"I only want the best for you, which is what you deserve, Victoria," he replied. "If Mother and Father were still here, they would insist on exactly that, too."

Tori sighed with disappointment. Gordon had become her square-toed big brother again and had shut tight the briefly opened channel of real communication they'd just shared. He said good-night to her brusquely and departed.

She picked up her book again, but the words floated past her eyes without leaving the slightest dent in her mind. What she really saw in her mind's eye was the image of Serge and Ginger leaning toward each other in lively conversation at the sedate Ritz Bar. Had they gone on to dinner together? she wondered. She slept little that night, but she'd become used to insomnia ever since she'd first laid eyes on Serge Zhdanov.

Chapter Ten

Despite how little sleep she'd been getting, Tori arrived at the Museum of Fine Arts bright and early the next day to keep her date with Serge. Her mood was less than bright, though. She waited for Serge in the vast marble foyer, the heels of her soggy pumps clicking impatiently as she paced. She'd stepped directly into a puddle when exiting from her taxi. "Perfect!" She'd shouted.

Rain continued to pour over the city, and Tori was beginning to think that the black cloud hanging over her head was the cause of it.

The fact that Serge was twenty minutes late didn't improve her frame of mind. She was remembering the time she'd waited on the park bench, heart fluttering, only to feel deflated when he never appeared. That seemed centuries ago to her now. So much had happened since then. The man had taken her on a roller-coaster ride of emotions. Because of him her heart had soared in ecstasy, then plummeted in disappointment. Yet as she waited for him now it began fluttering again.

Serge spotted her the moment he entered but held back before approaching her. The loose Burberry raincoat she was wearing did nothing to accent her tall, elegant build, but he knew in intimate detail the charms it was hiding. He stood very still, captivated by the graceful way she moved.

"Like a Degas ballerina," he mused, not as ignorant about art as he'd led her to believe.

Sensing his presence almost immediately, Tori turned around. "So there you are," she said crisply, without a glimmer of a smile to show her relief. "Finally."

"Sorry I'm late, but it couldn't be helped."

"Yes, I know what a busy man you are, Mr. Zhdanov. I'm sure the last thing you want is a boring art-appreciation lecture from me." She wished he'd stop looking at her so intently. She was quite sure she must look like a drowned rat or something equally unattractive.

Actually, he was comparing her to a pink rose after a spring shower as he took in her natural freshness. But the last time he'd blurted out a flowery compliment to her, he'd felt foolish, and he kept this image to himself. "A deal is a deal," he told her. "I'll get to bore you with my expertise, too."

Hardly! she thought, remembering his expertise on a more personal level that had nothing to do with finances. But she'd promised herself she wasn't going to think about *that* anymore. She glanced at her watch, a frown creasing her high, smooth brow. "Let's get started, shall we? It's almost eleven. I'd about given up on you."

"I got held up in traffic," he said tersely to explain his tardiness.

He'd also been delayed in the waiting room of the veterinary clinic, where he'd decided to take Duke first thing that morning. Concerned with the dog's lack of appetite and listlessness, he wanted his old pal checked out. The vet had suggested running some tests and keeping Duke overnight.

Now Serge was even more concerned. He'd always felt a little silly about his inordinate love for the husky. Sentimentality embarrassed Serge, so he made a point of keeping his own deep Russian streak of it hidden most of the time. As he did now, not even touching on the subject of his ailing dog with Tori.

Despite the nagging little worry in the back of Serge's mind and Tori's irritation and wet shoes, they both ended up having a good time touring the museum together.

As exhaustive as Tori's knowledge of art was, her natural reserve kept her from showing off about it. She didn't even mention, as they passed a Gilbert Stuart portrait of a Colonial patriot, that she was a descendant of the subject or that her grandfather had donated the priceless work to the museum. In fact, Serge had to prompt her with questions to keep her talking. He enjoyed listening to her clear light voice with its variety of musical nuances. She was one of the few women he'd ever known who he wished would talk more rather than less.

It was his perceptive questions that made Tori realize that Serge was more receptive to art than she'd assumed. She wasn't especially surprised; it seemed that every assumption that she'd been so quick to make about him had proved false. Of course that was as much his fault as hers, she reminded herself. He was such a difficult man to get to know.

"I think I'm suddenly getting a sensory overload," Serge said to her, touching her shoulder to halt their slow march through the French Impressionist section of the gallery. He loosened the knot in his tie to demonstrate his discomfort.

Tori laughed. She'd often had the same sensation in the heady atmosphere of so many vivid Monets. The colors absolutely vibrated off the canvases, and it was enough to take anybody's breath away. "Let's go visit some Greek athletes and Roman generals," she suggested. "I'm sure you'll feel right at home with them."

He bowed, not at all displeased by her observation. "Lead me to them," he said.

As they passed through the upper rotunda he took her hand. His friendly gesture comforted her. His grip was strong and warm. "My hands are like ice," she said, a little self-conscious. She'd been longing for some physical contact with him since they'd met at the entrance.

He briefly brought the one he was holding to his lips and skimmed a kiss across her knuckles. "Colds hands, warm heart, so they say."

The brief touch of his lips against her skin more than warmed Tori's heart. She wished that she wasn't so susceptible to it still. "Cold hands, cold *feet*," she contradicted. "I'm afraid I waded right into a puddle when I got out of my cab."

Serge, who'd been paying as much attention to the fine form of her legs as he had to the rest of the art in the museum, had neglected to notice her wet shoes. "Come on, honey. We'll go to the Members' Room. You can slip off those shoes and have a hot cup of coffee there."

Tori was rather pleased by his concern. So he was back to calling her honey, was he? She hated to admit it to herself, but she liked the sound of the endearment coming from him.

"Wait a minute. If you know about the Members' Room you must be a museum supporter," she said.

He shrugged. "Just a tax write-off," he said to explain his rather substantial donations. In truth he contributed for more sentimental reasons. When he was a boy, he used to roam around the museum on rainy days such as this one because the admission was free. It had opened up new vistas for the tough city kid with a foreign accent.

"You probably know your way around here as well as I do," Tori guessed correctly. "While I've been leading you around, you've been leading me on!"

"Hell, I haven't been back here for years," he said to defend himself. He liked the way the color came to her cheeks so quickly when she was miffed. "And I really don't know much about art. I've learned a lot from you today."

Tori was somewhat mollified. She'd enjoyed his companionship this past hour or so and had almost forgotten that she now considered him her adversary. Almost, but not quite. "You're as tricky as they come, Serge Zhdanov. I could never trust you to really level with me."

"What do you mean? I've always been straight with you." His low, gravelly voice took on an offended tone.

That was a bit too much for Tori. Despite the fact that they were standing in a public place, she decided to have it out with him once and for all. All the resentment she'd been feeling toward him bubbled to the surface. "You call stealing half my business being *straight* with me?" He was still holding her hand, and she snatched it from his. "I may be forced to be civil to you now, but that doesn't mean I have to like you."

"You'll come around to seeing things my way," he replied easily. He was quite sure she would. Now that he had a say in running things, that little gallery of hers was really going to take off. He only wished that she'd stop being so obstinate about it. Was he going to have to drag her kick-ing and screaming toward financial success?

"I can't understand why you want to hurt me so much," she said, not seeing things his way at all.

"Hurt you?" He looked a bit stunned by the accusa-tion. "Why would I ever want to do that?" He reached out to touch her cheek.

She twisted her face from his touch. "Because I'm a Langford," she replied. "You've resented my family for years, and now you're using me to get back at them."

"That's crazy! You're way off base, Tori."

"Am I?" She clutched her hands together tightly, pray-ing the tears she'd held back ever since she'd believed it was so wouldn't come now. "Wasn't that the real reason you made love to me? Just to somehow even the score?"

Serge stepped back as if she'd struck him, and his icy blue eyes glittered with anger and confusion. Her accusa-tion made him want to howl with outrage. At the same time, self-doubt gnawed at him from someplace deep in-side, eating through all his rationalizations. It was true that he'd used her gallery business as an excuse to have some kind of hold on her. But not because she was a Langford, and certainly not to hurt her. He'd simply been afraid of losing her.

He couldn't admit this to her, though. He could barely admit it to himself.

"I made love to you because I found you very lovely, very fascinating," he told her in his deep husky voice. The muscles in his wide, lean face were tightly drawn. "How can you accuse me of using you, dammit? I didn't even know your name when I became attracted to you."

"But once you did, it complicated everything between us," Tori insisted.

Serge groaned. "Only in your own mind, lady." He brushed his hand across his eyes, as if suddenly exhausted. When he looked back at her, they were filled with resignation.

They stared at each other a long moment as people passed by them. Caught in each other's desolate gaze, they could have been the last two people on earth. Two people with nothing left to say to each other.

Then one more thing did occur to Serge—the only thing he could say that would please her, he thought with bitter regret.

"Our partnership is null and void as of now. My lawyer will be in touch with you as soon as possible." With that, he walked away.

Stunned by the absolute simplicity and abruptness of his final words, Tori watched him head down the rotunda's marble stairway with unblinking hazel eyes. The green sparkle in them had died out completely when she realized that she would probably never see him again. She felt nothing but a cold, bleak numbness. It seemed to invade her entire body. And she knew that it wasn't her stupid wet shoes causing it.

Tori returned to Back Bay Gallery to discover more customers milling around than had come in all week. Ginger rushed up to her, a little breathless. "It never rains, but it storms," she said.

"Pours," Tori said, automatically correcting her. "And let's just hope a few sales result from this unexpected downpour."

"Not to worry. There are some serious buyers rubbing shoulders with the usual gawkers today. See that lady in the fuchsia turban..." Ginger jerked her head to the left. "She's enthralled with the Cholewa watercolors and can't decide which one she likes best. And those three Japanese businessmen over there in matching three-piece suits..." Ginger rolled her eyes to the right. "They're very interested in our geometric abstracts. Why don't you go chat with them while I try to convince Fuchsia Turban that a grouping of Cholewa's watercolors would look *simply divine* in her drawing room."

Tori nodded and smiled with approval as Ginger headed off. Her assistant had everything under control as usual, despite her rather way-out appearance. Today Ginger was wearing skintight leopard-printed pants and a voluminous top in a zebra pattern. Her silver earrings were nearly the size of pie plates. Ginger's style of dressing blended right in with the avant-garde art Tori featured in her gallery, and Tori appreciated her friend's vivid taste in apparel although she certainly didn't share it.

She hung up her raincoat in the back closet, smoothed down the pleats of her basic navy skirt, then patted her neatly coiled chignon for good measure. After retying the prim bow of her creamy silk blouse, she returned to the showroom and approached the three Japanese businessmen. As she sailed toward them on a cool wave of poise, a pleasant smile on her full lips, she looked like a woman in total control of her surroundings and life. But inside she was aching, and her head was throbbing with the knowledge that she made a terrible mistake. She had not stopped Serge Zhdanov from going down the museum staircase.

She bowed back to the three gentlemen. The pleasant smile was still stuck on her face as she politely spoke of the paintings in which the men were interested.

Eventually they decided to purchase six. Tori didn't so much as blink when they announced this, but she was secretly jumping up and down, hooting, and clasping each of them in a hearty bear hug. "You've made excellent choices," was all she said, coolly hiding the fact that such a big sale as this wasn't an everyday occurrence.

After closing time Tori checked over the sales receipts in her office, pleased with the way they added up. She only retained a portion of the income since the biggest chunk went to the artists; but even after she subtracted that and operating costs, she figured that what was left would at least make a little dent in the debt she owed Serge. The sooner she got that off her books, the sooner she'd get him off her mind—or so she hoped.

She brewed a pot of Darjeeling tea and brought it out to the showroom to share with Ginger. It was an aromatic, full-bodied beverage, and as Tori drank in the comforting warmth of it, she was somehow reminded of Serge. Which was silly, she told herself, since he disliked tea so much.

"By the way, Ginger," she said as casually as she could, "Mr. Zhdanov and I are no longer business partners." Or any other kind, she added silently.

Ginger's face fell. "That's too bad! I was really looking forward to working with him."

"I'll just bet you were," Tori murmured dryly.

"No, really. We discussed a lot of good ideas he had for the gallery over drinks last night.

Tori set down her teacup with a sharp click. "Oh, Ginger, he doesn't give a damn about the gallery. He was using it to get back at me."

"Why? What did you do to him?"

"It's not a matter of what I did, but who I am," Tori replied after a moment.

"I don't get it." She waited for Tori to explain, but nothing followed except silence. Ginger went on. "Anyway, he could have fooled me with his enthusiasm. And one of his ideas is obviously paying off already."

Tori paused in the motion of pouring herself more tea. "What are you talking about?"

"Those Japanese businessmen, of course. Didn't they mention to you that Serge suggested they come here?"

"No, his name never came up. Are you sure about this, Ginger?"

"Yes, they told me Serge convinced them to invest in art for their new corporate headquarters off Route 128. Serge likes the idea of corporations supporting gifted artists. He figures everybody benefits in the end." Ginger plopped a lump of sugar in her cup. "He was pretty hot on the subject last night."

"Rest assured he's lost interest since then," Tori stated in a hollow voice. "He'll be staying out of my business from now on."

Ginger looked doubtful. She blew on her tea to cool it. "He was pretty hot on the subject of you, too, by the way."

Tori's heart jumped at the bait. "What did he say about me?"

Catching her interest, Ginger smiled. She took a tiny testing sip before replying. "Not much. He expected me to do all the talking. All he did was bombard me with questions about you." Ginger laughed good-naturedly. "I should have been ticked off when I realized he wasn't the least bit interested in me. But since you're my best friend, I didn't really mind. It's about time some terrific man came into your life, Tori."

"I'm afraid that man isn't Serge Zhdanov." Tori looked down at the tea leaves in her empty cup. If she knew how to read them she was sure they'd predict a rather bleak future for her.

There was a knock on the front door, and Ginger jumped off her stool. "I'll tell them we're closed," she said. "Unless it's the man under discussion." She gave Tori a hopeful look.

But it turned out to be Gordon. Ginger let him in anyway. She glanced at her reflection in the glass protecting a watercolor and fluffed up her hair as he chatted with his sister.

Tori wondered what urgent matter could have taken Gordon away from his work and brought him here in the middle of a rainstorm. There didn't seem to be any though. He had very little to say for himself and appeared to be interested in Tori's recounting of the day's happenings at the gallery.

"And then they announced that they'd buy all six of them!" she said, concluding her story about the Japanese businessmen.

"Who?" Gordon asked, giving her a blank stare, and Tori realized that he hadn't been listening to her at all. His attention had strayed to Ginger, who was bouncing around the showroom turning off display lights.

"Never mind, dear," Tori said with an understanding smile. "Why don't you go help Ginger turn off the lights while I lock up in back?"

She'd finally guessed the urgency of his visit. Jealousy had driven him to the gallery, and she was sure it had been a very bumpy journey. Seeing Ginger with Serge Zhdanov the evening before had lit a fire under him, or at least rekindled his interest in her.

Tori took her time straightening our her office. But when she returned to the showroom, Gordon and Ginger had begun to argue.

"I'm not taking you out to dinner dressed like that," he was telling her, critically eyeing her clashing zebra-and-leopard attire.

"Listen, buster." Ginger's full, pretty face was set stubbornly. "I'm not changing the way I dress or talk or act to suit you." She tossed her head angrily and her big silver earrings flashed. "We've gone through all this before. If you're embarrassed to be seen with me, then go eat alone."

"But I want to have dinner with you," Gordon insisted.

"I don't understand why."

"Because you drive me crazy, and I miss that feeling when you're not around, that's why." Sighing deeply, he raised his hands in a gesture of surrender, "You win, Ginger. You look perfect just as you are."

Ginger's smile was more relieved than triumphant. Observing them from the doorway, Tori was also relieved that her brother hadn't blown it this time. If anyone could pull him out of his reclusiveness, she was sure Ginger could. Hurrying them out of the gallery before they started another argument, she fervently hoped they'd pick up where they left off a few months ago.

She was anxious to leave the gallery herself after they departed. She wasn't comfortable alone there ever since the incident with Ugly. She bent down to leash Mr. Jiggs. He hadn't proven himself to be much protection against intruders. She could understand the little spaniel being intimidated by someone as nasty as Ulger. What she couldn't understand was his sudden adoration of the biggest intruder of all—the man who'd invaded her heart and mind—Serge Zhdanov.

Tori looked deeply into her dog's lustrous brown eyes, wondering if Jiggs knew something she didn't. Nonsense, she told herself, straightening up. Serge had confirmed all her suspicions about his motives by walking out on her at the museum that morning. Still a nagging thought kept nipping at the back of her mind. Although Serge had told her that their partnership agreement was no longer valid, his lawyer hadn't contacted her yet. Was he just playing games with her? He'd given her no reason to trust him. Yet she hadn't missed the hurt in his eyes when she'd accused him of using her. As hard as she tried to block it from her memory, it kept coming back to haunt her.

"Let's go home, Jiggs," she said, a sense of loneliness pervading her spirits. He eagerly pranced to the front door and waited for Tori to open it. When she did she came face-to-face with a tall, dark-haired figure in a tan trench-coat. His slanting blue eyes looked directly into hers.

"I was just about to knock," he said.

Her heart resumed it's normal beating. "You're Serge's brother, aren't you?"

He smiled and nodded. "Alexander. We met at my mother's restaurant," he reminded her. "Did I catch you at a bad time, Ms. Langford?"

"Well, the gallery's closed. I was just leaving."

"Could you spare a few extra minutes?" he asked politely.

Puzzled, she gestured for him to enter and turned on a few lights. "Did Serge send you here?"

"Actually, his lawyer did." He went to the counter and placed the attaché case he was carrying on it. "I work for him part-time. I'm a law student." He opened the case and took out some papers. "We just need your signature, and then I'll be out of your way. Sorry to hold you up like this. I meant to get here sooner, but two of Mama's waiters called in sick and I had to help set up for the dinner crowd." He glanced around the gallery. "Wow, this sure is a neat place."

Tori wasn't about to be deceived by his boyish, easy-going demeanor. Being a Zhdanov, he was sure to be tricky. "I'm afraid I can't sign anything without *my* lawyer looking at it," she said sharply. "I made that mistake once, but I won't again."

"No problem," Alexander readily agreed. "That's always the wisest course of action." He laughed. "Listen to me! I already sound like a staid legal adviser. Anyway, I'll leave this with you. It's a fairly simple document stating that you and Serge are no longer business partners."

Tori turned on another light and read it over. "But there's no mention of the loan here."

"I don't know anything about that, Ms. Langford. My instructions were just to deliver this to you today. I'm sure glad I caught you in time."

"So am I. It appears your brother is a man of his word."

Alexander seemed surprised by her remark. "Well, of course he is. He's a Zhdanov." He closed the attaché case and tucked it under his long arm. "Well, I'd better get back to the restaurant. We're booked solid tonight, as usual."

"I can understand why. I've never eaten such delicious food," she said, recalling the excitement of sharing that meal with Serge. She could almost feel his leg pressed against hers, and the touch of the rose petal as he stroked her cheek with it.

"Not to mention the excellent service," Alexander put in.

"Yes, you were a very solicitous waiter."

"I figure whenever Mama needs me to fill in, it's the least I can do." He laughed self-consciously again. "Listen to me! Now I sound like a saint. The truth is—the tips are damn good."

What a nice boy, Tori thought . . . and how he reminded her of Serge at times. "It was nice seeing you again, Alexander," she said, walking him to the door. She doubted that she ever would again, considering the way things stood between her and Serge.

"Same here, Ms. Langford. Mama, Neda and I were all hoping to see a lot more of you after Serge brought you in." He looked a little abashed after stating this. "Not that Serge's affairs are any of our business," he hurriedly added. His face reddened. "I didn't mean to imply that you and my brother are having one. Just a figure of speech." The color deepened, and he groaned. "I'd better shut up and get out of here before I say one more stupid thing, right?"

He left, but a moment later he was back, knocking on the door. Tori let him in again. "Did you forget something?" She glanced toward the counter.

"Yeah, I was supposed to deliver a personal message to you, too."

Tori's heart picked up a few beats, expecting it to be from Serge.

"Mama would like you to join her for brunch at the restaurant Sunday." Perhaps he sensed that Tori was about to refuse because his voice became more earnest. "It would mean a lot to her. She's been talking about your family since she last saw you. Mama is real sentimental about the past."

Remembering Mrs. Zhdanov's warmth and kindness when she was a child, Tori accepted the invitation. "Of course, I'll come. Please thank her for asking me."

Sunday brunch at Mother Russia's was a festive occasion, and the restaurant was alive with chatter and clatter and the music of strolling violinists when Tori arrived at eleven. Mrs. Zhdanov managed to spot her in the midst of the happy chaos the moment she entered and came immediately to her side.

"Little Victoria!" she cried, taking both Tori's hands in her tiny, soft ones.

Tori smiled at the greeting, being at least six inches taller than the older woman, and automatically bent down to kiss her cheek. It seemed such a natural thing to do. Mrs. Zhdanov exuded a warmth that was contagious.

"Come, come, little one," she said, keeping a firm hold of Tori's hand and leading her to the long buffet table set up in the middle of the restaurant. She handed Tori a plate rimmed in gold. "First you eat. Then we chat."

Tori had never seen so much food in one place at one time—all of it beautifully presented. At Mrs. Zhdanov's urging, she took a sliver of goose pâté, a sample of both the smoked duck and haddock, and a serving of lobster Newburg. The chef in his high white hat waited to cut her a juicy slice from one of the succulent roasts of veal, beef or pork, or better yet a slice of each. His two assistants suggested she try the chicken with truffle sauce and the sweetbreads. Then, of course, there were the Russian specialties to sample: plump *pirogi*, pickled herring, savory stuffed cabbage leaves, beef Stroganoff, mushrooms in sour cream, and . . .

"My *Kulebiaka*, darling," Mrs. Zhdanov said, kissing her fingertips. "I made it with my own two hands when Alex told me you were coming today."

Tori took a wedge of the brioche filled with a salmon-rice mixture and added it to her laden plate. Her usual meal at this time of day would have been a boiled egg and a slice of toast, and she hoped she could do justice to this feast as she followed Mrs. Zhdanov to a table in back. Recognizing it as the same table that she and Serge had once shared, Tori felt a little tug at her heart. She slid onto the red velvet banquette.

Mrs. Zhdanov sat across from her and folded her lovely hands on the white linen tablecloth. Apparently she intended to eat nothing, but devoured each bite Tori took with her merry blue eyes. "Is it good?" she kept asking, then ate up Tori's enthusiastic compliments. It was obvious that her chief pleasure in life was feeding others.

At last Tori placed down her fork, amazed at her own hearty appetite. Mrs. Zhdanov, though, was a little disappointed when she refused seconds. Then her face brightened. "But of course, you must save room for all the desserts! Come. I'll help you select."

Tori's stomach groaned silently in protest. "Not quite yet, if you don't mind."

"Not at all, darling. We can talk for a while and catch up." She reached across the table to pat Tori's hand. "Serge told me about your dear parents' tragic boating accident. I was so very sorry to hear of your loss. And you still a child when it happened." She squeezed the hand she was patting. "If only our families hadn't lost touch. If I'd known, I would have come to comfort you during that sad time, little one."

Tori soaked up the sympathy radiating from the other woman and thought what a true comfort she would have been during that time. "I wasn't completely alone. I had my brother," she said.

"Ah, yes. Gordon." The sadness in Mrs. Zhdanov's eyes receded, and they began to twinkle again. "I remember him well. Such a proper young gentleman, even as a boy. I hoped some of his good manners would rub off on Serge." She threw up her hands. "But to no avail. I'm afraid the opposite occurred, and my little hooligan brought out the less refined side of Gordon's nature. Those two used to fight like cat and dog, no matter how hard your mother and I tried to encourage friendship." She sighed. "Little boys can be very obstinate."

So can grown men, Tori thought. But she certainly wasn't going to tell Mrs. Zhdanov that they'd never outgrown their dislike for each other.

"Tell me, Victoria. How *is* your brother? No doubt he has his own family by now."

"No, Gordon isn't married. He's very involved in his work." She hoped that didn't sound too vague, but in truth she only had a hazy idea of what he did with all his time and energy. So far none of his inventions had amounted to much.

Mrs. Zhdanov clucked her tongue, not needing further explanation. "Just like my Serge. Work, work, work! There's more to life, I tell him. It's time you found a good woman to marry, I say." Her incisive blue eyes latched onto the young woman across from her. "One who would do him proud."

Tori shifted uncomfortably under her gaze. "Yes, that's what I hope for Gordon, too," she said to deflect attention away from herself.

It didn't work. "And what about you, young lady? Don't you plan to settle down one day?"

"Oh, I'm quite settled," Tori replied. "I still live in the old house on Beacon Hill, and I have my own business. An art gallery."

"So my Alex tells me. Serge, he tells me nothing. I have to get all my information about him second hand from my other two. Alex and Neda are much more open. Maybe that's because they were born in America. Serge is more guarded. Much like his father, God rest his soul." Mrs. Zhdanov smiled sadly. "Ah, well. He could do worse than be like his father."

A silence fell over the table. Tori twisted the napkin in her lap. There was something she wanted to ask Mrs. Zhdanov about, something that had been bothering her ever since the first time she'd visited the restaurant. She cleared her throat.

"Why did you and your husband leave, Mrs. Zhdanov?"

"Oh, so many reasons. Politics and ambitions." She laughed. "Even in-law troubles. We were lucky to get out of the Soviet Union, and I know we made the right decision to immigrate to America. Life here has been good."

"I'm sorry. I didn't make myself clear," Tori said. "What I want to know is why you stopped working for my parents once you came here. Did they fire you because Serge and Gordon couldn't get along?"

Mrs. Zhdanov looked a little startled. "Whatever gave you that impression, darling?"

"Something Serge said. Something about giving my brother a black eye while they were playing."

"Yes, he did do that," Mrs. Zhdanov readily admitted. "And that hooligan would've been punished for it, too, if your mother and I hadn't been there to witness that it had been an accident."

"Did my mother overreact, though, and order you out of the house?" Tori prodded.

"Certainly not." Mrs. Zhdanov sounded more than a little put out. "I recall that your mother was upset. She tended to baby Gordon a bit. But she never held it against *us*. We did leave shortly after that incident, but our reasons had nothing to do with it. We'd saved enough money to start a little diner and wanted to be on our own. Your parents understood. We parted amicably."

Tori was greatly relieved to hear that. "But why does Serge believe that you were fired because of him and Gordon?"

Mrs. Zhdanov shook her head in puzzlement. "He's never discussed that with me. If he had, I'd have set him straight. It was a difficult time after we left. Mr. Zhdanov and I struggled night and day to make a success of the diner... I'm surprised that Serge must have somehow thought it was his fault. Maybe he even blamed your parents for it all these years. I'll have to talk to him about it."

"What was he like as a little boy?" Tori wanted to know.

His mother smiled fondly. "Much as he is now, I suppose—a stoic. He never complained about anything, although I'm sure he was homesick when he first came here. Then, when Mr. Zhdanov passed away, he took over the responsibility of caring for his family. I have Serge to thank for this restaurant. He knew it was my dream, and he gave me the money to make it possible."

"You must be very proud of him, Mrs. Zhdanov."

"But of course!" She beamed, then looked at Tori seriously. "I want him to have his own life, though. He needn't worry about his mama or brother and sister anymore. You tell him that, Victoria."

"Me?" Tori let out a little laugh. "I hardly have the right to tell Serge anything. The truth is, Mrs. Zhdanov, your son and I aren't on friendly terms any longer."

Mrs. Zhdanov pursed her lips. "You looked friendly enough when he brought you here for dinner. 'That young lady,' I remember telling Neda, 'means something special to your brother.'"

"Did you?" Tori's eyes lit, but dimmed almost immediately. "I'm afraid I'm very confused about what Serge feels for me."

"Yes, love can be so confusing in the beginning," the older woman said, placing her little hand against the black silk of her dress in the general area of her heart.

Tori laughed nervously again. "Who said anything about love?"

"Your eyes, darling, that's who." Mrs. Zhdanov's own laugh was more robust. "Don't be afraid, Victoria. Serge would never hurt you. It's clear to me that you two have had some kind of misunderstanding. Go to him right now and straighten it out. It's as simple as that." She waved her hands in the air.

"Mrs. Zhdanov, shame on you. You are a blatant matchmaker."

The small, silver-haired woman looked shocked at such an accusation. "What nonsense, darling," she said. "I never interfere in my children's lives." Then she gave Tori her elder son's address.

Chapter Eleven

The moment Serge opened his door Tori knew she'd made a dreadful mistake. She should never have followed Mrs. Zhdanov's suggestion and come to talk things over with him. At the very least she should have called first. The expression on his wide, lean face was hardly inviting. He looked almost dour.

"Have I come at a bad time?" How she wished that she hadn't come at all! Spontaneous gestures like this always backfired. Her visit was so obviously unwelcome.

"Yeah, it's a pretty bad time," he replied. He was wearing a blue terry robe. His hair was uncombed, and there was a shadow of dark beard on his high cheeks. There were shadows under his eyes, too. Those eyes, usually so clear and piercing, were bloodshot.

Had he been partying all night? Tori wondered. It was early afternoon now, and for all she knew, there was someone inside his apartment with whom he was still partying. "I'm sorry. It was stupid of me to drop by out of the blue like this."

"There's no need to apologize." He made a great effort to smile but didn't quite carry it off. "I'm the one who should apologize. I must look like hell."

If she refuted that, she'd be lying. "I can come back some other time," she said. Her pale cheeks pinkened. "Or better yet, not come at all. It's clear that you don't want to see me."

He rubbed his rough chin. "The truth is I don't want to see anyone right now."

"I'm sorry," she muttered again and turned to go.

But he stepped out into the hall and grabbed her upper arm, halting her impulse to flee. "Wait a minute, Tori. Don't go off without telling me why you came in the first place."

She hardly knew herself. She had longed to see him again, that's all. And now that she had, she regretted it. One thing she knew for sure—she wasn't going to stand in the middle of a hall and try to work out what was wrong with their relationship. Serge obviously had no intention of inviting her in. She gave him a quick once-over, noting how the loosely tied belt of his robe was just barely keeping it closed. Her feminine instincts told her that he was naked beneath it.

"It can wait, Serge," she said coolly.

"No, it can't." Tightening his grip on her arm, he gave it a none-too-gentle yank. "Since you've come this far, you might as well come in."

"Such a gracious invitation." Tori muttered, but accepted it.

When she stepped into his living room she was amazed at the size and airiness of it. She walked directly to the wall of windows and looked down at the city. The rooftops were shiny with rain, but the heavy clouds seemed to be thinning. A pale glimmer of sunlight penetrated through them.

"I think it may clear up," she said.

"Who knows." He shrugged, uninterested.

"This is quite a view you have, Serge."

"I like it."

Ignoring his taciturnity, she maintained a polite smile as her eyes swept the room but avoided his. Everything in it was totally modern. And terribly expensive, Tori recognized. The molded leather chairs were by Eames, the high-standing bookcase no doubt a Wormley, and the hand-woven area rug displayed on the shining parquet, a vivid zigzag pattern of purples and blues, was a Vida Baptista creation for sure. Tori knew because she'd displayed Baptista's stunning textiles in her gallery.

In fact the feeling of the room, so classically simple and functional, very much reminded Tori of her gallery. She was far from feeling at home in it, though. Serge was doing nothing to put her at ease. He was just standing there, watching her in gloomy silence.

Her polite smile faded. "I won't comment on the decor," she told him. "I'm sure you don't want to talk about that any more than you do the weather or the view."

"I'm sorry, Tori. I'm in no mood for chit-chat." Serge ran his hand through his dark, uncombed hair, ruffling its thickness even more. "I wasn't expecting a little social call from the proper Miss Langford." He gave her a hard stare. "Especially after you accused me of using you."

The bitterness in his tone made her tense up even more. "Perhaps I misjudged your motives, Serge, but—"

"You got that much straight, lady," he interrupted.

"But I'm not a mind reader," she continued in her own defense. She turned to gaze down at the view again.

"Anyway, I received the papers from your lawyer, and that's why I'm here."

"I figured as much." Serge kept his distance from her. "You couldn't wait to sign and deliver them and officially end our brief business association, could you, Tori?"

"Now you're misjudging *me*," she threw over her shoulder. "I haven't signed anything. You can't just give up your share of the gallery without making conditions for me to repay the loan, Serge. As it stands now, I'd be free and clear of any debt."

"So? That's my problem, not yours." He stuffed his hands into the pockets of his robe.

She faced him, ready to argue about it, but could clearly see that he wasn't up to it. "What's wrong with you, Serge? Are you ill?"

"I'm okay," he insisted. "If you're going to stay, at least sit down. I'm going to get myself a beer. You want one?"

He didn't bother to wait for her reply but padded off to the kitchen on bare feet. Strangely, his gruff manner, which bordered on rudeness, didn't put Tori off. She sat down on the softly molded sofa, determined to find out what was really upsetting him. He was obviously still angry about what she'd said in the museum, but that didn't explain the deep undercurrent of sadness she could feel emanating from him.

It seemed to her that he stayed in the kitchen a very long time and when he returned he was empty-handed. He plopped down on the sofa beside her and his robe opened enough to display a muscular thigh. Tori stared at it, then glanced away, trying to ignore the tug of arousal the sight produced deep within her.

"No beer," Serge informed her succinctly.

"It doesn't matter. I didn't want one anyway." She attempted to move a little away from his heady nearness but he'd inadvertently sat on the full skirt of her dress. She pulled at it.

"Oops, sorry about that," he said, shifting his body to free it. "Hope I didn't wrinkle it too much. I like that dress on you. I remember you were wearing it the first day we met in the Public Garden."

She was touched that he remembered. "And you weren't wearing very much at all that day," she said. "I thought you were a professional athlete of some kind. And I thought your dog was a wolf!" She glanced around. "Where is Duke, by the way? I've been expecting the big brute to pounce on me at any moment."

Serge turned his face away. "Duke died yesterday, Tori."

She was stunned for a moment. Serge had reported this news so matter-of-factly that it took a moment to sink in. But when it did, Tori understood completely how much he was suffering from the loss now, and how hard he was trying not to show it. He kept his face averted, but she'd already seen the misery in his eyes. She wanted desperately to comfort him, but words seemed to be insufficient. She placed her hand on his shoulder. He tried to shrug it off, but she wouldn't let him. She began to stroke his back. His muscles were tense beneath her fingers.

"I'll be all right," he said in a muffled tone. "It just takes some getting used to. Old Duke and I go back a long ways."

"It's okay if you want to cry," Tori told him.

He straightened his slumped shoulders, shifting his back away from her gentle strokes. "I'm not going to cry over a dog, dammit."

But Tori surmised that he'd been doing exactly that all day. Her visit had interrupted his mourning. She didn't doubt that he'd prefer her to leave so he could get on with it in private, but she couldn't bear to leave him alone like this.

"Let me hold you, Serge," she said. Leaving herself open to rejection, she wrapped her arms around his neck and kissed his beard-roughened cheek. It was damp against her lips. Tears of compassion sprang to her own eyes. "I care for you, Serge," she murmured softly. "Very much. Please don't hide your feelings from me. Let me comfort you."

She felt him melt in her arms as his muscles relaxed, and she pressed his head against her breast. He wept silently for a while as she combed back his thick unruly hair with her slender fingers. Tori's heart went out to him completely. She loved him, she realized. It was as simple as that.

"Oh, God, I feel like such a fool," he said at last, regaining his control.

Tori continued to soothe him with her gentle touch. "Why? Because you have deep emotions? It's only fools who don't, Serge."

Neither of them spoke for a long time after that, but the silence they shared said enough as they held on to each other's warmth. Breathing in Serge's unique, pleasurable scent, Tori cared little about their past differences or even about problems she foresaw between them in the future. It was as if her arms contained the very essence of this complicated, sometimes impossible man. She treasured him then as much as she treasured her own true self.

It was the sunlight streaming through the wall of windows that finally broke through their mutual silence and made them aware of their surroundings once again. The room suddenly lit up with brightness.

Serge stood up and led her to the window. "Look," he said, pointing to the heavens. "A rainbow. Let's go out to the terrace, Tori. We'll be able to see it better from there."

He opened the sliding-glass door that led out to it. When Tori walked out she had the sensation that she was standing on a cloud as she looked up at the arc of colors hanging over the city.

"How magical rainbows are," she said.

Serge wrapped his arm around her and kissed the tip of her uptilted nose. "You're the one who's magical," he told her. "How else could you have known how much I needed you today?"

Her eyes left the rainbow and met his vivid blue gaze, which she found even more enchanting. "It wasn't intuition, if that's what you mean. I had no idea what you were going through. My only thought was that I wanted to make contact with you again."

"You mean this kind of contact?" He dipped his face to hers and kissed her lips softly.

"Any kind of contact." Tori kissed him back with the same sweet swiftness, then walked to the end of the terrace. She rested her elbows on the rail of the balustrade that enclosed it.

Looking down at the city traffic below from such a height, she experienced a sudden vertigo. Serge encircled her in his arms from behind and the world stopped whirling beneath her. He made her feel safe.

She leaned her back against his solid chest. "Is this the highest building in Boston?"

"Just about." He brushed his lips against her hair. "No one can see us up here, you know. We can do anything we want to."

She shivered at the huskiness in his voice. "We could do anything just as well in the bedroom," she pointed out.

"But there's no rainbow in the bedroom, Tori."

He left her standing alone on the terrace before she could come up with any more sensible suggestions and returned in a matter of minutes with a thick silky quilt. He laid it before her feet on the flagstone.

"Our flying carpet," he said and sat down on it. He raised his arm, offering Tori his hand. "Care to take a trip on it with me, lovely one?"

Tori hesitated, all the inhibitions that had been bred into her coming back full force. "I've never made love alfresco before."

"You'd never made love in a bathtub before, either," Serge reminded her. "And you seemed to enjoy that." He grabbed her by the waist and pulled her down to him. "Didn't you?" he whispered, his breath hot in her ear.

"As if you didn't know I did," she replied, allowing him to slowly unbutton the front of her demure orchid dress.

Her pretty pink bra was also demure but that didn't stop Serge from sliding down the straps of it with his teeth to expose her soft white breasts to the sun. He playfully nipped at the rosy tips, then rubbed his lips against them as they hardened. Soon the lightest pressure of his tongue against each pleasure point was enough to send shocks of desire throughout her body.

Tori moaned, wanting more, and Serge pushed her down on the satiny quilt. The coolness of its texture against her bare back contrasted with the heat of the sun on her flushed face and throbbing breasts. He pulled off her dress and underthings, then lay down beside her to fondle and caress the beauty he'd uncovered. Tori soaked up the pure pleasure of his touch, wondering how she could have managed without it for so many days. The sun beat on her flat, smooth belly as a burning passion radiated from within.

She slid her hand down the rough texture of his terry robe, then untied the loosely knotted belt and pushed it away from his long, lean body. She'd guessed correctly. He was naked beneath it. "You might as well get sunburned along with me," she joked.

"Don't worry, honey. I'll shield that delicate skin of yours from the burning rays," Serge promised, shucking off the robe. He covered her milky-white body with his golden-brown one.

Their kisses were long and lingering, deep and probing, and Tori lost herself in a whirlwind of sensuous delight. Eyes closed, she imagined that they were floating high above the city on the silvery-blue quilt. She arched against Serge, ready for more thrills. The pressure of her soft palm against the smooth muscles of his back was demanding.

He answered that demand and entered her. "Open your eyes, love," he commanded.

Tori complied and saw the glorious rainbow overhead. It seemed his special gift to her as he slowly gave of himself. Serge took Tori over the arc of the rainbow again and again. All the colors of it shimmered as if from within her own pulsing body as he paced himself to give her more and more pleasure.

"Come with me this time," she urged when he brought her to the top of the arc once again.

He silently accepted her invitation and let go of his control. They sailed through the sky together with furious speed. There was no stopping now, no turning back. And when they could go no higher, they spiraled back to earth, clinging tightly to each other. It was a breathtaking landing for both of them.

Serge took a big bite out of the crunchy apple, then offered it to Tori, who was sitting cross-legged on the plush quilt and nibbling cheese. She accepted the apple.

"I don't know why I'm so famished," she said around a mouthful.

He smiled, thinking that she looked absolutely adorable in his terry robe. He'd insisted that she wear it rather than get dressed again. Actually, he'd begged her to stay nude while they picnicked on the terrace, but she'd refused to go along with that. For the sake of her propriety rather than his own modesty, Serge had slipped on his white running shorts. The rainbow had faded away, but the sun continued to beat down on them, warming their backs.

"Why shouldn't you be famished?" he asked her. "We burned up a lot of calories a little while ago."

His smile was so smug that she threw a cracker at him. It bounced off his chest. "Maybe so, but I ate a gigantic meal at Mother Russia's this morning."

Serge raised his thick eyebrows in surprise. "What inspired you to go there?" His boyish grin return. "Hopes of seeing me, I suppose."

She threw another cracker, which hit him square on his blunt chin. "It so happens your mother invited me. We had a cozy tête-à-tête. Mostly about the past. I must admit that your name did pop up in the conversation, though."

"What did Mama tell you about me?"

"That you were a hooligan as a child. That you work too hard." Tori paused and adjusted his big robe around her slender frame. "That you would never hurt me."

Serge shifted his position on the quilt to kneel before her and cup her face in his hands. "Never, Tori," he said softly. "At least not intentionally. I was wrong about butting my nose into your business, but my inflated ego convinced me that you would benefit from the partnership. I never intended to take advantage of you."

"I believe that now," she replied, looking into the depths of his crystal-blue eyes. "And since you refuse to let me pay back the loan, you might as well remain my partner. For the time being, anyway. It may not work out at all.''

"Then again, it may." He touched his lips to her cheek. "Did you mean what you said before, Tori? Or were you just being kind when you told me you cared for me?"

She ruffled his hair. "You shouldn't even have to ask."

"Spend the night with me," he said.

How typical of him, Tori thought, to make it more a demand than a request. Still, she was tempted. She could easily get used to waking up in his arms. But she shook her head. "I didn't bring a toothbrush."

"No problem. I have an extra one." He slid his hand beneath the robe and began to caress her softness.

"No, Serge. Really, I can't." She stopped his roaming hand before she weakened under its persuasion.

"Why? Give me one good reason." His other hand inched up her leg and began massaging the tender spot behind her knee.

"It wouldn't look right," she explained feebly.

"Don't be silly." He dipped his head to kiss her knee. "Who would even know or care?" He left a trail of kisses up the inside of her thigh.

"My brother would."

Serge stopped fondling her. "You've got to be kidding?" His laugh was harsh. "What does Gordon have to do with it?"

"He would worry about me if I didn't come home tonight." She tensed, ready for the argument she knew was coming.

"You're a big girl now, Tori. You shouldn't give a damn if Gordon approves of me or not."

"And I don't!" she insisted, jumping up from the quilt. "This has nothing to do with you personally, Serge."

"Oh, really?" He stood up, too, and walked to the terrace railing. "Funny, but that's not the way I see it."

Tori sighed with frustration and stared at the tautly muscled back he had turned on her.

Such a stubborn back, she thought. And such a beautiful one, too—so sleek and broad and brown. She loved the way his wide shoulders seemed molded from bronze, and the way his white shorts rode low beneath his tapered waist.

"Serge, please listen to me." Since he refused to turn around and face her she went to him and pressed her cheek against his sun-warmed back. "What we share together *is* personal. But that's my point. It's nobody else's business but ours. Certainly not my brother's. Maybe I'm too discreet, but that's my nature. Can't you accept that?"

"I suppose I'll have to." There was still a residue of irritation in his voice, but when he took her into his arms his hold was gentle. "May I take you out to dinner tomorrow evening like a proper suitor, Ms. Langford?"

"I'd like that. Why don't you pick me up at the gallery around seven."

Serge immediately released her. "Instead of your home so Gordon won't know you're going out with me?"

"You're impossible! I thought it would be more convenient for both of us, that's all." Irritated herself now, Tori plucked up the plate of cheese and crackers from the quilt and headed toward Serge's kitchen.

Her mood changed the moment she entered it and spotted Duke's water and food bowls, both still filled, in the middle of the shiny tile floor. It was as if Serge expected his old pal to return at any moment.

Tori emptied and cleaned the bowls, then put them out of sight deep in a cupboard, shedding a few tears for Duke herself as she did so. She hadn't been terribly fond of the husky but could certainly empathize with his master. Wiping her eyes, she looked up to see Serge in the doorway.

"Thanks for doing that," he said. "I didn't have the heart to. And thanks for putting up with my surliness when you first came here. I thought I wanted to be alone, but what I really needed was to be with you, Tori."

She was glad that she'd stuck it out instead of taking umbrage and leaving before she knew what was bothering him. "Will you be all right alone after I go?" she asked him.

"If I said no, would that induce you to stay the night with me?"

"Probably," she admitted.

"Don't worry. I won't stoop to using emotional blackmail on you, honey." He gave Tori a wan smile. "Yeah, I'll be all right."

Tori was relieved to hear it. "Are we still on for dinner tomorrow? If you'd really prefer to meet at my house, it's perfectly fine with me."

"No, you were right. The gallery's more convenient for both of us. But after dinner I intend to bring you back here and ravish you madly."

Tori reached out and ran the tip of her finger down his chest. "I would be terribly insulted if you didn't."

For the next two weeks Tori led a frantic existence. She worked hard all day organizing the upcoming gallery exhibition, had dinner every evening with Serge, and made love with him every night until midnight. She always insisted on spending what was left of the night in her own bed, though, and although Serge grumbled about it a great deal, he always complied with her wishes and drove her back to Beacon Hill. Neither one of them was getting much sleep.

And neither one of them could get enough of the other. Serge would often meet Tori in the Public Garden in the morning and walk with her and Jiggs. They met for lunch whenever their busy schedules allowed. They called each other often, for the slightest reason, or for no reason at all but to hear the other's voice. Serge had one perfect pink rose delivered to the gallery for Tori every day.

It never occurred to Serge that he was courting Tori in the manner that he'd always thought ridiculous and unnecessary with other women. If someone had accused him of being a romantic, he would have energetically denied it. He simply felt like being with her all the time, and it happened to please him to do nice things for her.

"Why don't you do us both a big favor and move in with me," he suggested late one night as she stumbled out of bed and began dressing. "This silly business of your going home every night is wearing me out, honey."

"I've told you time and again that you don't have to drive me home, Serge. I can as easily take a taxi."

"Like hell you will! No woman of mine is going out alone past midnight."

"I'm not your woman, darling." Tori stepped into her lace-edged panties.

Serge watched her pull them up from the bed, a regretful expression on his face. "Yes, you are," he insisted.

Tori wasn't going to argue semantics with him at that late hour. She hung the silk kimono he'd bought for her back in his closet and put on her peach shirtwaist dress. She was a bit bleary-eyed and had trouble with the little buttons. Serge got out of bed to help her but wasn't much help at all. He began unbuttoning instead, tugging the material away from her shoulders to kiss them.

"I'll never leave at this rate," she told him, ready to abandon herself to him all over again as his lips slid across her sensitive flesh.

"That's the idea." Serge cupped her buttocks and pressed her closer to his naked body. "What do you say, Tori? Why not move in with me?"

That he made it sound so simple, so casual, irked her. What did he think she was, a Gypsy? She'd never lived anywhere but Beacon Hill. How could Serge expect her to tear up her roots for his convenience? They'd made no commitment to each other. They hadn't even declared their love in words. She pushed away from him a bit impatiently.

"Where did I leave my shoes?" she mumbled, and then went off in the direction of his living room to search for them.

Serge glared at her slender, retreating figure. He'd just asked her to live with him, and her only response was concern over her damn shoes! His jaw was set hard as he dressed. He wasn't going to ask her again, dammit. He could do very well without her as his roommate. She couldn't even cook!

He went to the closet for his jacket and brushed against her silk kimono. Bringing the sleeve of it to his face, he inhaled the lilac scent of her still clinging to it. He knew that by morning the scent would fade, and he would start yearning for her all over again. But Victoria Langford was as elusive as her delicate perfume. Was their romance as fleeting as springtime in Boston? he wondered, a tightness in his chest. She called from the front door, and he hurried to her, afraid she would leave without him.

They spoke very little in the car, both of them sleepy and irritable. As always, Tori insisted that Serge drop her off and not bother to walk her to her door. As always he double-parked on the narrow street and escorted her anyway. He liked to give her one last, lingering kiss, pressing her back against the door, before she went inside and disappeared from his life until the next day. Expecting and very much desiring this last kiss of the night from Serge, Tori lifted her face to him, lips half parted, eyes glowing under the soft light of the iron streetlamp.

But this time they were interrupted by a honking horn. Frowning, Serge glanced toward the street. Traffic on Beacon Hill was rare after midnight. His double-parked car, he saw, was blocking the way of a little red sport car.

"That's Gordon," Tori said. She gave Serge a quick kiss on the cheek instead of their usual long, drawn-out one. "I guess you'd better move so he can get by."

"Your brother's timing stinks," Serge grumbled, leaving her with gruff regret.

Tori watched as the two men ignored each other. Gordon sat rigid in his car, looking straight ahead as Serge approached. Serge didn't so much as glance at him as he passed by to get to his own car. Tori shook her head sadly and went inside.

Jiggs trotted down the stairs to greet her with wild cries of joy. She bent down to let him wrap his front paws around her neck and lick her face. Although the little spaniel spent all day by her side at the gallery, Tori felt guilty about dropping him off at the house every night before going off with Serge. Mr. Jiggs wasn't used to his mistress leaving him in the evening. He yelped sharply in her ear to show that he didn't like it one bit.

Gordon came in shortly, after parking his car. From the look on his face Tori expected him to start yelping at her, too. He asked her to come into the parlor with him for a little talk. Exhausted as she was, Tori complied. She and Gordon had barely spoken to each other all week. She sank down on the sofa. When he began his pacing back and forth in front of the fireplace Tori knew what was going to come next. Sure enough, he got right to the heart of the matter.

"What could you possibly see in a man like Serge Zhdanov, Victoria?" Gordon asked her in his most exasperated tone.

"He makes me happy," she answered simply.

"Well, you certainly don't look very happy to me."

Tori wearily folded her arms across her chest. "At this particular moment I'm not, Gordon. I don't want to sit here and listen to you put down the man I . . ." She left the end of her declaration hanging in the air.

"You love?" Gordon guessed. "You *love* that Russian peasant? Has it come to that?" He threw up his hands but said nothing more, apparently flabbergasted at such a turn of events.

"Yes, it's come to that," Tori told him. "Why can't you accept it?"

"I want the best for you, that's why. Not some pushy, second-rate parvenu who'll end up hurting and disappointing you."

"You're the one who's hurting me now, Gordon." She stood up to stare down her brother. "And what's more, you disappoint me, too. You're a snob. A horrible snob."

He backed away from Tori's fierce glare as if it were physically piercing him. "Zhdanov's already turned you against me," he said. "I was afraid he would. He's always turned people against me. And now my own sister!"

Tori's expression softened. "Serge has done no such thing. Can't the two of you forget past differences for my sake?"

Gordon looked doubtful. "You're asking for the impossible, I'm afraid. I simply cannot tolerate the man."

"If you insist on keeping such a closed mind, it's pointless to continue this discussion," Tori declared.

"Very well." Her brother nodded stiffly. "Good night." He left the parlor without another word.

It pained Tori to be at odds with her brother. She remembered that they had disagreed years ago—when Gordon had tried to warn her about the man she was engaged to marry. She'd refused to listen to him then, and just as he'd predicted, she'd been badly hurt. She'd kept a tight lid on her emotions ever since. Until now. Was she making the same mistake all over again? Should she heed her brother's warning this time?

No, she couldn't believe that. Love for Serge filled her heart with such warmth that the cold doubt melted away. She refused to allow memories of what had happened in the past taint that love. It was the present that mattered.

Tori went to stand before the portrait of her great-great-aunt and namesake. "Poor dear, you never gave yourself a second chance at happiness," she said softly.

Chapter Twelve

Going out with Serge again tonight?'' Ginger asked Tori as they closed up the gallery the next day.

Tori nodded and smiled as she tucked the rose he'd sent her that morning into her chignon.

"Why don't the two of you join Gordon and me for dinner?'' her friend suggested.

"There's nothing I'd like better,'' Tori replied wistfully. "But I doubt either man would agree to that.''

Ginger smiled impishly. "What if we all met somewhere accidentally on purpose? You tell Serge you want to go to a certain restaurant, and I'll suggest the same one to Gordon. We'll act real surprised when we see each other there and insist that we all sit together.''

Tori laughed, shaking her head. "That sounds like a plot from an *I Love Lucy* rerun, Ginger. We're not dealing with Ricky and Fred, though. This little plan of yours is sure to backfire.''

"No, it won't. Sharing a civil meal will break the iceberg between them. Don't you want Serge and Gordon to be on friendly terms?"

"Of course, I do. More than anything." Tori pressed her palms together. "But I think we should leave well enough alone, for now."

"Except it's not well enough," Ginger pointed out. "Those two have to learn to get along if they're going to be brothers-in-law, don't they?"

Tori laughed again, but this time her laugh was a little strained. "You're jumping way ahead of things, Ginger. Serge and I have never come close to discussing marriage."

"I bet he's asked you to move in with him, though."

"How do you know that?" Tori stared at Ginger, astonished.

"It doesn't take a genius to figure it out, sweetie. I see the way you look at each other every night when he comes by to get you—as if you've been parted for years instead of hours. You might as well live with him, Tori. It'll save you both a lot of time and energy."

"I can't be so nonchalant about it," Tori told her. "Serge's invitation was a little too casual for me to take seriously."

"Oh, don't be a goose. If all Serge wanted was a good time, he certainly wouldn't have picked you for his playmate, Miss Prim."

"Thanks a lot!"

Ginger patted her friend's back. "That wasn't meant as an insult, Tori. It's obvious to me that you and Serge are serious about each other. It's time for Gordon to accept that, too. He and Serge have to forget about some silly grudge left over from the past."

Since Tori agreed wholeheartedly, it didn't take Ginger much longer to convince her to go along with her little scheme. They decided to meet at an Italian restaurant in the North End, each with her recalcitrant man in tow.

But an hour or so later, when she and Serge entered the cozy little restaurant, Tori had second thoughts about the wisdom of such a ploy. She was tempted to tell Serge that she'd suddenly changed her mind and wanted to eat Chinese food instead. It was too late, though. Ginger had spotted them and was waving madly from a corner table.

"Well, look who's here," Serge said blandly.

"What a coincidence," Tori murmured, feeling pangs of guilt rather than hunger.

"What a setup, you mean," Serge corrected. He flashed his wide smile and waved back at Ginger while Gordon glared.

"I'm sorry, Serge. This was a dumb idea," Tori admitted. "We don't have to sit with them. We can even go somewhere else if you prefer."

"You think I'd leave just because of your brother's presence? Of course, we'll join them." He took Tori's arm in his firm grasp and led her to their table. "Let's hope Gordon doesn't bolt, though. Or strangle us with his linguine."

Gordon did neither. In fact, he behaved like the perfect gentleman he considered himself to be. He rose as Tori and Serge approached and asked them, coldly but civilly, to sit with him and Ginger. Serge accepted with the same polite stiffness.

Surprisingly enough, things began to warm up after that, thanks to the good food and cheering bottles of Chianti. Tori threw Ginger an appreciative glance across the red-checkered tablecloth. Her idea, it seemed, hadn't been so dumb after all.

Ginger winked back, her round cherub face flushed with wine and goodwill. "Isn't this fun?" she cried. "We're like the Four Musketeers! All for one and one for all forever after!" She raised her glass.

"Don't get carried away, angel," Gordon cautioned.

"But isn't it wonderful that things have worked out so well for all of us?" Ginger's baby blues were glazed with sentimental tears. "You and I are back together, Gordie. And your sister has finally found the man of her dreams. Who turns out to be an old family friend!"

"Not quite that," Gordon corrected a bit caustically.

Ginger waved away his objection with her wineglass, spilling some of the garnet liquid. "He's the best friend you ever had, Gordie. Thanks to Serge, your debt to Ugly got paid off." She lifted her glass even higher. "Here's to happy endings. And to Serge, who came through when it counted.

No one else joined in the toast or so much as moved a muscle. As a silence fell over the table, Ginger's open face slowly registered understanding of her blunder. She muttered a soft expletive over her own lack of discretion and gave Tori an apologetic look. "I guess I sort of let the cat out of the box, didn't I?"

Tori's anger with her flashed bright and hot, then dissipated. "That's all right, Ginger. It was wrong of me to ask you to keep it a secret from Gordon in the first place." She turned to her brother. "I was afraid you wouldn't take the money if you knew it came from Serge," she explained feebly.

"So you lied." Pale as a ghost, Gordon carefully put down his fork, then carefully refolded his napkin and placed it on the table. "You deliberately lied to me, Victoria. I find that difficult to accept, let alone forgive."

"Oh, come off it, Langford," Serge interjected angrily. "Your sister was only trying to help you out of a difficult situation."

"By getting me into a worse one?" Gordon locked eyes with Serge. "A Langford indebted to a Zhdanov. How acutely ironic. You must find it as amusing as I find it distasteful."

Serge threw down his own napkin. "Actually, I find your attitude damn insulting, Gordo. You mean you'd prefer to still owe money to a lowlife like Ugly?"

"Anything would be better than having my sister in your clutches, Zhdanov." Gordon looked back at Tori, pain and anger dulling his gray eyes. "You sold yourself to this Russian bear, didn't you?"

She was horrified at the accusation and deeply ashamed of her brother for making it. But before she could even open her mouth to object Serge had leapt up from the table, tipping over a few wineglasses in the process.

"That's it, Langford. We'll settle this outside," he told Gordon.

"Oh, no, you won't." Tori jumped up and grabbed Serge's arm. "Please, darling. Don't fight with Gordon. It'll only make matters worse."

"How the hell could they be worse?" Serge wanted to know.

The manager of the restaurant came rushing to their table, which was now the center of the other diners' attention. "What's wrong? What's wrong?" he asked, wringing his hands. "Is it the food? Is it the service?"

"It's the rotten company," Serge told him. He took out his wallet and threw some bills down on the table. "That remark wasn't addressed to you, Ginger," he added.

"It should be. This is all my fault," she said, tears sliding down her plump cheeks.

"It was my sister who deceived me, not you," Gordon told her. He remained rigid in his chair, stiff with rage.

"I couldn't stand by and let Ugly make good his threats, Gordon," Tori said, her voice trembling.

"Don't try to reason with that ingrate," Serge advised her gruffly, pulling her away from the table. "Come on. We're getting out of here right now."

"If you leave with him, you needn't come back home, Victoria," Gordon warned.

Tori had blanched as pale as her brother. "If that's your ultimatum, then I'll move out tonight. Goodbye, Gordon."

"You're making the biggest mistake of your life, Victoria!" Gordon shouted after her as she and Serge walked out of the restaurant together. Tori was sure that her brother had never raised his voice like that in a public place before.

Lone wolf that he was, Serge had never had a roommate before. In the past he'd rarely asked a woman to even spend a weekend with him. He disliked the awkwardness of breakfast small-talk. He found it tiresome to share toast and eggs and sections of the Sunday Boston *Globe* with someone else. He was an extremely private man, even with his family. But after living with Victoria Langford for a week, Serge realized that she was even more private than he, more guarded about her personal space. Serge didn't mind that as much as the way she tended to tiptoe around *his* personal space. He sorely wished that she would make herself more at home and stop acting like a very proper but very temporary guest. He didn't want the situation to be temporary.

It gave him a kick to see the few things she'd brought with her around his place—from her engraved silver hairbrush to her red plastic toothbrush. Some of her clothes now hung in his closet along with the silk kimono he'd bought her. Not *all* her clothes, though. Every day or so Ginger would bring over a few more articles. Serge had suggested packing up all of Tori's belongings in one fell swoop and moving them to his place, but she had resisted the idea.

She'd brought Mr. Jiggs with her, of course. And despite his prejudice against silly toy dogs, Serge was becoming inordinately fond of the mutt. He even let Jiggs share the king-size bed with Tori and him as long as he stayed at the foot of it. The little spaniel snored even louder than Duke had. Lying in bed waiting for Tori to come out of the shower, Serge was now breaking the rule he'd laid down about Jiggs by allowing the dog to sit on his chest.

She walked into the bedroom on the balls of her feet, which she tended to do when she was barefoot. That never failed to delight Serge. What delighted him even more was that she was only wearing one of his plush white towels and her skin was still rosy and damp from the hot spray of water.

He pushed Jiggs off and sat up in bed. "Come here," he said, smiling his lopsided grin and opening wide his arms to her.

Tori let the towel fall to the carpet and quickly got under the covers to nuzzle against him. She loved the touch of his hard muscle against her soft flesh, the scent of him mingling with the smell of the clean sheets and her own feminine scent. She adored being in bed with him, not just to make love but to rub shoulders and knees and simply be close.

"Let's stay in all morning," Serge suggested. "I'll call Sonya and tell her to cancel all my appointments."

"But I can't, Serge," Tori whispered with regret into his ear, then kissed it to make amends. "I have an important collector flying in from New York."

"Can't Ginger handle that?" he asked a bit petulantly.

"Well, I suppose. But there's also a young artist coming from the Cape. I've promised to take a look at his work."

"Let Ginger handle that, too." He nuzzled his cheek against the slope of her white shoulder.

"Serge!" Tori protested—not the nuzzle, but the suggestion. "I happen to be the one running Back Bay Gallery, not Ginger. And lately I've been dumping too many of my responsibilities on her."

"Come on, honey. Stay in just this one morning," Serge urged, doing some rather wonderful things to her with his hand under the covers. She was about to agree as her body turned to putty, but he made the mistake of continuing to talk. "If I can take the time off, surely you can, Tori."

"Because what you do is so much more important than my work?" she asked sharply, shifting away from his touch.

They'd had this discussion before. Serge didn't like Tori working late at the gallery. It didn't matter to him that he was the one who was usually late. He tried explaining to her how that was different; his career was more demanding and high-pressure. Tori refused to accept that.

"Let's make love, not war," Serge pleaded with her now, not wanting to lose sight or touch of her soft, supple body.

"We'll have all night together," Tori reminded him. She'd gladly let her question drop, not wanting to argue with him, and was smiling again. She was remembering last night together and wondering how they could top it.

"Not tonight, we won't," Serge reluctantly informed her. "Or the rest of the week, for that matter. I'm leaving for LA this afternoon."

"Oh?" Tori propped herself on her elbow and looked down at him, annoyance in her expression, disappointment in her eyes. "Why didn't you mention this to me sooner?"

"Because I just decided while you were in the shower. I've been delaying it too long." He left unsaid that the reason for this was her presence in his life. "One of my investments out there could use some closer monitoring from me."

"I see." Tori got out of bed, truly annoyed now. "So you expect me to change my entire morning schedule to suit your sudden change of plans. I'm not your little geisha, Serge."

He took in her pale, smooth nakedness through narrowed eyes. Even when he was angry with her, he still found her beautiful. "That you certainly are not, lady," he agreed adamantly. "You never let me forget for a minute that what you are is my honored guest." He got up too and began stomping toward the closet for his robe.

That was hardly an insult, but Tori sensed it was meant as a criticism. She put her hands on her slender, naked hips. "What's that suppose to mean?" she asked him.

"This!" he shouted, throwing open his closet door. He pointed to her clothes hanging at one end of it. "Four dresses. A couple of pairs of shoes. And your underthings still in your suitcase, dammit! Talk about a temporary situation. Why, it would take you less than five minutes to clear out of here!"

Tori wasn't quite sure what Serge was shouting about. "I didn't think you'd care to have my things strewn all over the place," she said.

"But I would." Serge's broad chest heaved with a deep sigh. "I want you to feel at home here, not like you're visiting some foreign country. If you don't feel comfortable in these surroundings, change them. Move in some of your antique furniture. Like that vanity of yours. Or even that four-poster bed if you miss it."

"You think I miss that old stuff?" Tori threw back her long neck and laughed. Then she looked around Serge's sleek, functional bedroom with all its modern, streamlined comforts. "This environment suits me much better. Not that it couldn't use a bit of a woman's touch."

Serge forgot about getting his robe and walked back to her. "That's exactly what I mean, honey. It seems to me that you've gone out of your way to leave my home untouched. Jiggs has left more of an impression. At least he sheds hair on the furniture!"

"Well, I don't shed, and this isn't my home," Tori answered, still unsure what he was driving at. "But if I haven't expressed how much I appreciate your letting me stay here until—"

"Until nothing!" Serge was shouting again. "I find your incessant politeness an insult, Tori." With that he headed for the bathroom and turned on the shower full blast.

Tori sat down on the edge of the bed and contemplated what had just occurred between them. Had it been an argument? A misunderstanding? A complete lack of communication? She turned to Jiggs, who'd been watching her intently from the foot of the bed.

"You heard it all, Mr. Jiggs," she said. "Did you understand any of it?"

Apparently not. The toy spaniel's only response was to roll on his back and wait for his fuzzy belly to be scratched. For once Tori ignored his plea for attention, sensing she'd had a more urgent, if indirect, one from Serge. She went into the bathroom and threw open the smoked glass shower-stall door. She could barely make out Serge in all the thick steam. He'd lathered his body from head to foot.

"You look like the abominable snowman," she laughed.

Growling, he hooked his long arm around her waist and yanked her in. "Now you know my little secret, lovely one," he whispered hoarsely, nibbling her ear as the hot water gushed over them both. "I *am* the abominable snowman."

"My hair is never going to dry in time for work," she said, not terribly upset over his revelation. "Did we just have a fight, by the way? If so, I want to make up before you leave for the Coast."

"Not a fight, exactly." He held her to his soapy chest as the spray beat against his broad back. "But I don't like to think that the only reason you're staying here is because your brother forced the issue."

"And I don't like to think that the only reason you want me here is because it's more convenient for you."

"Well, it is more convenient," he admitted.

"And my brother did force the issue," she replied.

"But more important, I happen to be in love with you," he went on.

"And I wouldn't be here if I didn't love you, Serge."

They separated and backed away from each other as much as they could in the cramped space of the stall. They stared at each other, wide-eyed.

"I think we may just have established something pretty important," Serge finally said.

"And it's about time, too," she agreed. "I never thought I'd hear you say it."

"Say it? Hell, I'll sing it."

And so he did. Serge sang out his love for Tori with gusto, and the off-key melody reverberated off the tile walls of their enclosed space. Tori joined in with her own version of the made-up love song. And Jiggs began to howl outside the bathroom door.

"Stop!" Tori finally cried. "We'll get evicted."

"Impossible. I was one of the initial investors in this building complex."

"That still may not stop your neighbors from calling the police, and I for one don't want to be dragged to the station in my birthday—"

He silenced her with a kiss, always an effective method. "I love you," he said, a mere whisper this time.

She whispered the same thing back to him. "And I want you right now," she added.

"Aren't you getting to be the adventurous one," he said, chuckling.

But the shower stall proved to be a less than ideal choice for prolonged lovemaking, and they were forced to move their dripping bodies to the bed. Not that the interruption made them lose their stride or break their rhythm. They knew each other's bodies too well; they wanted each other too much. What they both found so amazing was that the more times they made love, the deeper the sensations became. They'd already become an ingrained habit to each other, their mutual passion their drug.

Later, as Tori and Serge crossed each other's path and brushed against each other in the intricate dance of dressing for work, she returned to a subject he'd brought up earlier.

"I really do feel comfortable living here," she said, pulling on one pale silk stocking and hooking the top to her garter belt. Serge always stopped whatever he was doing to watch this particular performance each morning.

"I like the simplicity of this place and don't miss the clutter of memorabilia in the Beacon Hill house at all. The only thing I truly do miss is that old marble bathtub."

"I sure did, too, this morning," Serge agreed. "That shower isn't half as romantic...or comfortable. We should have turned on the Jacuzzi."

"It's not the same thing," Tori replied wistfully, remembering the magnolia blossoms floating in the marble tub. She began to pull up the other stocking.

"God, I'm going to miss you while I'm away," Serge sighed as he watched. "Why don't you come with me, honey?"

His simple request vexed her because she longed to take him up on it. "You know I can't very well drop everything and follow you across the continent, Serge. I have a business to run."

"Right," he replied dryly. He took out his suitcase and began to pack.

Tori stayed his motions as he was folding a shirt and wrapped her arms around him. "I love you, Serge," she said once again. She thought it bore repeating since they would be parted for a few days. And she took such great pleasure in saying it.

Serge called her three, sometimes four times a day while he was away, occasionally forgetting the difference in time zones and waking her up. Tori liked those calls best, when his low, husky voice would pull her out of the dreams she was having of him.

When she wasn't dreaming about him, she was thinking about him constantly. How could she not? Instead of his usual daily pink rose, he was having one delivered to the gallery every hour on the hour, eight a day.

"What is it about you that inspires men to send flowers, Tori?" Ginger asked, more amused by Serge's excesses than envious. "Gordon never sends me flowers. Once he gave me a prickly cactus, which I did not find particularly humorous." She laughed anyway. "Of course, your brother does have a pretty dry sense of humor, as you well know, and..." Ginger's voice drifted off. "Sorry," she muttered.

"You don't have to apologize for bringing up Gordon," Tori told her. "I like to hear how he's doing. He's well, I hope."

"Healthy as a mule and as stubborn as one," Ginger replied. "He doesn't like to hear about how well *you*'re doing. And God forbid I even mention Serge. He'll stalk right out of the room." Short and plump as she was, Ginger did a fairly good imitation of tall, thin Gordon stalking. Then her shoulders drooped. "I'm so very sorry about all this, Tori. I'm surprised you're still speaking to me."

"Forget it, Ginger. Everything's worked out for the best. And if Gordon refuses to understand my actions, so be it." Although Tori truly meant what she said, her heart was still heavy with regret over the breach with her brother.

Ginger took in her friend's sad expression. "Maybe I can get him to come to the opening-night party of the gallery exhibition."

Tori gave out a humorless little laugh. "I doubt it very much. I doubt Gordon will set foot in this gallery ever again."

"We'll see," Ginger replied, a determined set to her round features.

When Serge returned home from his West Coast trip he noticed a few welcome changes. There were some striking paintings from the gallery hanging on the living-room walls. Tori's pear-shaped silver teapot and flowered china cups were on the glass-and-chrome dining table. Her collections of Jane Austen and Henry James nestled beside his books on the bookcase, and in the bedroom's walk-in closet, her wardrobe crowded his. He opened a few drawers of his built-in dresser until he found what he was hoping to see—her lingerie neatly folded and scented with lilac sachets.

"You told me to make myself at home," Tori said, entering the bedroom, Jiggs close at her heels. She'd just returned from work and was delighted to find Serge back from his trip.

Serge opened his arms wide to her. "Home is where the heart is, Tori." He held her close, breathing in her delicate scent, not wanting to ever let her go. But he did release her. He'd made special plans. "We're going out to dinner tonight," he announced,.

Tori shook her head. "I'm keeping you all to myself tonight, Mr. Zhdanov. I've been deprived of your company for way too long." She wrapped her arms around his neck and smiled up at him. "You're looking at one lusty lady, mister."

Serge moaned, unable to resist her teasing, musical voice or her parted, waiting lips. All his well-laid plans flew out the window as Tori began unbuttoning his shirt, this time with a great degree of finesse. She'd made her own plans for the evening, plans she'd thought about all week as she lay in Serge's big wide bed, yearning for him.

"Funny," she said, unbuckling his belt. "I've slept alone all my life without any trouble. But it seems I'm unable to perform such a simple task anymore. I couldn't sleep a wink without you by my side, Serge."

He stared down at her shining, smoothly parted hair as she slowly unzipped his conservative gray trousers and began tugging them down his hips. "But you're not suggesting we take a nap now, are you?" he managed to ask as his stomach muscles contracted with desire.

Tori placed her palms flat on the hard wall of his chest and pushed him down on the bed. "Maybe a little nap later," she said. "Much later." Then she undressed them both.

This time she was the one who led them in their dance of love, and Serge didn't mind one bit. Her gliding touch over his body had the power of knowledge in it, the knowledge of how to drive him wild. Yet he managed to hold on to his sanity, managed to endure all her sweetly tormenting caresses without losing control or taking it.

"I've taught you well," he murmured into her ear in a feverish daze.

Tori smiled to herself but said nothing. She was the one teaching him now by allowing the latent force of her female power to bloom within her. She gave to him in wild abandon, knowing that her energy could trigger and even surpass his. She took him to the brink, pulled him back, took him there again. And again. What amazed her was that he let her set the pace. They both knew that he had the physical strength to take them both over that brink if he chose.

When she slid her sleek, hot body along his muscled limbs and took him inside her, Serge groaned with relief. But still he followed her lead, her rhythm, her maddening pace. And in the end it was worth the wait, the patience, the self-control. They moved together, arrived at the peak of pleasure together, and laughed together afterward.

They ate take-out Chinese in the kitchen at midnight, after the nap they'd discussed hours earlier. Serge pushed aside the cardboard containers to make room for a small purple velvet box. He'd planned on a more romantic setting, but this would have to do. He couldn't wait.

"What's that?" Tori asked, chopsticks poised midair with sesame noodles dangling from them.

"Open it and see." Serge couldn't help smiling at the thought of the millions of men and women who had had this exact conversation. Of course he still considered Tori and himself unique. No one, as far as Serge was concerned, could ever love as much or as well as they did.

Tori laid down her chopsticks and opened the box. A square-cut emerald blazed within it. She stared at it for a long, breathless moment, then looked across the table at Serge, her own large eyes blazing green.

"A little something I picked up for you on Rodeo Drive," he said, trying to sound casual and unassuming but not carrying it off particularly well. "Why don't you try it on?"

"Which hand?" she asked.

"I was going to leave that up to you."

She arched her lovely eyebrows. "Oh, were you now? And do you expect me to propose to myself, too?"

"I want you to have the ring whether you want to marry me or not," Serge explained awkwardly.

Tori prodded him with a chopstick. "But do you want to marry *me*?"

He opened his mouth to say something gruff or to make a joke—anything to deflect the seriousness of the moment. Yet it was this moment that he'd been constantly thinking about during the long flight home. How many times had he reopened the box to look at the ring during those hours, just to make sure the quality of the emerald was good enough for her. He'd spent a small fortune on it, but still he was worried.

"Yes, I want to marry you," he replied gravely. "I had a little speech that I rehearsed on the plane, but I'll be damned if I remember it now. I was going to take you to Mother Russia's and order the exact same meal we had that first night together; and if you accepted me, I was going to have Mama and Neda and Alex join us to celebrate with champagne. That's how I imagined it, anyway. But it seems that in reality I'm a bumbling, unromantic fool."

"No, you're not," she said beaming. "What you just described is perfect."

"Too bad it didn't work out that way."

"But it will!" Tori cried. "We'll do it exactly the way you planned tomorrow night. And make sure all your family will be there for the toast, because I'm going to accept."

His face filled with joy as he took her left hand, kissed it, and slipped the ring on her finger. "Oh, honey, we're going to be so happy. And you're going to love California."

"This is the most beautiful ring I've ever seen," she said. Her hand was trembling. Her voice was, too. The momentous decision they'd just agreed on was beginning to hit home to her. "Yes, I know we'll be happy. We *are* happy," she went on. She touched his dear, handsome face with her fingertips. "What's this about California? Is that where you want to go for our honeymoon?" She didn't really care where they went, or if they went anywhere at all. But she did think they should at least talk about it together.

"Honeymoon?" Serge frowned. He hadn't even considered one. But if she expected one, of course he would take the time—somehow. The upcoming months were going to be extremely busy. "We'll go anywhere you want, Tori. As soon as I can get away. But what I meant is that you're going to love living in Los Angeles. That's where I'm relocating my business.''

The blissful smile on Tori's face froze. "You expect me to move out there? What about *my* business?''

"Don't worry, honey.'' Serge patted her hand—the one sporting the big emerald. "I'll help you set up another gallery on the West Coast.''

"I don't want another gallery. I want to keep the one I have. It's my life. You can't expect me to walk away and leave it behind, Serge.''

He got up and went to the refrigerator for a beer. He said nothing until he'd opened it and poured some in a glass. "The gallery is your life?'' he asked with hurt in his voice. "Then, where will your husband fit in? Don't you think I should come before your business, honey?''

She slapped her hand on the table impatiently. "And shouldn't I come before your business? Boston is my home. Yours, too. Why should we uproot? You make a good living here, don't you?''

"I could make more money out there,'' he informed her.

"Is that all you care about?''

"You know it isn't.'' He took a deep swallow of beer. "At least, I hope you do.''

"Well, I'm confused right now.''

"Then maybe you'd better sleep on it, Tori. Maybe you'll see everything more clearly tomorrow.''

She stood up and carefully closed the Chinese-food containers. "You mean see things your way, don't you, Serge?''

They had very little to say to each other after that, and went to bed without so much as kissing each other good-night. They easily avoided touching in the big bed. They could have been sleeping a hundred miles apart, Tori thought. They'd never gone to bed angry before. She brushed a tear from her eye. Why did her hand feel so heavy? Oh, yes. The engagement ring. She took it off and placed it on the nightstand.

Chapter Thirteen

Serge got up early and made omelets for them the next morning, hoping that would appease Tori. It occurred to him that the last time he'd made omelets there'd been a major breach in their relationship. But he wasn't going to start getting superstitious about a couple of scrambled-up eggs.

It was his mind that was scrambled, that's what, he thought. Why had he assumed that Tori would just go along with his plans? He hadn't handled that well at all, he allowed. Would serving her breakfast in bed help? Or would that be a precedent he'd come to regret a few years into their marriage? He had already determined during the long, lonely night that there would be a marriage. No matter what, he would have the woman breathing so softly beside him for his wife. Even if that... Serge folded the omelet and gave out a sigh of resignation. Even if that meant giving in. He supposed she had as much a right to decide their future together as he had.

Tori came upon him silently, barefoot, walking on the tips of her toes. She paused by the kitchen doorway to watch him a moment, and despite her troubled frame of mind, a little smile flitted across her full lips. It was the same smile that he'd inspired the first time she'd laid eyes on him in the Garden. He was wearing his brief white running shorts and nothing else. Tori had been surprised to learn that he didn't even own a pair of pajamas. He was a man totally at ease in his nakedness, and she knew he'd slipped on the shorts in deference to her sense of decorum.

"Good morning," she said, wrapping the silk kimono more tightly around her slenderness.

He looked up at her, a certain wariness in his ice-blue eyes. "Is it?" he asked. "It sure was a hell of a night."

"I guess Jiggs was the only one who got any sleep."

"It was that damn snoring of his that kept me up," Serge declared.

"Was it?" She walked up to him as he stood by the stove and put her arms around him. "We have to talk, Serge."

"I know." He took her hand and touched his lips to her palm. "You're not wearing the ring I gave you!"

She took it out of the deep pocket of her kimono and offered it to him. "It felt so heavy last night."

He stared down at it. He was shocked and hurt that she would give him up so easily, without further ado, because his plans didn't suit her. Whereas he'd been willing to do more than compromise: he'd been willing to see things her way completely.

"You want me to take it back?" he asked in a strangled voice, deeply disappointed in her because of her inability to yield in the slightest. That rigidity must have been bred into her, he thought, through generations of intolerant Langfords.

She was shaking her head, though. "I want you to put it back on my finger," she told him a bit sadly. "I'll soon get used to the weight of it. And who knows, I may even get used to Los Angeles. I'm willing to give it a try at least."

"What about Back Bay Gallery?" His slanting eyes registered surprise and relief.

"I'll offer Ginger the position of manager."

"I object to you letting somebody else run it. That wasn't the deal when I bought in as your partner, lady."

His attitude totally confused her. "I can't very well run things if I'm thousands of miles away, Serge."

"And what if we decide to have children?" he asked out of the blue. "How is my mother going to manage to interfere with the way we raise them if we're that far away? Poor Mama! It would break her heart."

"Serge, this was your idea," she reminded him. "You said the West Coast offered you more business opportunities."

"I can be successful anywhere I please," he boasted. "So we're staying right here in ole Beantown, Tori. I don't want to hear another word about it."

How very like him, Tori thought, eyes shimmering as she gazed up at his proud Slavic face. He could even make a concession sound like a demand.

"Not another word," she agreed as tears of relief slid down her cheeks.

"And no crying, either," he commanded. He snatched up the ring she still held in her palm, and knelt down on one knee before her. "Let me do this right this time. Will you marry me and be my love, Miss Victoria Langford? For better or worse, but always in Boston?"

She nodded. Her heart was singing with happiness. "You know I'd follow you to the ends of the earth, don't you, Serge?"

"I do now." He put the ring back on her finger and still kneeling, pressed his face against her abdomen. "And I'll never make you regret loving me. Never, honey," he promised her.

Serge had reason to doubt his ability to keep his promise to her the following week. He should have expected something unpleasant to occur to mar their happiness. There was a streak of pessimism, or perhaps fatalism, in his Russian nature that made him wary of total bliss. But he hadn't seen it coming at all. In fact, as he and Tori dressed for the opening-night reception at her gallery, he was so filled with optimism that he could barely contain himself—or keep his hands off Tori, who was having trouble dressing because of those teasing hands of his.

"Darling, when I asked you to zip my dress I meant up, not down," she told him.

His mouth slid down the vertebrae of her bare back, and his tongue flicked at the dimple indenting the small of it before he complied. It was a form-fitting gown of silver sequins that molded to her body like mermaid scales.

Tori moved away from him just in time to prevent him from unzipping her enchantress gown again. "Serge, you'll make me late for the party," she reprimanded softly.

He smoothed down the lapel of his dinner jacket and straightened the black bow tie. She'd been getting ready for the past hour. He'd dressed in ten minutes flat.

He watched her nervously fumble with a silver earring and thought of the present he'd bought her for their wedding day the following month. He decided to give it to her now, instead. He couldn't resist. He went into the living room, retrieved the black jewelry box from its hiding place high on the bookshelf, and returned to the bedroom.

"Perhaps you'd like to wear these tonight," he said, handing over the box, his smile wide and boyish.

Tori opened it to discover a pair of large diamond earrings winking at her. "Oh, no, Serge! This is too much," she cried.

"Not for the future Mrs. Zhdanov, it isn't. Go on, Tori. Put them on. They'll go with that dress of yours," he urged gruffly.

She did. They were perfect. As far as Serge was concerned, everything was perfect. But looking back later that night, he realized how nervous Tori had been, getting dressed. At the time he'd thought little of it. Why shouldn't she be nervous before the opening-night party of a big exhibition she'd been organizing for months? There would be art critics there. And important collectors. To say nothing of the unpredictable artists her gallery represented.

What Serge hadn't known was that Tori was on pins and needles because she was hoping her brother Gordon would attend the reception after receiving the note she'd sent him. It would be such a perfect time for a reconciliation. Serge and she planned to announce their engagement that evening. They hadn't even told Ginger about it yet.

The reception proved to be a huge success. Early into the evening many of the paintings on exhibit had red stickers beside them to signify that they'd already been purchased. The artists were happy. The collectors were happy. Even some of the serious, hard-to-please critics looked relatively happy. Words of praise flowed along with the champagne.

Serge was content to stay on the sidelines, observing Tori in her element. How confident she was in this environment, he thought. And how admired and respected she was, too. He appreciated more than ever that she would have been willing to give it up for him. He was more sure than ever, too, that he'd made the right decision to stay in Boston because of her. It made him feel good to care about her ambitions as much as he cared about his own. Yes, he was feeling pretty good about himself, and Tori, and life in general at that moment. And it was at that moment that Gordon Langford walked in.

Both Serge and Tori saw him at the same time. Serge's eyes narrowed suspiciously. Tori's face lit up as she rushed to her brother.

"Welcome," Tori told him softly. She tilted her cheek, expecting his usual kiss, but received none. She continued to smile graciously, not missing a beat. "You look well, dear. How's your work coming along?"

"Fine, thank you," Gordon replied curtly. "And you look well too, Victoria. Did Zhdanov give you those flashy diamond earrings?"

Tori touched one of them with her fingertip, feeling self-conscious. "Yes, he did," she replied, her gentle eyes beseeching her brother to be kind.

But Gordon's expression remained aloof and cold. "They're a bit ostentatious, don't you think? Not that I expected a man from his background to have good taste."

Serge appeared at Tori's side at that moment. "I think you should leave, Langford. Tori doesn't need any more aggravation from you."

"Actually, you're the one I wanted to see," Gordon replied, slipping his hand inside his jacket. For a mad instant Tori feared he was going to pull out a gun and shoot Serge. Instead he extracted a harmless-looking envelope. "A check for fifty thousand dollars," he explained in precise syllables, handing it to Serge.

"Where in the world did you get the money, Gordon?" Tori asked in amazement.

"In the best part of the world there is," he replied. "Beacon Hill. I sold the house, Victoria."

Gordon's simple announcement produced a rush of emotion within Tori—a combination of both relief and regret that he'd manage to break from the past. But what she felt most was concern for her brother.

"Oh, Gordon!" she cried, reaching out to him. "That must have been difficult for you."

He pulled back from his sister's touch. "Less difficult than remaining in that man's debt." He jutted his sharp Langford chin in Serge's direction. "He's out of my life completely now."

Tori raised her own chin. "Only if you want me to be, too. Serge is going to be my husband, Gordon. My partner for life."

Tori held her breath, waiting for his reaction. Confusion clouded Gordon's previously haughty expression. Then she saw his eyes widen as if he finally understood her love for Serge. For a moment Tori thought her brother had come around to accepting it all, but then his expression hardened again.

"You actually intend to marry this Russian peasant? To become Mrs. Zhdanov?" His voice quivered slightly, sounding hurt as well as angry. "Good Lord, I bet you can't even spell your new last name, Victoria!"

He left the gallery, slamming the plate-glasss door behind him. A stunned silence followed his exit, and Tori realized that most of the guests had witnessed the altercation. She was at a loss as how to handle the situation.

But Serge wasn't. He lifted his champagne glass and waved it around the room. "Now that we've got your attention, Miss Langford and I would like to take this opportunity to announce our engagement. And I do believe her brother's right about one thing, folks. I don't think Tori knows how to spell Zhdanov yet! So what? She's got the rest of her life to learn how."

With that he turned and kissed Tori as the guests laughed and applauded. She clung to him, more than ever appreciating his strength.

Serge knew that she was crying in the bathroom. Did Tori think she could fool him by running the shower like that? He couldn't stand knowing that she was crying her heart out and there was nothing he could do about it. He'd promised her happiness. He'd promised her that she'd never regret loving him. And he'd failed on both counts.

No, it wasn't his fault, he told himself, pacing the thickly carpeted bedroom floor. Jiggs followed in Serge's tracks for a while but soon wearied of the senselessness of it and went back to sleep on the bed. No, Tori's unhappiness was Gordon's fault, not his, Serge tried to convince himself as he paced. He stuck his hands in the pockets of his tuxedo pants and balled them into fists. Damn Gordon! He loathed him more than ever now for making Tori so miserable.

"Good riddance!" Serge said aloud, immediately getting Jigg's attention. "She's better off never seeing that jerky brother of hers again." He glared at the dog. "Isn't Gordon a jerk? Isn't she better off?"

Jiggs tilted his head to the side and looked puzzled.

"I've got my own pride," Serge continued. "I'll be damned if I'm going to go to Gordon and plead with him to accept me."

Jiggs watched with big saucer eyes as Serge threw off his dinner jacket, ripped off his silk bow tie, and began unbuttoning his white pleated shirt with the same unnecessary vehemence. Then Serge stopped and muttered under his breath. Jiggs tilted his head again. These were words he'd never in his sheltered life heard before.

Serge grabbed his jacket, slung it over his shoulder, and headed for the door. He paused on the way out to scrawl a note for Tori.

He found a parking spot right in front of the Langfords' Beacon Hill town house. This must be my lucky day, he thought sardonically. He hurried out of the car and up to the door before he could change his mind about what he intended to do. He almost collided smack-dab into Ginger, who was just coming out.

"What are you doing here, Serge?"

"What do you think? I've come to see Gordon."

Ginger frowned and blocked his entrance. "You mean to have it out with him, don't you? Leave it alone, Serge. One of these days Gordon will see reason and come around."

"Yeah, when hell freezes over." He gently touched Ginger's shoulder. He had nothing against her. "Move aside, please. You can't spend your life protecting Gordon, Ginger."

"Why not?" Her little Kewpie-doll face was guileless. "Someone has to protect him from himself. He's his own worst enemy, Serge. He doesn't need some big hulk like you as one, too. What do you plan to do? Beat him up?"

"It wouldn't be as easy as that," Serge told her. "You underestimate Gordo. He can be pretty tough when he wants to be. He was one of the toughest competitors on the Harvard crew team. He never said die." Serge couldn't believe what he was hearing, mainly because it was coming from his own mouth! Was he actually defending Gordon?

"Does Tori know you're here?" Ginger asked him.

"She's taking a very long shower. She doesn't want me to hear her bawling her eyes out because her brother's turned his back on her."

"If you hurt him, Tori will never forgive you," Ginger warned.

"Run along now, Ginger," Serge said in his low, husky voice. "I only intend to do what has to be done."

He went in the front door and called out Gordon's name. He got no response and went searching. When he reached the kitchen he heard banging beneath his feet. He opened the basement door and shouted down the stairwell. "Hey, Langford? You down there?"

The banging stopped. Gordon came up the stairs, fight in his eyes, a mallet in his grip. Showdown time, Serge thought.

"We've got to settle things between us right now, Gordo."

"Every time you call me that I want to strangle you by that thick neck of yours, Zhdanov."

Serge shrugged. "Hell, it's just a nickname. You called me a lot worse than that when we were kids. You used to ridicule me all the time when my parents worked here."

"Someone had to keep you in your place. You would have taken over the whole house if you thought you could get away with it. You were always the pushy kind. Still are. You pushed yourself right into my sister's heart, didn't you?"

"You make it sound as if I forced her to love me."

Gordon tapped the mallet against his palm. "I'm not going to discuss Victoria with you, Zhdanov. If she wants to throw her life away, that's her business. Now get the hell out of here."

There was nothing Serge would have preferred to do, but the image of Tori's unhappy face at the gallery show made him stay put. Swallowing a big chunk of his pride, which almost got stuck in his throat, Serge continued to try to reason with Gordon.

"You're the one throwing away something valuable, Langford... Your sister's affection and regard. The last thing I want to do is alienate her from you."

"Hah! You've already done just that."

Serge looked at Gordon's face and saw the defeat and pain in it. "No, only you have the power to do that injury to yourself, pal," he told Gordon softly. "I could never influence Tori against you and would never try. Can't you understand that all I want is to make her happy?"

Gordon stopped tapping the mallet against his palm, and he studied the other man closely, as if seeing Serge for the first time. "She believes you can, apparently." He shook his head over the wonder of it. "You of all people."

"Yeah, me of all people," Serge agreed. "That's why I've come here to beg you to shake my hand and forget about the dislike we have for each other. Put the past in the past, Gordon. I have. Let's not let it ruin the future."

Surprise flickered in Gordon's gray gaze as he stared at Serge's extended hand. "I didn't expect this from you. You were always so damn stubborn and proud."

"And you weren't?" Serge smiled, keeping his hand out. "Maybe our problem is that we're too much alike."

That made Gordon laugh a little ruefully. "And maybe you have a little more class than I do in the end, Zhdanov. As much as my sister means to me, I wouldn't have come and begged you for a truce."

"Not a truce, Gordon. A friendship. For Tori's sake."

"I won't stand in the way of her happiness anymore," Gordon stated, laying the mallet on the kitchen table. "I accept your offer, Serge. It's about time we became friends. And not just for Tori's sake. Maybe we owe it to ourselves after all this time." Without further hesitation, he shook Serge's hand.

"Will you give the bride away at the wedding?" Serge asked him. The request had come out unexpectedly, but the moment Serge had spoken he sensed how right it would be.

Apparently Gordon did, too. "It'll be an honor," he said, and at last he smiled. "Victoria Zhdanov," he murmured. "Well, I suppose I'll eventually get used to it."

Serge laughed good-naturedly and slapped Gordon's back. "Admit it, Langford. You already are." He was tempted to give him a big Russian bear hug but thought better of it. It would take years before the reserved Gordon Langford got used to the Zhdanov exuberance. "What were you doing down in the basement, by the way?" he asked curiously. "Building Frankenstein's monster?"

Gordon carefully regarded Serge before replying. "You're probably one of the few people who can appreciate what I *am* doing down there," he said. "Remember the problems we used to have with those damn wooden oars when we raced?"

"Yeah?" Serge's eyes glinted with interest. "Have you invented a better one?"

"It's a space-age oar, Serge," Gordon told him enthusiastically. "Made of fiberglass and plastic instead of Sitka spruce."

Serge withheld his own enthusiasm although he felt that little spark of excitement he always did when someone approached him with a good, marketable idea. "Synthetic oars have been tried before without too much success," he reminded Gordon.

"Not like this one! Come on down. I'll show you."

"I hope they haven't come to blows yet," Ginger said as she and Tori hurried down the cobblestoned street toward the house.

"No, of course they haven't," Tori replied in a tense voice. "Serge and Gordon are two intelligent, civilized, well-educated adults."

"Adult *males*," Ginger amended.

"I'm sure they won't resort to violence to settle their differences," Tori insisted, silently praying that they wouldn't. The note Serge had left her had only stated that he was seeing to unfinished business and would be back shortly. If Ginger hadn't come by to tell her where Serge was, she'd still be guessing.

The two young women entered the house, each calling a different man's name. Neither received a response for her trouble.

"I'll make some tea," Tori said, heading for the kitchen, as if that magical brew would conjure them up. Ginger followed her.

They heard male voices in the basement and looked at each other with apprehensive eyes. "You think they've decided to fight it out down there?" Ginger asked.

"If so, we'll have to stop them," Tori suggested.

The two men barely glanced up as they came down the stairs. "Oh, hi," Gordon said with total disinterest. Serge merely nodded, then went back to examining the sweep oar that he'd taken down from one of the racks lining the basement walls. He was examining it intently.

"I can't believe you've manufactured all these oars down here in this limited work space," he told Gordon.

"And I can't believe you're here!" Tori interjected.

"Just a minute, honey," Serge replied distractedly. "So light and well balanced," he observed to Gordon.

"Cheaper and more durable, too," Gordon pointed out.

"Do you think they're talking about us?" Ginger asked Tori.

"They don't even know we're here," Tori said with a sigh.

"I've got more orders than I can fill," Gordon went on. "But there's a catch: I need staff and space to produce more, yet I can't afford to expand."

"That's where I come in," Serge said, smiling.

"Here's where we get out," Tori told Ginger. "Let's go back up where it's more comfortable. We won't be missed down here." She tried to sound annoyed, but in fact she'd never been more pleased to be ignored in her life. Not only were the two most important men in her life on speaking terms, they seemed to be on friendly terms. Possibly even business terms!

Tori and Serge's small wedding reception was held in the Langford town house at Gordon's insistence. Mrs. Zhdanov catered it, at her insistence. Everybody was having a marvelous time. Even the dour portraits of Langford ancestors hanging in the front parlor seemed to be expressing their approval of the match—or so Tori fancied through the shimmer of her happiness.

"Let's slip away," her husband whispered in her ear, his hot breath sending shivers up and down her spine.

"We can't, Serge. Not yet. It would be rude to leave so early."

"Just for a minute," he insisted, wrapping his strong fingers around her slender arm and ushering her out to the foyer, away from the crowd. He dipped his head to graze his lips across hers. Tasting honey, he kissed her again, more deeply. "There's something I want to show you upstairs," he said.

Tori laughed and blushed. It surprised her that Serge could still make her blush like a schoolgirl; could still make her tingle all over like one, too. Would she be blushing and tingling like this when their hair had turned gray? She certainly expected to be.

"There's nothing to see upstairs, Serge. All the furniture's been moved out," she said. "Including the beds," she added with emphasis. "If that's what you had in mind."

"What kind of insensitive brute do you take me for anyway, wife?" he asked. He tugged at her slender, pale hand. "Come on. It's a surprise."

She could never refuse him when he gave her that boyish lopsided grin of his. Picking up the skirt of her ivory damask wedding gown, the same simple, elegant gown her mother and grandmother had been wed in, Tori climbed the curving staircase with Serge. The echo of their footsteps ricocheted off the ceiling.

Except for the front parlor, all the rooms were empty. Gordon had moved to Cape Cod, where he'd set up a small oar-manufacturing company. Serge was a partner in the venture. The town house was scheduled to be completely remodeled the following week. Gordon had sold it to a condominium developer. Instead of two people knocking around too many rooms, there would soon be three families in separate apartments at the Beacon Hill address.

"Are you sad that the house isn't in the Langford family anymore?" Serge asked Tori as he led her down the upstairs hall.

"The sentimental part of me is," she replied. "But it's really for the best. I'm glad the burden of it is off Gordon's shoulders and he can get on with his life. He loves living at the Cape. It was always his favorite place. I know he can't wait to close up the house for good today and go back."

"Yeah, and he'd better. He's got a business to run out there," Serge said gruffly.

It didn't put Tori off. She stopped and threw her arms around his neck. "Thanks to you, he does."

Serge kissed the top of her head, his nose brushing against the spray of lilies-of-the-valley entwined in her chignon. "Thanks to me, baloney. I can't take credit for Gordon's inventiveness—especially after underestimating him all these years."

"Now that he's making a success of his life, do you think he'll ask Ginger to marry him?"

"I don't know, honey." He lightly tweaked her long, lovely nose. "Just because we got married today, we can't expect the whole world to, can we?"

"Not the whole world. Just my brother and my best friend," Tori replied wistfully.

But Serge wasn't interested in matchmaking. He was only interested in his own mate at the moment. He led her into the bathroom.

"Oh, no!" Tori cried, staring at the gap in the tiles that had once been filled by the big marble tub. "They've already moved it out." She looked up at Serge, her expression dismayed. "This isn't the surprise you were talking about, I hope."

"Nope. The surprise is waiting for us at home."

"I don't get it," Tori said a bit impatiently, beginning to worry about leaving all their guests downstairs. But then her hazel eyes lit up green with understanding. She laughed with delight. "You had the tub moved there!"

"And hired as many men as it took to install it this morning while you were out getting married, Mrs. Zhdanov."

"To the most thoughtful, most wonderful, most considerate man I—"

Serge gently placed his finger on her lips. "I did it for myself as much as for you, lady. This is a wedding present I intend to enjoy as much as you do. Now, why don't we say goodbye to all our guests and go home?"

Not only did Tori agree, she even induced Serge to sneak down the back stairs to save time. She figured she could forget about good manners and protocol for once in her life. It was her one and only wedding day, after all, and the temptation of a luxurious bath for two was just too much to resist.

*   *   *   *   *

Silhouette Romance™
Legendary Lovers Trilogy

BY DEBBIE MACOMBER....

ONCE UPON A TIME, in a land not so far away, there lived a girl, Debbie Macomber, who grew up dreaming of castles, white knights and princes on fiery steeds. Her family was an ordinary one with a mother and father and one wicked brother, who sold copies of her diary to all the boys in her junior high class.

One day, when Debbie was only nineteen, a handsome electrician drove by in a shiny black convertible. Now Debbie knew a prince when she saw one, and before long they lived in a two-bedroom cottage surrounded by a white picket fence.

As often happens when a damsel fair meets her prince charming, children followed, and soon the two-bedroom cottage became a four-bedroom castle. The kingdom flourished and prospered, and between soccer games and car pools, ballet classes and clarinet lessons, Debbie thought about love and enchantment and the magic of romance.

One day Debbie said, "What this country needs is a good fairy tale." She remembered how well her diary had sold and she dreamed again of castles, white knights and princes on fiery steeds. And so the stories of Cinderella, Beauty and the Beast, and Snow White were reborn....

Look for Debbie Macomber's *Legendary Lovers* trilogy from Silhouette Romance: *Cindy and the Prince* (January, 1988); *Some Kind of Wonderful* (March, 1988); *Almost Paradise* (May, 1988). Don't miss them!

SRT-1

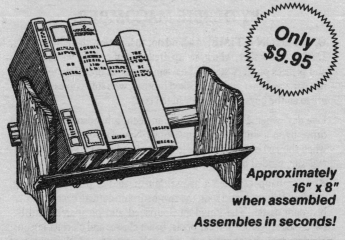

Silhouette Special Edition

COMING NEXT MONTH

#445 THROUGH ALL ETERNITY—Sondra Stanford
Upon colliding with luscious Lila Addison, big Jeffrey Chappel found the
former model kind to strangers but cautious about commitment. He vowed to
win her precious trust, but could he truly offer her his own heart?

#446 NEVER LET GO—Sherryl Woods
Though Dr. Justin Whitmore acted hard as nails, hospital psychologist Mallory
Blake had glimpsed his softer side. As professional awe turned to personal
ardor, Mallory longed to crack Justin's icy facade—and rush right into his
heart.

#447 SILENT PARTNER—Celeste Hamilton
Fiercely independent Melissa Chambers needed bucks, not brainstorms, to
launch her new restaurant. But headstrong Hunt Kirkland, her far-from-silent
partner, was full of ideas... for passionate teamwork!

#448 THE POWER WITHIN—Dawn Flindt
Strongman Joe Rustin had saved Tina's life. He then became her exercise coach
and devoted companion—but *not* the lover she longed for. How could she
convince Joe to unleash his powerful inner passions?

#449 RAPTURE DEEP—Anne Lacey
When lovely, treacherous Stacey reentered Chris Lorio's life, buried rage
surfaced... as did memories of rapture in each other's arms. For the long-ago
lovers, the past held bitterness, secrets and, somewhere, sweet promise.

#450 DISARRAY—Linda Shaw
In small-town Finley, Arkansas, little went unnoticed—especially not "good
girl" Barbara Regent's canceled wedding, compromised reputation and
budding romance with a mysterious, untrusted outsider.

AVAILABLE THIS MONTH:

Silhouette Intimate Moments

THIS MONTH
CHECK IN TO
DODD MEMORIAL HOSPITAL!

Not feeling sick, you say? That's all right, because Dodd Memorial isn't your average hospital. At Dodd Memorial you don't need to be a patient—or even a doctor yourself!—to examine the private lives of the doctors and nurses who spend as much time healing broken hearts as they do healing broken bones.

In UNDER SUSPICION (Intimate Moments #229) intern Allison Schuyler and Chief Resident Cruz Gallego strike sparks from the moment they meet, but they end up with a lot more than love on their minds when someone starts stealing drugs—and Allison becomes the main suspect.

In May look for AFTER MIDNIGHT (Intimate Moments #237) and finish the trilogy in July with HEARTBEATS (Intimate Moments #245).

Author Lucy Hamilton is a former medical librarian whose husband is a doctor. Let her check you in to Dodd Memorial—you won't want to check out!

IM229-1R